FORTUNE FURLOUGH

A Miss Fortune Mystery

NEW YORK TIMES BESTSELLING AUTHOR
JANA DELEON

MISS FORTUNE SERIES INFORMATION

If you've never read a Miss Fortune mystery, you can start with LOUISIANA LONGSHOT, the first book in the series. If you prefer to start with this book, here are a few things you need to know.

Fortune Redding – a CIA assassin with a price on her head from one of the world's most deadly arms dealers. Because her boss suspects that a leak at the CIA blew her cover, he sends her to hide out in Sinful, Louisiana, posing as his niece, a librarian and ex–beauty queen named Sandy-Sue Morrow. The situation was resolved in Change of Fortune and Fortune is now a full-time resident of Sinful and has opened her own detective agency.

Ida Belle and Gertie – served in the military in Vietnam as spies, but no one in the town is aware of that fact except Fortune and Deputy LeBlanc.

Sinful Ladies Society – local group founded by Ida Belle, Gertie, and deceased member Marge. In order to gain membership, women must never have married or if widowed, their husband must have been deceased for at least ten years.

Sinful Ladies Cough Syrup – sold as an herbal medicine in Sinful, which is dry, but it's actually moonshine manufactured by the Sinful Ladies Society.

CHAPTER ONE

I FINISHED MY INSPECTION OF GERTIE'S PURSE AND LOOKED down at her small travel suitcase. So small, in fact, that she wouldn't even have to check it.

"That's it?" I asked.

"She can't make it through security with her usual arsenal," Ida Belle said. "That reduces her gear by at least half. But I agree, that still looks a little light."

"I have toiletries, sandals, four bikinis, cover-up, shorts and tees, and an evening gown," Gertie said. "There's a washer and dryer in the condo. What else do I need for a week on the beach?"

Ida Belle had been staring at her best friend with a horrified expression ever since the word "bikinis" had passed her lips. She probably hadn't even processed the formal wear yet.

"Why an evening gown?" I asked. I absolutely refused to address the bikini thing. There weren't a lot of things in this world that scared me, but Gertie's wardrobe choices made the list. Since I planned to wear really dark sunglasses and drink a lot, I figured I could manage. Ida Belle, however, might need more help adjusting.

"The evening gown is in case I meet a man and he wants to whisk me away somewhere fancy," Gertie said.

"There's no place on the Key fancy enough to require an evening gown," Ida Belle said. "But let's move back a bit and discuss this bikini thing."

Gertie clapped her hands. "I started shopping as soon as we booked the condo. I got a leopard print, a red sequined, black mesh, and one that is the same color as my skin. So I'll look like I'm completely nude."

"Remember the drinking part," I said to Ida Belle.

"There's not enough alcohol in Florida to make me unsee Gertie in a nude bikini," Ida Belle said. "Or any other bikini for that matter. Don't you have a one-piece? Maybe we can find you one of those swim burkas on Amazon and have it delivered right to the condo"

"A wet suit would work," I said. "We can probably pick one up in Florida."

Ida Belle shook her head. "Too tight. It would take both of us to get her in and out of it. I'm barely recovered from the butt-wrapping events at Halloween."

"Good point," I said.

Gertie sighed. "The two of you really need to work on your sense of adventure. It's another state. We don't know anyone there. Go crazy with your wardrobe. It's the perfect opportunity."

Ida Belle snorted. "What are you talking about—opportunity? You've known everyone in Sinful for a thousand years, and it's never stopped you from wearing crazy crap here."

Gertie threw her hands in the air. "Whatever. The bottom line is that the two of you will have to deal with it. Because I plan on flashing my goods to every available man on the beach."

"It's the flashing of the bottom line that has me worried,"

Ida Belle said. "Please tell me you don't intend to go into the water. You know there's actual surf, right? One of those waves could rip a bikini right off of you."

"That's why I'm bringing four," Gertie said. "Plenty of backup."

"I give up," Ida Belle said.

"You should have given up a hundred years ago," I said. "It would have saved you an untold amount of time and energy."

"I keep hoping God will let me off for time served," Ida Belle said.

"Apparently He has a large sense of humor," I said. "Or you did something terribly wrong in your youth."

"Short of betraying Jesus, I'm not sure what would earn this," Ida Belle said.

Gertie gave her the finger and started rolling her suitcase to the front door. "I heard Carter pull up, so you two better decide quick what is more tolerable—another boring week in Sinful or the potential of seeing me lose my bikini and enthrall every man on the beach."

Ida Belle and I looked at each other, and I know we were both weighing the drinking against the potential for permanent blindness. Ultimately, the drinking must have won out because we both grabbed our suitcases and headed for the door.

"We can always wear sunglasses *and* close our eyes," I said as we walked.

Ida Belle nodded. "And if that doesn't work, we can poke them out with those little umbrellas that come in the drinks. After a couple, we won't even feel it."

Carter met us at the porch and smiled. "Ready for the big trip?"

"As ready as we're getting," Ida Belle said.

"What's this place again?" he asked. "Quiet Key?"

Ida Belle nodded.

He grinned. "Quiet Key, huh? Did you warn them that you guys were coming?"

"No," Ida Belle said. "They might not have allowed us across the bridge."

"Good call." Carter reached down for Gertie's suitcase. "Is this all you're bringing?"

"That's a question you really don't want to hear the answer to," I said.

Immediately, he lifted the suitcase and whipped around, leaving Gertie no time to respond. Given some of the attire Gertie had worn around Sinful, he probably knew where the conversation would go. No one needed those images in their mind. Especially my boyfriend. It might ruin the romance mood for a month or better.

Carter tossed the suitcases in the back of his mom's SUV, we all climbed in, and we were off.

Swamp Team 3 was officially on vacation.

―――――

I OPENED THE SLIDING GLASS DOORS AND WE STEPPED OUT on the huge balcony overlooking the beach. Gertie gazed over the railing, squealed, and clapped her hands.

"Do you see that buffet of men down there?" Gertie asked.

"God's waiting room," Ida Belle said. "That buffet is long past its expiration date."

Gertie waved a hand in dismissal. "More for me."

Ida Belle grimaced and I couldn't help smiling. There was a definite advantage to having a boyfriend. No pressure to troll for old buffet items. I had a feeling Ida Belle wouldn't get off so easy, especially if the menu items traveled in pairs.

"This is going to be great!" Gertie exclaimed. "We've barely just gotten here and I've already been felt up."

"He tripped over a potted plant and was blind as a bat," Ida Belle said. "He probably thought he was clutching the drapes."

"My boobs do *not* hang like drapes," Gertie protested.

"Well, I guess we'll find out soon," I said. "Let's hit the beach."

Gertie squealed again and ran back inside. Ida Belle let out a long-suffering sigh and followed her. I closed the sliding door and glanced around. It was a really nice setup. Three bedrooms, each with its own bath, so that eliminated a lot of potential issues. A good-sized living room with two couches and a wall of glass overlooking the beach. And a smallish kitchen, but the only thing that was really relevant was that it had a refrigerator. I didn't cook in Sinful. I certainly wasn't going to come all the way to Florida to start.

I headed to my bedroom and smiled. I'd taken the one meant for kids, so I had a double bed and a set of bunk beds. That meant I had three different places to sleep depending on my mood. Ida Belle had taken the smaller of the two remaining bedrooms—my guess was because it was in the corner and didn't share a wall with an adjoining unit. That left Gertie with the master suite, which was right up her alley, complete with the spa tub.

I donned my bright blue one-piece and white cover-up that Ally had insisted on while we were online shopping for my vacation wardrobe. It looked sorta like a really short sundress with a plunging neckline and a hem that barely inched past the bottom of my bathing suit. Ally thought I would look hot in it, so I headed for the bathroom and did a mirror assessment. I decided that the outfit worked, but it felt a little weird. I wasn't much of a beach baby, although I really enjoyed the water. It was just that most of my swimming had been done in a wet or dry suit. Still, I supposed I didn't look too bad and the hours spent on my laptop had made Ally happy, so it appeared to be a win for both of us.

Ally had also insisted on a mani-pedi, so my fingers and toes sported the hot pink polish she'd picked out. Carter had smiled so big when he'd seen them that I thought he was going to laugh. He managed to restrain himself, but he knew how much I avoided the girlie stuff. However, he also knew how much I loved Ally. So hot pink nails and sexy swim cover-ups had won.

I slipped on a pair of silver flip-flops—Ally said they'd match everything—and headed back into the living room. Ida Belle was already standing there, wearing wide-leg blue linen pants, a blue-and-gray-striped polo shirt, and hiking sandals. It was the most casual I'd ever seen her dressed. Until now, I'd been convinced that she slept in jeans, button-up shirts, and tennis shoes.

She gave me the once-over and nodded. "I see the online shopping went well. Surprised you didn't go for a suit that matched the nails."

I raised one eyebrow and she grinned. Then I heard Gertie's room door open and the grin disappeared completely.

"No way," Ida Belle said, shaking her head. "You are not walking out of here dressed that way."

I looked over and let out a strangled cry. The red sequined bikini consisted of a halter top and a string bikini bottom. Clearly the designer had saved on the sequin expense because there wasn't a lot of fabric to cover. Which meant we saw a lot more of Gertie than either of us wanted to. Then there was the added bonus that since a good bit of Gertie was usually covered up with regular clothes when she was outside, her tan did not extend to all the parts not covered by the bikini. So she was an odd mix of tanned legs below the knee and tanned arms to the shoulders, but the rest was bright white, making the red bikini appear as if it were glowing.

"Isn't it great?" Gertie asked, beaming. "There's even tassels on the boobs. Bet I can make them swing around in circles if I do some sexy dancing."

I'm pretty sure that if she'd had her gun on her, Ida Belle would have shot Gertie right then. I could abstain for the statement, but if she started any actual tassel swinging on the beach, I might have to improvise.

"You could grab a boob with your hand and swing it around just standing there," Ida Belle said. "And when you get down to the beach and take a hike far from Fortune and me, you are free to twirl whatever body part you feel like. But I am *not* walking through the lobby with you dressed like that."

"At least I'm not dressed like I'm going to the library," Gertie said. "How in the world do you consider that beach attire?"

"The shirt has short sleeves," Ida Belle said. "I'm going to get a bedsheet for you to wear."

"Why not just get a towel?" I asked.

"I'm afraid it wouldn't hide enough," Ida Belle said.

"This was the discreet lady version of the suit," Gertie said. "The other one was really racy."

Ida Belle stared, somewhat horror-stricken.

"Don't you have a cover-up?" I asked. "Ally told me that only hookers and gold diggers walk around the resort with their bathing suits exposed."

Gertie frowned. "Hmmm. There are some advantages to that, but I suppose my good upbringing ultimately wins out. I'll go grab my cover-up."

"Thank the Lord and her mother for the good upbringing," I muttered as she walked back into the bedroom.

"That woman is going to be the death of me," Ida Belle said. "One way or another."

Given the type of items Gertie usually hauled around in her purse, Ida Belle's statement wasn't really all that far-fetched.

"You're not planning on swimming in that, are you?" I asked Ida Belle.

"Of course not. I have on board shorts, a sports bra, and a tank top, but decency is decency. I'm not about sporting my kneecaps through a lobby. That sort of thing belongs on the beach or around a pool."

I grinned. "Those must be the sexiest kneecaps in the Americas if you're afraid to let random lobby people see them."

"At least they don't have tassels."

Gertie came strolling out of the bedroom again. She was wearing a cover-up, but the crocheted dress didn't really hide much of anything. Still, it was harder to make out the tassels, so it was going to have to do, because I really didn't feel like starting my vacation off rolling Gertie up in a bedsheet like a burrito. She was also carrying a beach bag that could have held a torpedo launcher. I knew she hadn't been allowed to carry anything of the sort on the plane, but I still gave the bag a suspicious eye.

"Should we be worried about the contents of that bag?" I asked.

"It's necessary beach stuff," Gertie said.

I looked over at Ida Belle, who was holding a towel. I was holding a towel and the room key. We both had sunglasses on our heads. Clearly, Gertie had a whole different set of needs at the beach than either of us.

Ida Belle let out a long-suffering sigh and headed for the door. "They serve drinks on the beach, right?"

"Oh yeah," I said, and followed her out.

"I bet if I swing my tassels, I could score us some free ones," Gertie said.

"If you swing those tassels, you'll knock out the waiter and we'll never get a drink," Ida Belle said.

"Then you best order before I get in a swinging mood," Gertie said, and stepped into the elevator.

"We're going to have to make them doubles," Ida Belle said.

I nodded. We hadn't even made it outside and Ida Belle and I were already planning on drinking away the pain. And Gertie was only getting started. Because I was absolutely certain she would improve on the terror once she hit the beach and started flaunting her wares in front of the sea of old men out there. Sinful didn't exactly offer up a lot of options in that arena. Florida was practically a farmers' market of goods. Mostly overripened, from what I'd seen, but perfect for Gertie and her tassels.

Surprisingly, we managed to get all the way through the lobby and past the pool without incident. I actually heard Ida Belle's sigh of relief as we set out on the sand toward a trio of chairs sitting under a blue-and-white-striped umbrella. I clipped the reservation tag on the umbrella and plopped into one of the chairs, using my towel as a pillow, then looked around for the drink server. Ida Belle sat in the middle chair next to me and Gertie stood, hands on her hips, frowning at us.

"That's all you're going to do?" she asked. "Sit there?"

"No," Ida Belle said. "We're going to drink."

I nodded.

"You're not going to swim?" Gertie asked. "Why did we come all the way here if we're not going to swim?"

"I came to drink and lie around and not see another dead body," I said.

A couple sitting next to us looked over at me.

"Professional assassin," I said.

They snapped their heads back in place.

Ida Belle chuckled. "Imagine how they'd have reacted if they knew it was the truth."

"Not exactly," I said. "I'm retired from that line of work now. Now, I am a professional busybody and servant to a cat."

"So you're not swimming?" Gertie asked again.

"Oh hell, woman," Ida Belle said. "You're not swimming either. You're going to wade out into that surf, get knocked down and dragged around on the sand for a bit, then you're going to wind up right back here with us. We're just being efficient about it."

I looked out at the water and nodded. "She's right. None of us are interested in actual swimming, and those waves are high enough to make standing around and chatting difficult."

"Not to mention that we'd spill our drinks," Ida Belle said.

"Fine," Gertie said. "Then you two can sit here and bake, but I'm getting in the water to cool off and do some mingling. I see several targets. Get me a margarita on the rocks. I'll be back before it melts."

She pulled off her cover-up and headed toward the water, lumbering in the sand as if she were wearing cement boots. And even though I hadn't thought it possible, the red bikini covered even less in the back than in the front.

"Those sequins are going to give her a rash on her butt," Ida Belle said before leaning back in her chair.

I nodded. "Add that to the total body exfoliation she's about to get in that surf and there might not be enough lotion in the pharmacy to handle it."

A cute blond guy with a dark tan and bright green eyes popped up next to us. "Can I get you ladies anything?"

"Piña colada for me," I said. "I want something with a slice of pineapple and an umbrella."

"Straight scotch," Ida Belle. "The good stuff. Nothing cheap. And a margarita on the rocks for the crazy one who went swimming."

He beamed a giant smile of white teeth at us and winked. "I'll be right back with those."

Ida Belle watched as he walked away. "That is one good-looking young man. Gertie should have stayed on shore."

I grinned, slightly surprised to hear Ida Belle talking about good-looking men. But then, we *were* on vacation.

"One toss about in those waves and Gertie will landlock herself until we get a green flag," I said. "Yellow-flag surf is just too rough to relax in."

"Got that right. And I certainly didn't come here to exercise. We get enough of that back home."

"If we stopped going to the Swamp Bar, we could probably cut the exercise portion of our residency in half."

"Or if we left Gertie in Florida." Ida Belle looked out at the water. "There she goes. Any bets?"

"No point. We'd both be betting on the same thing."

"I'm just hoping her dunking doesn't involve any disrobing. That bikini is the worst thing she could be wearing."

I nodded, and we watched as Gertie took a couple of hesitant steps into the water. Standing in six inches of surf must have bolstered her confidence, because she threw her shoulders back and pushed ahead.

Ida Belle shook her head. "Here we go."

CHAPTER TWO

I ROSE FROM MY CHAIR AND PULLED OFF MY COVER-UP. A couple chairs down from us, a group of college-aged guys whistled.

Ida Belle looked up at me and raised an eyebrow. "You're going swimming?"

"Not by choice, but someone might have to pull her out."

"That's what the lifeguard is for."

"If things go as expected with that bikini, I'm afraid he'll hesitate on the extraction."

"Good point." Ida Belle jumped up and pulled off her pants and shirt, exposing a pair of black board shorts and a solid black tank. I paused for a second, trying to remember if this was the first time I'd seen that much of her legs, but decided my musings would have to wait.

We started across the sand toward the water, but realized quickly, we'd waited too long to make our move. With her newfound confidence, Gertie had lunged headfirst into water above her waist. Literally headfirst. One second, the sun was glinting off her white hair. The next second, it was glinting off her white butt. I broke into a run—as fast as one can run in sand—thankful that I'd caught a flash of red when Gertie upended. At least the bottom of that ridiculous bikini was still in place.

For the moment.

Gertie's head bobbed up for a second and she let out a strangled cry, waving her hands in the air. One hand was clutching something red.

"Oh good God," I mumbled as I reached the water.

A crowd had gathered at the edge of the ocean to watch and film Gertie's potential death, and I had to shove my way through them to get to the water. I dodged two kids on floats and one drunk who was toasting Gertie with his beer and dived below an oncoming wave. I swam underwater until I spotted a swath of red around white legs and then I popped up.

Gertie was a couple feet away and upright, but a huge wave was barreling toward us and I was afraid when it hit, that bikini bottom was going to head out to sea with the undertow. I yelled at her to duck and she frowned, but unfortunately, my warning didn't register soon enough. She turned around just in time for the wave to slam her right in the face. Then her head went under and she disappeared.

I ducked and dived in time to miss the wave and as soon as I surfaced, I scanned the surf, looking for her. About twenty feet away, I spotted something red floating and took off swimming that way. I saw Ida Belle coming from the other direction, the lifeguard in tow. I reached the red floating object and snagged it from the water. It was Gertie's bikini top.

Panicked, I ducked under the water and looked, but I didn't see her anywhere. I surfaced and yelled at Ida Belle and the lifeguard.

"She went under somewhere around here!" I said. "I can't see her. Fan out."

Ida Belle and the lifeguard immediately went in the opposite direction, scanning the water for any sign of Gertie. A couple seconds later, I heard coughing and a man shouted.

"Over here!"

I spun around and caught a full face of saltwater wave, but I got a glimpse of a man with a float. I started that direction, wiping the salt water from my eyes, and was relieved to see a partially clad Gertie coughing on top of a blue floatie. Even more fortunately, she was lying on her stomach. The man with the float had thinning silver-and-black hair and was struggling to keep the float from tipping in the surf.

Sixtysomething. Five foot ten. One eighty-five. Too tan. Too flabby. Why is he wearing a T-shirt in the water? No threat until Gertie is conscious enough to spot her hero.

I made my way over and grabbed one end of the float.

"Let's get her in before the next set comes," I said.

He gave me a grateful nod and moved to the other end.

"Are you okay?" I asked Gertie as we pushed through the waves.

She coughed and gave me a thumbs-up. That was good enough. At least she was breathing and recognized a question.

We were almost to the shore when the next big set of waves moved in. The first one swept under the float and pitched it up, tearing it from our grasp. I heard Ida Belle yell just before the wave sent me crashing into the ocean floor. The strength of the wave and the undertow rolled me a couple of times before I could get my feet planted on the bottom and launch up again. Gertie's rescuer was struggling to stand next to me, and I grabbed his shoulder and yanked him upright.

Gertie was still on the float, riding the top of the wave toward the beach. But now, she was completely conscious and her lungs were working just fine. She clutched the sides of the float, head lifted, and let out an excited hoot as the wave tossed her straight at the lifeguard. I heard her laughing as she pitched off the float and flattened the lifeguard on the beach.

Ida Belle ran as the horrified lifeguard launched out from under the semi-naked woman who'd landed on him.

"What?" Gertie asked. "No mouth-to-mouth?"

"Good God, woman!" Ida Belle said. "Cover those things up."

"I lost my top," Gertie said.

"You've got hands!" Ida Belle looked around frantically, then grabbed two plastic pails from children standing nearby and plopped them on her chest. "Show's over, people. She's alive and no one else needs to see what's under those buckets."

Gertie clutched the buckets and laughed hysterically as her rescuer and I made our way over. The lifeguard just stood there, no idea how to handle the situation. I was going to hazard a guess that his training hadn't covered anything like half-naked seniors, even though it seemed it should have.

Gertie looked over at me as I walked up. "Did you save my top?" she asked.

I shook my head. "I lost it in one of the fifty times I got rolled." I motioned to the lifeguard. "Let's get her up."

He gave me a look like a five-year-old who wanted to protest having to eat his vegetables but must have decided it was easier to comply.

"Shoulder and elbow," I said. "I don't want those buckets slipping."

We each grabbed a shoulder and elbow and hauled her to her feet.

"Are you all right?" the rescuer asked Gertie. "I'm sorry if I touched anything inappropriate getting you onto the float."

Gertie perked up. "What do you think you touched?"

"I'm not really sure," he said.

I didn't even want to think about all the things that simple sentence covered.

"Well, thank you for saving me," Gertie said. "I don't really care what you touched to do it."

The man looked pleased. "As long as you're all right."

"Oh, I'm fine," Gertie said. "This isn't even the most exciting thing that's happened to me in the past month."

"I like a woman of adventure," he said. "I don't suppose you'd let me take you to dinner tonight?"

"Of course. Maybe we can revisit that touching thing," Gertie said and winked.

Ida Belle closed her eyes and shook her head, then turned around and headed up the beach toward our chairs. I trailed behind her. I was looking forward to the seafood buffet tonight and didn't want Gertie's romantic talk ruining my dinner.

The drinks had arrived while we were gone and mine was already melted, but it didn't matter. Ida Belle downed her entire glass, then whistled for the bartender and pointed to the glasses, signaling the need for another round. Then she picked up Gertie's margarita and downed it as well. I took a big swig of my fruity drink. It wasn't as good as it would have been frozen, but at that point, alcohol in the system was the goal. I really needed to take things down a notch. Or ten.

I heard giggling and we looked up to find Gertie plodding through the sand toward us, still clutching the plastic pails over her chest. A bit behind her, a man of about thirty years of age stomped up the beach, glaring at her back.

"You took toys from my children?" he yelled as he approached.

Gertie turned around and the man locked in on the toys and the reason for their acquisition.

"Sorry," Gertie said. "You can have them back."

"No!" The man's expression instantly shifted from angry to horrified, and he put his hands up in front of him and took a step backward. "I'm sorry. I didn't realize. I'll buy new ones."

He spun around as quickly as one can in the sand and hurried back down the beach, probably trying to work up a good way to explain to his kids why they were never, ever getting those buckets back.

"If you're not going to go back to the room, put on my shirt, for God's sake," Ida Belle said as she tossed her shirt over Gertie's head. "You're scaring the vacationers and spoiling my buzz."

"Your shirt doesn't match," Gertie said, her voice slightly muffled since the shirt was covering her head.

"Shirt. Now." Ida Belle waved a hand in dismissal. I didn't want to point out that it really didn't help, as one, Gertie couldn't see her wave, and two, she also couldn't see to walk. I climbed out of my chair and yanked the shirt off her head.

"Come with me," I said. "The bathroom is right behind us. You can change there. Trust me, the shirt will clash less than the plastic buckets."

"I'll borrow the shirt," Gertie said, "but only long enough to get back upstairs and change. I can't be seen looking like a hobo, especially not now."

"Why the heck does it matter now?" Ida Belle said. "You just flashed half of Florida. Calls to therapists' offices and drug dealers probably went up fifty percent in the last ten minutes."

"So I'm stimulating the economy," Gertie said.

"Don't ever use the word 'stimulating' when talking about yourself," Ida Belle said. "You owe me that much."

Gertie gave her the finger and stalked off toward the resort. Our waiter arrived about five seconds later.

"I missed your friend again," he said. "I heard she had a mishap."

"If by mishap you mean losing half of her clothes and almost drowning, then yes, she had one," Ida Belle said.

He shrugged. "Happens several times a week. Is she all right?"

"She's fine," Ida Belle said. "Everyone who got a good look might not be."

He nodded. "Drink orders have gone up in the last couple minutes. I have to run."

He hurried off and I grabbed my frozen fruity drink and took a sip. "Well, we've been here an hour and Gertie has almost died and flashed at least a hundred people."

"So...just like being back home," Ida Belle said.

"Except I see your knees. I never see them in Sinful."

Ida Belle grinned. "I don't want to give people the wrong impression."

CHAPTER THREE

I WAS AWAKENED THE NEXT MORNING BY BRIGHT SUNLIGHT shining directly in my eyes. I groaned and turned over, pulling the pillow over my head, but it was as if the entire room was glowing. I cursed myself for forgetting to close the blinds but figured it probably had something to do with all the whiskey shots Ida Belle and I had knocked back the night before. With Gertie out on her "hot date," Ida Belle and I had decided to do our favorite thing—stay in.

So instead of a night filled with strangers, resort music, and watered down drinks at the seafood buffet, we picked up a good quality whiskey and a pizza and spent the rest of our conscious night playing an HGTV drinking game. It had sounded simple enough when Ida Belle explained it—every time someone complained about the paint color, lack of granite countertops, or desire for real hardwood flooring, you took a shot.

We were drunk before a single episode finished.

The amount of complaining that people were willing to do on television amazed me. They all looked like spoiled babies. But on the plus side, the pizza was good, the whiskey was excellent, and since we'd both gotten a ton of sun, we'd headed to bed at a fairly early hour. Gertie was still out and unless we heard from her or the police, we had decided to assume that everything was still within legal limits.

It was a wide-reaching assumption, but one that didn't require getting off the couch or putting on pants. We'd headed to bed around midnight. Gertie was still out on the town, but we'd gotten a text earlier telling us not to wait up, so we'd followed her advice. About an hour later, I'd heard her open the front door, giggling like an idiot and whispering too loudly —I assumed to her date. I was just happy to hear a single set of footsteps going to her bedroom.

It was useless to close the blinds and try to sleep more as I was already too awake, just not necessarily energetic. So I flung back the covers and headed into the kitchen. Ida Belle joined me as the coffee was just finishing up. She looked as alert as I felt.

"I'm surprised to see you up this early," I said. Ida Belle's window faced west, so blind positioning wouldn't make a difference for her.

"Old habits," she said and slid onto a barstool at the kitchen counter. "What's your excuse?"

"Forgot to close my blinds. Did you hear Gertie come in last night?"

"Yes. I thought the giggling would go on forever. We're going to have to listen to her recount that date all day long, aren't we?"

"Probably," I said as I poured us both coffee. "But I draw the line when it gets to any states of undress."

"My line is when she walked out of the room to meet him."

I laughed. "I don't think you're going to be able to pull that one off."

"Well, at least I want to get in a cup of coffee, or maybe

ten, before she wakes up. A bottle of aspirin wouldn't be a bad idea, either."

I nodded and pulled the bottle out of my shorts pocket. "Got you covered."

"That's what I like best about military trained individuals. The preparation."

"Well, enjoy the aspirin, because I've got nothing for everything else that's coming our way."

"More whiskey?"

I groaned. "Maybe I'll just go for cotton balls in my ears. Or running. As soon as our hangovers are gone, we can outrun her."

"That's true."

"Maybe we could sneak out before she wakes up. We could have breakfast in peace, anyway."

Then we heard what sounded like yodeling coming from the master bedroom.

Ida Belle sighed. "Too late."

A minute later, Gertie emerged, looking like someone had given her an energy drink. Her hair stood on end, her face was flushed, and she practically bounced into the kitchen, beaming at us like a cheerleader. All she lacked was a set of pompoms. And about fifty years off her knees.

"I had the best night ever!" she exclaimed as she sat on a stool next to Ida Belle.

"I'm sure," Ida Belle said. "Fortune and I figured you could tell us all about it while we're at the beach."

Gertie laughed. "I'm not hanging out with you two today. I have a beach date planned with Otis. We're going to oil each other up and work on our tans."

I spit out my coffee at the oiling part of the conversation, and Ida Belle whacked me on the back as I coughed.

"So I guess I'll have to tell you all about it now," Gertie

said, completely ignoring my hacking. "First, he took me to dinner at the Italian restaurant downstairs. It's overpriced, but the food isn't bad. They didn't have any high-quality wine, though."

"You wouldn't know high-quality wine if the grapes were growing in your backyard," Ida Belle said.

"I don't always drink my wine out of a box," Gertie protested. "Anyway, after dinner, we took a walk on the beach and he kissed me under the moonlight. It was so romantic."

Ida Belle rolled her eyes. "If Otis is so perfect, why were you in so early? Heck, why did you come home at all?"

Gertie gave her an indignant look. "You can't just give everything away the first night. You have to play hard to get."

Ida Belle stared. "At your age, you should be playing 'get it before you both stop breathing.'"

"I'm going with Ida Belle on this one," I said. "Not a lot of options in Sinful, and then there's the judgment police flapping their jaws. What happens in Florida stays in Florida. And we're only here a week."

Gertie shook her head. "You two are hopeless. I'm building the sexual tension. It's always better if you dance around it for a bit."

Ida Belle cringed. "I don't want to hear about dancing around sexual anything. You are absolutely forbidden to give us any details that involve you not wearing underwear."

"I wasn't wearing underwear last night at dinner," Gertie said.

I said a silent prayer of thanks—again—for the lack of available firearms. But Ida Belle was dangerously close to a spoon. I'd done plenty of damage with less equipment. Before Ida Belle could make whatever move she was contemplating, someone banged on our door.

"Sheriff's department," a man's voice shouted. "Open up."

Gertie's eyes widened. "Is there some law about not wearing panties to dinner that I don't know about?"

I frowned and headed for the door. "I don't think the cops here care about undergarments. People are half to mostly naked on the beach every day."

I opened the door just as the man outside was about to bang on it again. He dropped his hand and gave me the tough-guy look that was meant to intimidate.

Five foot eleven. Two hundred twenty pounds. If the elevator broke, he'd be stuck on our floor forever. Zero threat unless he shoots me for smirking at the tough-guy look.

"Can I help you?" I asked.

"Sheriff's department," he said, clearly confused as to why I wasn't cowering in a corner somewhere.

I nodded. "That's what you said. Badge, please."

His jaw flexed and he pulled his ID out and showed it to me. Deputy Sidney Benton.

"You got a problem with law enforcement?" he asked.

"Sometimes," I said. "Especially when they have a problem offering proof of identity and are dressed like a tourist."

The jeans and tropical print top didn't exactly play into his attempt to look threatening.

"It's Florida," he said. "Everyone dresses this way."

"No. Vacationers dress that way," I said. "I'd expect more from law enforcement, but honestly, I can't work up the effort to care. So I'll ask again—can I help you?"

He reddened a bit and I could tell he was pissed, but he had also figured out he wasn't going to get anywhere with me. "I need to speak to Gertie Hebert."

"I knew it," Gertie said. "There *is* a panty law."

I waved him in Gertie's direction. "This is Ms. Hebert. What's this about?"

He stepped inside and walked toward Gertie, sizing her up

as he went. By the time he stopped in front of her, the determined look he'd worn before was replaced with one of confusion. "You're Gertie Hebert?" he asked.

Ida Belle threw her hands in the air, her patience for everything clearly shot. "Oh, for Christ's sake, it's her. Will you get on with it?"

He stiffened and pulled out a pad of paper and a pen. "Ms. Hebert, were you with Otis Baker last night?"

"Did he report the panty thing?" Gertie asked, slightly outraged. "That was supposed to be our sexy secret."

Benton looked pained. "I don't know anything about your undergarments. I'd just like some information about your time spent with Mr. Baker."

"What kind of information?" Gertie asked.

"Can you please run through your night with me?" he asked.

"You really don't want her to do that," Ida Belle warned. "Especially when it comes to the sexy part."

He grimaced. "Can you start with the last time you saw him?"

"When he walked me to the door," Gertie said. "Around one a.m."

"He walked you to this door?" Benton asked.

"What other door is there?" Gertie asked. "What is this about? He paid the bill at the restaurant. We didn't have illicit sex in the resort tent, although I considered it. We didn't take glass onto the beach. And we weren't loud. Might have been if the tent thing had gone down."

He waved a hand at her, probably trying to stop visions of Gertie and tents from rolling through his mind. "And he was fine when he left."

I stiffened. I knew where this was going.

"Of course he was fine," Gertie said. "Why wouldn't he be?"

Benton narrowed his eyes at her. "Because maintenance found him dead in his room this morning."

Gertie gasped. "Dead? No. You must have the wrong person. Otis told me he didn't have heart trouble."

"I never said it was natural causes," Benton said.

"Well, it wasn't a gunshot, because people would have heard it, awakened half the resort, and called the police last night," I said. "And since you didn't scan Gertie for defensive wounds, it wasn't a stabbing or choking or other form of attack that results in a struggle. So either the ME hasn't given a cause of death yet and you're just enjoying agitating people or the cause of death was something that left obvious markers."

Benton cut his gaze to me and stared. "You know an awful lot about murder."

"Former CIA agent," I said. "Comes with the territory."

His eyes widened and I could tell he didn't want to believe me, but there was something about my demeanor and tone that had him thinking I might just be telling the truth. "Anyway," he said, "I need Ms. Hebert to come down to the station and answer some questions."

"Is she under arrest?" I asked.

Benton hesitated, clearly aggravated at my blocking his play. "No," he said. "We just need her to clear some things up."

"What is there to clear up?" I asked. "Otis was alive and well when he walked Gertie to the door. I heard her come in. Clearly, something happened to him afterward and it has nothing to do with Gertie."

"We'll still need a statement," he said. "And I'm sure there will be other questions."

"And you know where to find us if there are," I said. "Now if you'll excuse us. We've got a full day planned."

"There's no reason to make this difficult," he said.

"Then don't," I shot back.

I headed to the door and opened it. He stared at me for a long time. I have no idea why. The CIA practically invented the stare-down. Finally, he blinked and went stomping out. I watched until he got on the elevator, then closed the door and looked at Ida Belle and Gertie.

"Houston, we have a problem."

———

IDA BELLE, GERTIE, AND I STARED AT ONE ANOTHER, NO ONE speaking. Then we all began to speak at once.

"What the heck is going on?" Ida Belle asked.

"Why Otis?" I asked.

"I really thought this was going to be about flashing everyone at the beach yesterday," Gertie said. "Or some weird panty law."

"I get the flashing thing," I said. "But why on earth would there be a panty law?"

"Sinful has one," Gertie said.

"Of course it does," I said. Sinful had all kinds of unusual laws.

"You're not allowed in public places without underwear unless you're height-weight proportionate," Gertie said.

"That seems a bit politically incorrect," I said.

"But it saves a lot of money on therapy," Ida Belle said. "Just think of all those times we've seen Celia's underwear. Now imagine that law didn't exist."

I cringed.

"Exactly," Ida Belle said. "But all talk of undergarments—

missing or otherwise—aside, we *do* have a problem. So what's our move?"

I grabbed my phone off the counter. "First things first. We find out how to proceed in case the sheriff's department decides to take this to the next level."

I dialed Carter's number, dreading the "I told you so" that I knew was coming.

"You in trouble already?" he asked when he answered. "That has to be some kind of record. And you cost me twenty bucks."

"How?"

"A bet with Walter. He didn't give you twenty-four hours. I was feeling optimistic."

"Serves you right then. Age and experience for the win."

"How bad is it? Drunk and disorderly? Property damage? Indecent exposure?"

"All of those apply in some form and you could even throw in theft of private property if children's beach toys count. However, our current problem is murder."

"What?" All the joking was completely gone from Carter's voice. "Are Ida Belle and Gertie okay?"

"Yes. The three of us are fine, but apparently, Gertie's hot date from last night didn't finish up things as well as she did. We just had a visit from a local deputy."

"And he said it was murder?"

"No. He was cagey. I think he was under the impression that he was being smooth or intimidating. Honestly, I couldn't tell because neither was working for me. But he asked Gertie some questions about when she last saw her date and then said he wanted her to come down to the sheriff's department."

"Is she under arrest?" Carter asked, now sounding slightly panicked.

"That's exactly what I asked, and when the answer was no, I told him Gertie wouldn't be going anywhere."

He cursed. "Deputy Breaux went on vacation this morning, and Sheriff Lee has the flu. There's no way I can leave."

"That's okay. I've got everything under control."

"That scares me more than you'll ever know. Naples is the nearest bigger city, right?"

"I think so."

"There's a guy in Naples that I served with in the Marine Corps. He went into criminal law when he retired and is a barracuda. Let me get in touch with him and verify the correct way to handle things in Florida, and I'll get back to you with his contact information. It's early, so it might be a while."

"No problem."

"In the meantime, until they arrest Gertie, she doesn't leave the area. And if they do arrest her, she keeps her mouth shut."

"Got it."

"And Fortune?"

"Yeah."

"Do *not* launch an investigation in another state when the woman you're rooming with is suspected of murder. It has disaster written all over it. And I can't cover for you there."

"I know. We're just going to stay off radar. I figure if they can't find Gertie then they can't arrest her, right? So we'll leave and head down to the beach. Maybe set up camp some distance from the resort."

"That's a good plan."

He sounded slightly relieved, and I felt guilty for lying. Well, sorta lying. I did intend to stay off radar. But no way in hell was I going to sit on my hands and wait for Gertie to be railroaded for something she didn't do.

I hung up the phone and relayed what Carter had said to

Ida Belle and Gertie.

"I'm glad Carter has a contact," Ida Belle said. "I have a feeling we're going to need him before this is over. I didn't like that deputy. There was something off about him."

I nodded. "I'm going to guess that murder isn't something that happens often around here. The sheriff will be under a lot of pressure from the resorts that pay his salary to wrap this up quickly and quietly."

"And Gertie is the quickest solution," Ida Belle said.

"But not the quietest," Gertie said.

"Understatement," Ida Belle said and studied me for a moment. "I'm surprised Carter didn't read you the riot act about not getting involved in the investigation."

"Oh, he did," I said. "I just didn't tell you that part because I didn't figure it was relevant."

Ida Belle grinned. "Swamp Team 3 Investigations...road trip."

Gertie clapped her hands, far too enthusiastic for someone who was on the hook for a murder rap. "Where do we start?"

The grin slipped from Ida Belle's face and she sighed. "Good God, I never thought I'd say this, but we start with you recounting every excruciating second of your date with Otis."

"All the details?" Gertie asked. "Really?"

I nodded. "Unfortunately, at this point we have no way of knowing what might be important. It's best to get it all down while your memory is fresh."

"I've got full charge on my phone," Ida Belle said. "We should record this."

I nodded. "I'll grab my laptop and take notes. Plus, we need to poke around on the internet and find out more about this Otis. If he was murdered, there's a motive. And I'm guessing it won't be something he and Gertie discussed over dinner."

"I don't suppose we have time for room service?" Gertie asked. "I didn't eat a lot last night because I didn't want my stomach to pooch out."

"You'd have had to cut back on eating in 1972 for your stomach to not pooch out," Ida Belle said.

"I don't think we can risk staying here any longer than necessary," I said. "We need to put on bathing suits and cover-ups, stuff anything we might need into beach bags, and clear out of the resort."

"There was a café near the bridge where we came onto the island," Gertie said.

I shook my head. "You know cops and food. Our luck, that deputy eats there every day. Besides, anything local will be packed with tourists, and we need privacy. I say we head off the island to the nearest half-empty dive we can find and hole up in a corner. Once we get everything documented and saved onto the cloud, we can head to the far end of the island and beach it for a while."

Ida Belle nodded. "Let's get changed and packed. Hats and sunglasses are also a good idea." She looked at Gertie. "And for the love of God, will you please wear something least likely to attract attention?"

I raised an eyebrow. "Like the evening gown?"

"I have casual resort wear," Gertie said.

I had no idea what casual resort wear looked like but figured it probably still wouldn't meet Ida Belle's approval.

"You know what?" Ida Belle said. "Never mind. I'll lend you some of my clothes."

Gertie frowned. "Everything you own is some shade of black, gray, or navy blue. It's boring."

"Yep," Ida Belle agreed. "But then boring people are rarely sitting in jail."

CHAPTER FOUR

WE MANAGED TO CHANGE, PACK, AND GET OUT THE DOOR IN ten minutes. I was ready in one minute, ten seconds. Ida Belle in two minutes. That left Gertie commanding the remaining eight. Something to do with the foam cups in her bathing suit top needing adjusting. Ida Belle and I were both afraid to ask. When we exited the elevator in the lobby, everything went south.

I shoved Ida Belle and Gertie behind a set of fake foliage and pulled them down. "Benton just walked into the lobby and he's headed this way."

I scanned our options, but they were looking slim. Leaving our leafy hiding place in either direction left us completely exposed, but so did staying there long enough for Benton to get to the elevator. Directly across from us was a store with overpriced vacationer needs, but the front was all glass and there were no shelves to hide behind.

But I got an idea.

I dashed into the store and grabbed a float from a display near the counter. I tossed some money at the startled clerk, then ran back out and positioned the float on my shoulder, motioning for Ida Belle and Gertie to get behind me. I peered through the foliage and spotted Benton approaching the elevators from the right side. I angled us a bit and headed off to the left.

The downside of the plan was that if I was hiding behind a float, I couldn't watch Benton in case he made a change in direction. So I'd just have to hope he stayed the course and we could make it across the lobby without him catching sight of us.

It was a good plan. Until it wasn't.

We were just about to round a huge banana plant when two boys, about ten years old, dashed out of the store with water pistols. I heard yelling and peered around the float to see them blasting Benton right in the face with water. He flung his hands up in front of his face and made a hard turn, sending him right behind us.

I made a quick turn around the plant and pulled on the float, trying to get Gertie and Ida Belle to pick up pace. Ida Belle managed just fine, but Gertie must have banged her leg on the plant's pot because all of a sudden, the resistance on the float was gone. I heard a whoosh of breath and the unmistakable crash of a body hitting the ground. I did a 180 with the mat and slapped a valet right in the head with the now-empty end. He dropped the suitcase he was carrying on the foot of the woman walking next to him, who tripped and lunged forward, grabbing a column to steady herself.

Benton was rubbing his eyes to clear them of the pistol water, and I stopped walking and stared in horror when I saw Gertie on the floor right next to him, wedged between his legs and the plant. She was trapped. And as soon as Benton got his eyes clear, she was caught.

I started to launch forward with the float, figuring if I could take Benton out, then Gertie could head off in one direction and I could outrun him. Maybe with my hair up in the hat and the sunglasses on, he wouldn't recognize me. But before I could make my leap, Gertie reached up and pinched the butt of the woman who'd tripped over the suitcase the valet had dropped.

She spun around, eyes locked on Benton, then slapped him as hard as she could across the face. Benton's eyes widened and he stared at her as if she'd lost her mind. The valet rushed up beside Benton as an argument ensued. Gertie crawled away, and I dropped the float, yanked her up from the ground, and we practically ran out of the lobby.

Gertie and Ida Belle ducked into the car and lay low until I was pulling away from the resort. Then they both moved into an upright position and Ida Belle, who had taken the passenger seat, blew out a breath.

"That was a close one," Ida Belle said. "And not a good sign that Benton was back so quickly."

I nodded. "I think we have to assume that the lovely deputy was there to officially collect Gertie for questioning."

"That must mean they have cause of death," Ida Belle said. "And if they got it this quickly, then it was obvious."

"And not natural causes or Benton would have made a phone call and not stopped in first thing on a personal visit. He didn't strike me as motivated enough to inform in person out of the goodness of his soul."

"No," Ida Belle agreed. "He was definitely there for Gertie."

"Maybe there's someone else at the resort on his radar," Gertie said. "After all, we know I didn't kill him but apparently someone did."

"It's certainly a possibility," I said. "But not a lot of time has passed and I don't make Benton for one looking beyond the easy answer."

"I'm not sitting in some rinky-dink, hick sheriff's department for my vacation," Gertie said. "Fortune paid good money for this."

"Yes, she did," Ida Belle said drily. "And once again, your shenanigans have landed us in the hot seat. Next time, Fortune and I are sneaking off to vacation on our own."

"Without me along," Gertie said, "this entire vacation would have been lying like slabs of meat in the sun."

I glanced over at Ida Belle and nodded. "Sounds good."

Gertie flopped back in her seat. "Might as well move to a convent in a sunny area. The only change we'd have to make for you two is Fortune would have to wear something that covered her knees. Ida Belle already has the wardrobe."

"Convents probably frown on weapons," I said. "I don't think I'd like it there. And I wouldn't feel safe without my side piece."

"You don't have one now," Gertie said.

"Says who?" I asked and pulled my nine from my beach bag. "My CIA identification is still valid. The government is horrible at processing paperwork."

"So I couldn't bring one little gun in my luggage," Gertie said, "but you got to stroll on the plane with that?"

"Hey, I slogged through the desert for years, taking out the worst of humanity," I said. "I think I've earned a few perks."

"Fair enough," Gertie said. "And honestly, I feel better that one of us is armed. Especially if there's a killer on the loose."

Ida Belle nodded. "I'm afraid if Benton is an example of local law enforcement, I don't have much confidence that this will go in Gertie's favor. Or go anywhere, to be honest. So if we don't want to get stuck here on an extended non-vacation, I think we better find this killer quickly."

"Maybe we can have it wrapped up before Margarita

Night," Gertie said. "I was really looking forward to all the margaritas I could drink for free."

I rolled my eyes. "We'll do our best not to let a murder interfere with your party."

Ida Belle shook her head. "I'm a little surprised at you, Gertie. You were so hot for this guy and he was murdered. I figured you'd be a bit more upset."

"I'm just being pragmatic," Gertie said. "If someone followed him here and killed him, he probably wasn't a nice guy."

"Could have been a jilted woman," Ida Belle said. "Maybe you're not the first topless damsel he rescued. Maybe Otis made a habit of this sort of thing."

Gertie frowned. "You think some jealous woman might have snuffed Otis over me? That would suck. I mean, I'm a catch but I'm not worth dying over. Especially for a vacation fling."

"No one is worth dying over for a vacation fling," Ida Belle said.

"What about Jason Momoa?" Gertie asked.

I looked over at Ida Belle. "Maybe Jason Momoa."

Ida Belle waved a hand in dismissal. "Forget Aquaman. Here's the reality—either Otis was a real bad guy and someone followed up on business, or he was a playboy and crossed the wrong crazy woman."

"Cause of death might help us determine that," I said. "But short of sending Gertie in for questioning, I don't see how we're going to find out anything. And even then, I don't anticipate that Benton will be forthcoming with information."

"We definitely don't want Gertie to be questioned before we have an attorney lined up," Ida Belle said. "So I guess we need to pursue both angles until we have cause of death. Then we can see if that helps us narrow down one avenue over the other."

I nodded and pulled into a café on the mainland located in a shopping center on the edge of town. "So we start with Otis. With any luck, we can get some dirt on him for the attorney to use. Anything that can point the cops in another direction."

"If Benton is any indication of the department mentality," Ida Belle said, "they're not going to be easy to redirect. Unfortunately, most departments don't have someone with Carter's brains and ethics running the show."

"So we're agreed," I said. "We totally ignore Carter's directive and get right in the middle of a police investigation."

"Isn't that what we always do?" Ida Belle asked.

Gertie nodded. "I'm surprised we're even saying this out loud."

"Hey, I'm all for it," I said, "but we have to remember, this isn't Sinful. You don't know the place and these people like you do the ones back home. And the cops here are looking to make one of us guilty, not innocent."

"We're guilty a lot back in Sinful," Gertie said.

"Not on things that matter," I said. "A few purse explosions aside, we don't commit crimes. Not the kind that count, anyway."

Ida Belle frowned. "She's right. We don't have home field advantage here, and the cops are on the opposite side of what we usually deal with. This is a completely different situation and we need to be very careful. We can't afford a screwup here. There's no one to cover it up."

Even Gertie looked a bit sober as we made our way into the café. We found a table in the back that had unoccupied chairs around it and took our seats. We all ordered coffee and breakfast when the waitress appeared and I pulled out my laptop, ready to take notes as soon as the coffee arrived and the waitress had cleared the area.

"Okay," I said as I created a new Word document. "Give me all the particulars you have on Otis."

Gertie nodded. "His name is Otis Baker. He's from Oklahoma City and was in real estate development. Those strip malls, I believe."

"They have entire malls for stripping?" Ida Belle asked.

"That's what I thought too," Gertie said. "But it's those long buildings in a straight line with multiple stores in them."

"Oh, like where we are now with a Laundromat, pizza place, check-cashing store, and café all in one place?" Ida Belle asked.

"Exactly," Gertie said.

"Wife? Kids?"

"He was widowed two years ago, no kids," Gertie said. "He said after his wife passed, he didn't feel like keeping up with the business anymore, so he sold it. Said everything in Oklahoma City reminded him of his wife. She'd been his business partner and he said everywhere he looked, there was something they'd built. So he sold everything and moved to Florida."

"So he lived here?" I asked. "Then why was he staying at the resort?"

"He said he tried Miami first," Gertie said. "But it was too crowded and not relaxing enough. So he traveled around the state, stopping in different places for a while to see if it seemed like a good fit. He's been here for a month but only at the resort the past couple weeks. He said he got a good off-season rate."

"Probably true," I said. "Summer rates are almost double what I paid."

Ida Belle nodded. "And any developer worth his salt is

rolling in cash anyway. Plus, if he sold everything off...my guess is money isn't something he spent a lot of time worrying about."

"Then let's see how that checks out," I said and did a search on Otis's name along with Oklahoma City. I got a couple good hits immediately. One was an article about a new development that Otis's company was building on the outskirts of town. It was going to contain a low-income medical center, and part of the parking lot had been allocated to build basketball courts for the local kids to play in. There was a blurry image of Otis in the background, cutting a big ribbon strung between two posts in the dirt. I couldn't make out the facial features, but the receding hairline was the same.

The next hit was an obituary for Otis's wife, Marion. She'd died a little over two years earlier from cancer. No kids per the obit. Just a sister-in-law living in a nursing home in Connecticut. The last hit was an article in the business section of the local paper talking about the sale of Otis's company and his plans to retire "where there's sand at my feet and sun in my face."

"So far, he looks legit," I said. "At least, everything he told Gertie checks out."

"But no indication of why someone might want to kill him," Gertie said.

"Ha!" Ida Belle said. "Oldest reason in the book—money. Who gets all that money he cashed out?"

I sighed. "You know, I'm really tired of the money motive. Can't anyone be more original?"

"You mean, like kill people because they got orders from their demon dog?" Gertie asked.

"Okay, maybe not a Berkowitz, but a different motive would be nice," I said.

"I'm afraid money is at the root of most crime," Ida Belle

said. "This time is probably going to prove no different. Did the obituary list any other family?"

I scanned it again. "No. Just the wife's sister."

"I don't think I'm going to bet on a woman in a nursing home in Connecticut popping down to Florida to kill for some cash," Ida Belle said.

"It doesn't seem right," I said. "But some of you seniors can be wily."

Gertie laughed and even Ida Belle smiled.

"Still, I agree she's an unlikely candidate," I said.

"Which means we need to find some likely ones," Ida Belle said. "Unfortunately, the only place to start collecting information is around the resort. If Otis has been there a while, surely he's developed some friendships with staff or regulars at the bar."

I nodded. "But we can't exactly stroll around the resort asking questions about Otis without giving up Gertie to the local cops."

"I wonder if Carter talked to his lawyer friend yet," Gertie said.

My cell phone rang and I picked it up. "Speak of the devil."

"Please tell me you're sitting at the beach and drinking a cocktail," Carter said.

"Can't do that exactly. Benton showed up at the resort again and we had to jet."

Carter cursed and there was several seconds of silence. "The sheriff's department is moving fast."

"I imagine they want this cleared and off their desk. I don't think they really care as much about who did it as they do being able to say someone is under arrest."

"Yeah, I did some asking around about Benton and that sounds about right. Did he see you leave the property?"

"No. He was too busy trying to avoid a sexual assault rap."

"I'm not even going to ask."

"It was one of Gertie's better ideas."

"I'm sure. Well, I talked to my buddy. He's tied up in court today and can't get there until this evening."

"So we lie low until he shows. I can manage that."

"Since when?"

He had a point. My entire summer in Sinful was supposed to have been about lying low. God knows, I'd completely screwed the pooch on that one.

"I'm a work in progress," I said. "But the day I can't dodge one idiot is the day I give up everything and sit down to knit."

He sighed. "Fine, then. Stay away from the resort until Byron can get there. I gave him a rundown of the situation and your contact info. He's supposed to call you when he arrives. I'll text you his info."

"Thanks."

"And Fortune? Please be careful. I can't help you there."

Actually, he could help a lot if he was willing to run a background check on Otis. And I'd bet my eyeteeth that he would, to pass on to Byron. He just wasn't going to share that information with me. It was really exhausting, sometimes, how much time I lost because Carter insisted on following the rules.

"I am aware of my limitations," I said.

"Could have fooled me. Anyway, I'm going to make a few calls and see if I can get some information on the case from my buddies in Florida. Maybe one of them has an inside line with the sheriff's department there and Byron can get this handled through channels."

"Great. In the meantime, we'll spend the day playing the invisible tourists. Talk to you later."

I hung up and filled Ida Belle and Gertie in on the lawyer.

Gertie frowned. "We can't really find out anything about

Otis if we have to stay away. We don't know for sure that Benton was coming for me. What if he was there to see Otis's room, or talk to the staff, or question some other suspect?"

"It's certainly possible," Ida Belle said, "but is it a risk we're willing to take?"

I was about to answer when my phone started ringing. I checked the display and frowned.

"It's local," I said.

"Who would have your phone number here?" Gertie asked.

"The resort," I said. "I had to give them a number when I made the reservation. I'll let it go to voice mail."

I watched the phone, waiting for the ringing to stop, then waited some more to see if whoever was calling left a message. I was about to decide that they hadn't when the signal came through that a message was waiting. I accessed the message and hit Play.

"Ms. Redding, this is Fletcher Sampson, the manager at the Quiet Key Resort. I'm so sorry to bother you, but Deputy Benton is here and he'd like to talk to one of your party members, a Gertie Hebert. Of course, Quiet Key Resort frowns on any disruption to our guests' stay, but Deputy Benton has left me no choice in the matter. When you receive this, can you please contact the sheriff's department and make arrangements for Ms. Hebert to talk to the deputy? Thank you so much and again, I apologize profusely for this disruption to your vacation."

I sat the phone down and relayed the message to Ida Belle and Gertie. "Sampson sounds mad enough to spit," I said.

"Probably afraid we'll blast them on TripAdvisor," Gertie said.

Ida Belle nodded. "Or ask for a bigger discount. So what now?"

"Nothing," I said. "I never got the message. I left my

phone in the car while we were off doing whatever the entire day and didn't see it until this evening."

"Works for me," Ida Belle said. "So what are we going to do the rest of the day?"

Before I could answer, the bell above the door jangled and two local cops walked in.

CHAPTER FIVE

GERTIE SLUMPED IN HER CHAIR AND REACHED FOR THE napkin. Before she could do something suspicious, like drape it over her head, I put my hand on her arm.

"They're not with the sheriff's department," I said. "Just act normal."

"What if they put out an all-points bulletin for my capture?" Gertie asked.

"Oh, good God," Ida Belle said. "You're not the Unabomber. Sit up straight before your spine fuses in that position."

Gertie dragged herself upright. "Maybe we should leave."

She'd barely finished her comment when our waitress appeared with breakfast. As she shuttled food in front of us, I watched out of the corner of my eye as the cops took a seat at a nearby table. The last thing we wanted to do was draw attention to ourselves, and running out the door without taking a bite would rank high on the attention scale.

"This looks great," I said to the waitress and smiled.

"Can I get you anything else?" she asked.

45

We all shook our heads and she strolled over to the cops' table.

"Just eat," I said, my voice low. "And act normal. Talk about vacation stuff."

"I saw some young people surfing yesterday," Ida Belle said. "Not much waves compared to other places but they looked like they were having fun."

"I tried surfing in Hawaii once," I said.

Ida Belle and Gertie both stared, clearly unsure whether I was offering up real information or just contributing to the vacation conversation.

"Really," I said. "I met a surf instructor on the beach and he offered to give me free lessons."

Gertie giggled. "I bet he did. What was the after-lesson cooldown like?"

"Well, mine was driving back to the hotel in my rental car," I said. "I have no idea what his was."

"Tease," Gertie said. "So what was it like?"

"Hard," I said. "I have really good balance and I've snow-skied a good bit, but this was different. And scary. The waves there are huge."

I had been sneaking sideways glances at the cops. When they'd finished ordering, they'd been silent for a bit, and both of them had looked our way. I was certain they could hear what we were saying, but apparently it wasn't interesting, so they'd started their own conversation. I gave Gertie and Ida Belle a thumbs-up where the cops couldn't see it and they both nodded. I continued to regale them with tales of my big surfing day in Hawaii while we ate, and Gertie and Ida Belle told stories about learning to water ski. In between nodding, I listened to the cops.

First, they bitched about their boss, which was pretty standard fare for any human being who worked for someone else. Then one complained about his wife and the other bested him with an even bigger complaint about his mother-in-law.

"Did you hear about the murder on the Key?" Cop One asked.

Cop Two seemed surprised. "That was murder? I figured it was a heart attack."

Cop One nodded. "Me too, but my aunt is dispatch down at the sheriff's department and she overheard one of the deputies saying it was murder."

"What did the medical examiner say?" Cop Two asked.

Cop One shrugged. "They don't tell her anything. She just overhears things sometimes. Anyway, since the sheriff is out for back surgery that fool Benton is in charge of the investigation."

Cop Two snorted. "Benton is barely in charge of zipping his own pants."

"Yeah," Cop One said. "Apparently he went to the resort this morning to bring in one of the suspects and almost got hit with a sexual assault charge after being slapped by a woman who claimed he pinched her butt."

"Benton?" Cop Two looked confused. "He doesn't have the stones to do something like that."

"Oh, I know that," Cop One agreed. "But my aunt had to send another deputy down there to talk the woman off the ledge. It was a real mess. Then they got back to the sheriff's department and apparently someone had called the sheriff. Probably my aunt."

"Isn't he in the hospital?" Cop Two asked.

"Yeah, but he's still trying to run the show by phone," Cop One said. "And my aunt is aligned with him big-time. She has no use for Benton. Anyway, the sheriff got Benton and the other deputy on the phone and yelled for a good ten minutes.

The walls are thin. She heard every bit of the assault story given the speaking volume."

"Did Benton acquire the suspect, at least?" Cop Two asked.

"No," Cop One said. "That was part of the yelling. By the time they got the assault woman handled, the suspect was gone. The resort staff couldn't locate her, so now Benton is on the hot seat until he runs her down."

"Her?" Cop Two sounded surprised. "The suspect is a woman?"

"Hey, these days it's equal opportunity, right?" Cop One asked.

"I guess so," Cop Two said.

"The sheriff ordered Benton to walk every inch of the island until he finds her," Cop One said.

Cop Two laughed. "I give him an hour before he collapses. Benton hasn't seen a treadmill since high school football."

"Let's hope he manages longer," Cop One said. "You know if he can't find the broad we'll be called on to help."

Cop Two sighed. "Us and every other able-bodied cop in the area, and I hate walking in that sand with shoes on." He shook his head. "It's been a long time since they had a murder on the island. The mayor is probably having kittens."

The waitress showed up with their food and they broke off the conversation. They didn't resume it after she left, but it didn't matter. I was pretty sure I'd gotten all they knew, and that was enough to know we had to avoid the entire island until Byron arrived.

I looked over at Ida Belle and Gertie and could tell by their expressions that they'd heard the conversation as well. We'd already figured that sitting on the beach wasn't going to be an option. But clearly, not only did we need to avoid the island, we had to worry that Benton would collapse under the weight of his own lack of physical fitness and political pressure and put a call in to every law enforcement agency in the area.

"I have an idea," Gertie said and reached into her purse. She pulled out a tourist pamphlet and set it on the table.

Ida Belle looked at the pamphlet, then stared at Gertie. "You want to go deep-sea fishing?"

I considered it for a moment. "It's not a bad idea."

Benton would never find us on a boat, and neither would anyone else. And the cops couldn't argue that Gertie was hiding from them if she didn't know they were looking for her and we were simply doing something that normal vacationers did. It's not like we were leaving the area. Not really. In fact, the more I thought about it, the better it sounded, especially when the alternative was spending the entire day avoiding everyone with a badge. Just dodging Benton this morning had proven to be problematic and we'd already run into more law enforcement in the first place we stopped. I didn't want to push our luck.

Or the Gertie factor.

Ida Belle must have come to the same conclusion as me because she nodded. "Fishing it is."

I picked up the bill from the table and tossed some tip money down. Ida Belle and Gertie followed me silently to the front of the café and headed next door to the convenience store to pick up fishing snacks while I paid the bill. A couple minutes later, we hopped in the rental car and Ida Belle called up the fishing charter. Not only was the boat not booked, but since it wasn't high season, the captain gave us a discount on the cost when Ida Belle told him we were interested in a full day.

When she disconnected, Ida Belle looked up the location on her phone and directed me to the marina.

"It's on Quiet Key?" I asked, not as confident as I'd been a moment before.

"Yes," Ida Belle said, "but it's on the opposite end from the resort and on the sound side. Hopefully, Benton will be held up scouring the resort long enough for us to get out to sea."

"But he'll eventually make it to the dock," Gertie said.

"I rented the car with points," Ida Belle said. "So it won't come back to Fortune or you if he runs a check."

"What if he shows someone at the dock a picture and they tell him we're on the boat?" Gertie asked. "He can call the boat back in."

Ida Belle shook her head. "It's either this, run around looking over our shoulder all day, or you turn yourself in now."

"No way," Gertie said. "I'd rather run the risk of fishing."

"You realize there's no escape from that boat, right?" I asked. "Bailing into the ocean and swimming to Cuba is not an option."

Ida Belle looked back at Gertie. "I swear to God, woman, if you bail into that ocean, I will leave you for the sharks. I won't even throw you a life preserver."

"You act like I always need rescuing," Gertie protested.

No one answered.

"Wow," Gertie said. "You have one little date that ends in murder and everyone labels you as trouble."

"You've been labeled as trouble since the womb," Ida Belle said. "Your mother was bedridden her entire pregnancy. This tragic date is merely one blip in a long line of things you manage to get yourself into."

Gertie threw her hands in the air. "No one will have to fend off sharks or throw a life preserver. If Benton finds us before Byron gets here, I'll go happily with him, then proceed to drive them crazy down at the sheriff's department until they wish they'd left me on the boat. But they *will* regret holding me. You can bet on that."

I wasn't about to bet on that. Even without her purse, Gertie could cause more trouble than any ten people put together. And that was without trying. If she set her mind to push the sheriff's department to the edge, they'd all be jumping off it before the day was out.

"So we fish," I said. "Or go out on a fishing boat. I'm not fishing, though. Fishing is work. I came here to relax."

"Because solving a murder is so relaxing," Ida Belle said drily.

"It's more relaxing than my previous job," I said.

"The apocalypse will be more relaxing than your previous job," Ida Belle said. "Turn here."

She pointed to a dirt road that led away from the beach highway and into the weeds. Although here, they called them something fancy. Sea oats, I think. Still looked like weeds to me. I slowed as the car dipped in potholes. The road was a mix of sand and shells dumped there to make it passable, I assumed. They'd barely succeeded.

"I feel like I'm back in Sinful," I said as we hit a particularly deep hole and I bounced off the seat.

"Except we're not in Ida Belle's Time Machine of Death doing 180 miles per hour," Gertie said.

"I'm happy to drive slower as soon as we're not being chased by the police or someone who wants to shoot us," Ida Belle said. "I drive slow to church."

"You do not," Gertie said. "Last week, you slid into a parking space and jumped out of the car and took off while it was still running. Fortune barely hit the brake before we took out four Catholics."

"I was late for choir," Ida Belle said. "And I'd already

assessed the Catholics. None of them would have dented my bumper."

The car lurched through one last big dip and the sea oats disappeared to reveal a clearing that ran right up to the water and served as a parking area. To the right was a marina with rows of boats in slips. Directly in front of us was a boat launch and a small dock. An old cabin cruiser was tied off at the end.

"Are you sure that thing can float?" I asked.

"It's floating now," Gertie said.

"I'm not concerned about now," I said. "That's three feet of water with minnows in it. I'm more concerned about thirty feet of water with God knows what in it."

"It's pretty clear offshore," Gertie said. "You'll be able to see God knows what."

"Great," I mumbled. "I love knowing what might kill me."

Ida Belle grinned. "Boats last a long time unless Gertie owns them. Some peeling paint won't stop it from floating."

"Good thing," I said and climbed out. We retrieved our beach bags, stuffed the snacks inside, and headed for the boat. As we stepped onto the dock, a man emerged from the boat cabin and smiled.

Midthirties. Six feet tall. One hundred ninety pounds. Nose broken several times before. Has never used sunscreen. Surgical scar on right elbow and left ankle. Even without my pistol, those weaknesses gave me the edge. Threat potential medium unless he started hitting on me.

"You must be the ladies who called about the boat," he said. "I'm Deep Sea Dave."

"Nice to meet you, Deep Sea," Gertie said. "I'm Saltwater Sally. This is Crabby Cathy and Landlubber Lisa."

Dave grinned. "Well, you guys come on board. I've already got the fishing equipment loaded and picked out a good spot a ways offshore. Should take a couple hours to get there. Unless you guys want to stay closer to shore."

I struggled with the options. Farther out meant less likely to be seen or accosted and a longer ride in if Benton managed to track us down. But closer to shore meant the option of swimming to safety if things went south. And things always seemed to go south.

"I wouldn't mind staying closer to shore," I said. "You never know when an emergency will arise."

Dave nodded. "The sea is unpredictable. Lots of people prefer to stay closer in. Except the men escaping their wives, of course. They want me to go as far as possible. Would probably settle for Mexico."

"Their wives would probably settle for one of those uncharted islands inhabited by cannibals," Ida Belle said.

"Ha!" Dave laughed. "You guys are going to be a hoot. I'm going to grab the ice."

He jumped onto the dock and headed for an old pickup truck parked near our rental. We stepped onto the boat and headed into the cabin to take a look around. It was old but clean, which surprised me. Dave didn't strike me as the type of guy with a woman cleaning up after him, which meant he was doing the housekeeping himself.

The first room of the cabin was a small living area with kitchenette. It contained a mini fridge, a microwave, and a coffeepot. Basically, the things you had to have to live. Someone like me could move in and retire here. The front part of the boat was a bedroom and a tiny bathroom. And I mean airplane-size tiny. But you could sit on the toilet and take a shower at the same time. There was something to be said for efficiency.

As I popped back into the main cabin, Dave poked his head in. "I'm ready to shove off if you ladies are."

"We're ready," Gertie said and clapped her hands, the fact that she was suspect #1 in a murder investigation apparently long gone from her mind. Louisiana people really loved their fishing. It seemed to cure most any ill.

"Cool," Dave said. "I'll be driving from up top if anyone wants to come up and take in the view. It's a little tight, but two people fit up there well enough." He gave me a suggestive look and I struggled not to grimace.

"We'll probably unpack our snacks and then just lounge on the back until we anchor," I said.

Dave looked a bit disappointed but headed off.

"Looks like I'm not the only one picking up stray men," Gertie said, and elbowed me.

"I am not picking up any men, stray or otherwise," I said. "I already have a man, and that's one more than you guys recommend anyway."

"Got that right," Ida Belle said. "Besides, Landlubber and Deep Sea aren't exactly a good combo. Even if Fortune went blind, deaf, and dumb, I don't think Dave is on her list of things to do."

"That's because she's got Captivating Carter waiting for her back home," Gertie said and giggled. "I crack myself up."

"That's one person, at least," Ida Belle said. "And what's with calling me Crabby? I'm not crabby. I'm a pragmatist. It's not my fault most things swing toward the negative."

"Let's unpack," I said, interrupting the argument that I'd already heard a million times. "As soon as we round the end of the island and head into the Gulf, we can leave the cabin. But until then, I think we should stay put."

Ida Belle nodded. "Good idea. If someone spots us, they might pass along the information to Benton."

"You really think Benton is likable enough that people would want to help him?" Gertie asked.

"No," Ida Belle said. "He's obnoxious enough that people would give him information so he'd go away."

We put our sodas and some chocolate bars in the fridge and placed bread, peanut butter, chips, and peanuts on the counter, then flopped on the couch to wait.

"Do you think Dave is a local?" Gertie asked.

"Probably," Ida Belle said. "Why?"

"I was thinking he might know the local gossip," Gertie said. "You know how fisherman talk back in Sinful. Heck, fishing is an excuse to drink and gossip for most of them."

"But Otis didn't turn up dead until this morning," I said. "Even if he's heard about it, there hasn't been enough time for speculation to start."

"If there's been enough time to drink beer," Gertie said, "that's enough time for speculation."

"True," Ida Belle said. "But it sounds like the only leak in the sheriff's department is the dispatcher and they keep her in the dark as much as possible. If there's no gossip available, Dave couldn't hear it."

"No," Gertie agreed. "But he might have known Otis. He's been on the island for a while and he told me his favorite thing to do was deep-sea fishing. Dave might have taken him out before."

I nodded. "It wouldn't hurt to travel down that road. And it should be an easy enough conversation to start. It's not every day a tourist is murdered in a resort you're vacationing in."

Ida Belle sighed. "You mean we have to do the worrywart woman act?"

"If I can do it, you can," I said. "It's just one conversation. It won't kill you to pretend you're scared of something for a bit."

"I'm scared of plenty of things," Ida Belle said. "Uninsured motorists, the contents of Gertie's purse, seeing Celia's underwear again..."

I laughed and looked out the window. "Well, we've rounded the island and are headed for deep water. Let's get the heck out of here and avoid this carpet that smells like stale beer and fish."

We headed out of the cabin and stretched out across the benches that circled all three sides of the open deck. The sun immediately began to warm my skin. I lay back on the bench and sighed.

If it weren't for murder, this would be such a nice day.

CHAPTER SIX

A SPLASH OF COLD WATER HIT ME DIRECTLY IN THE FACE, jolting me upright. I sputtered, blowing the water everywhere, and blinked. Gertie stood over me, her hands dripping wet.

"Thought you could use a little cooling off," she said. "Your face was red."

"You could have fanned me," I said then looked around. "Are we there yet?"

Gertie nodded. "And anchored. Ida Belle went up front to help Dave haul out the fishing gear."

"Then that's my cue to break out my e-reader," I said, and ducked back in the cabin to snag the device from my beach bag. I wasn't addicted to fishing like other people in Sinful. Maybe it was part of their DNA.

Gertie was shaking her head when I came back onto the deck. "You'd really rather read than fish? I thought you'd grow out of that."

"I hate to tell you, but I'm sorta already grown," I said.

Gertie waved a hand in dismissal. "I'm a couple years older than you and I'm not grown."

Ida Belle snorted as she exited the cabin. "In dog years

you're still a decade older. And I took that 'grown' thing off the table a long time ago."

Dave stepped out beside Ida Belle and looked over at me. "You're not fishing?" he asked.

"No thanks," I said. "I'm big on eating fish. Just not so much on catching, cleaning, and cooking them."

"She's more of a hunter," Ida Belle said.

"Big game?" Dave asked.

I plopped down on the bench and stuck a pillow behind my back so I could lean against the cabin. "You could say that. Used to be, anyway."

He frowned. "Don't tell me those people from PETA converted you."

"Nope. I still love a medium-rare steak more than life itself," I said. "I just decided to exchange some of my more strenuous activities for more relaxing ones."

He nodded and handed Gertie a rod and a container of bait. "I gave up arm wrestling down at the Shark Bar. Doc said if I broke my arm one more time, he was going to have to replace it with a hook. I mean, that's kinda cool, but I don't see how I could cast with a hook for an arm."

"Maybe just hang it over the side of the boat and swish it around," Ida Belle suggested.

He brightened. "I hadn't thought about that."

Ida Belle closed her eyes and shook her head. "I didn't realize God had let some of you out of Louisiana," she mumbled.

"What?" Dave asked as he cast his rod and stuck it in a holder.

"Nothing," Ida Belle said as she sent her bait flying into the ocean. "I was just thinking about how you remind me of someone back home."

Dave winked at her. "Bet he's good-looking."

"Definitely reminds me of some people back home," Ida Belle mumbled.

"Tell us more about this Shark Bar," Gertie said as she baited her hook. "We have a bar back home that's outside the normal fare."

"Really?" Dave perked up. "Where you guys from?"

"Louisiana," Gertie said.

Dave nodded. "Louisiana's kindred sisters with Florida. We do things different than the rest of the country. Better, of course."

"Of course," Gertie agreed. "So, this Shark Bar..."

"It's on the mainland," Dave said. "You turn at the good tattoo parlor and follow the trail into the marsh. The bar's nothing much to look at but they price alcohol reasonable and they limit the crowd to two fistfights a night. Cuts down on repairs."

I stared at Dave, fascinated that the Swamp Bar was apparently a chain. "If they limit the number of fights, wouldn't everyone show up early so they could be one of the two?"

Dave grinned. "Real smart of the owner, right? Used to, most people didn't show up till nine or after. But when he put in the fight rule, everybody started coming around seven. I bet Booger doubled his profits. He's really smart at the business stuff."

Ida Belle frowned. "Booger?"

"Yeah, he owns the bar," Dave said. "He got the nickname because—"

Ida Belle held up a hand. "That's all right. Sometimes a little mystery makes things more interesting."

"That's what my old girlfriend used to say when she wouldn't tell me where she was going Friday nights," Dave said. "I suppose sneaking around with her ex-husband might have been more interesting for *her*, but I didn't get it."

"Maybe we'll check out the Shark Bar while we're here," Gertie said.

"No!" Ida Belle and I both responded at once.

Dave looked a bit confused at our strong reactions. "It's safe and all, if that's what you're worried about. Tourists find it quite a bit and all of them have made it out okay."

"That's not it," I said, trying to adopt the best worried-female look I could manage. "It's just that we rarely get away for vacation and then the police were at the resort this morning. One of the maids said a guest was murdered...it's a little worrisome that someone could be killed at a place like that."

Dave scowled. "That was all the talk this morning down at the bait shop. But whatever happened to Otis Baker, he had it coming."

I glanced over at Ida Belle, then looked back at Dave. Strong emotions usually came from a bad place, and thinking someone had death coming was a fairly strong emotion. "You knew the guy?" I asked.

"Yeah, I knew him. He took my mom out for a while. Took her for a bunch of money, too. Then disappeared."

I blinked. Nothing about what Dave had just said made sense.

"Disappeared?" I asked. "You mean he used to live on the mainland?"

Dave nodded. "Stayed at one of those cheap motels but the manager said he cleared out in the middle of the night. I've been looking for him a couple weeks now. I didn't think to look at the resorts. And here he's been under my nose all this time."

"You said he took your mother for a bunch of money?" Ida Belle said.

Dave nodded. "Gave her some sob story about not having the money for his chemo treatment. He was gone a lot. Always claimed he was in Naples at the clinic. I told my mom he looked awfully healthy for someone with cancer."

"Was he losing his hair?" I asked. Otis had sported a receding hairline, like a lot of men in his age group, but I was pretty sure it was his own hair. I mean, if you were going to get the fake stuff, wouldn't you get more of it?

"He had thin hair on his head, about like every other guy his age," Dave said. "But his back looked like a carpet. He was always sitting on his butt at my mom's pool. Grossed me out. It was like bigfoot was squatting there, you know?"

That explained why Otis was wearing a T-shirt in the water. I was going to hazard a guess that Dave's revulsion was partially the back hair but mostly that Otis was running a con on his mother. And I had no doubt it was a con because the story he'd given Dave's mom was completely different from the one he'd given Gertie. My guess was Dave's anger came from trying to warn his mom off, in his own charming, ineffective, redneck way, and he'd been shot down. Unfortunately, lonely senior women were easy targets for a charmer like Otis. But more importantly, we now had a motive for Otis's murder.

And a suspect.

Granted, Dave didn't rank high on my list of people who could have pulled off a murder, but then Benton wasn't high on my list of cops who were good at solving homicides, so it might be a draw. Which meant if we didn't get involved, Benton would make his case against Gertie and wash his hands of the entire affair until a defense attorney picked it apart. But now it wasn't going to be that easy. What we'd just learned cast a dark shadow over the victim.

"Dave?" Ida Belle asked. "I don't suppose you have heavier weights? I think I'm going to try for something larger."

He'd been scowling at the water, and Ida Belle's question

seemed to draw him out of his thoughts. "I think I've got some up front. I'll go get them."

As soon as he was out of earshot, Ida Belle and Gertie stepped over beside me. "If what Dave said is true, what are the chances that his mother was the only one Otis took to the cleaners?"

"Slim to none," I said. "All those cancer trips to Naples were probably time he was spending working other women."

"But he didn't give me the cancer line at all," Gertie said.

"Maybe he was working a different angle at the resort," I said. "Hard to work the 'broke and dying of cancer' routine when you're staying at an expensive resort and partaking of fruity drinks on the beach all day."

Ida Belle nodded. "I'm sure you're right. Which gives us an unknown number of suspects. I don't know whether that makes me happy or tired."

"Both," I said. "It gives Byron a reason to argue Gertie didn't do it, at least. She didn't know Otis long enough to give him money."

"Nor would I ever be that foolish," Gertie said. "I can be intentionally silly about a lot of things, but no man is ever going to take me for my hard-earned money."

"Dave's coming," Ida Belle said, and glanced over at Gertie. "Give him a sob story about your date with Otis to get more out of him. Fortune and I will play dumb on the dinner date."

They hustled back to their rods as Dave stepped back out on the deck. "Here ya go," he said, and passed Ida Belle the heavier weights.

"Thanks," Ida Belle said as she reeled in her line to make the replacement.

"Is everything all right?" Dave asked Gertie, who'd been staring out at the ocean and frowning.

"What?" Gertie turned around and gave him a blank stare

before zeroing in on him. "I'm sorry. I guess I'm a bit distracted. And somewhat aggravated with myself."

"Fishing is all about relaxing," he said. "Don't let it stress you out."

Gertie waved a hand in dismissal. "It's not the fishing. It's just that when you said the dead guy was Otis, I was stunned. I met him on the beach yesterday. He was really nice and invited me to dinner with him last night."

I gasped. "*That's* who you went to dinner with last night? Good Lord!"

"In my defense, I didn't know someone was going to kill him," Gertie said. "I was just trying to have a bit of fun on my vacation."

Ida Belle shook her head. "Wow. That's some kind of timing you have."

"It's really disappointing," Gertie said. "Not that he was killed, although I suppose I should be upset about it. But I guess I'm more bothered by the fact that I thought he was interested in me. I should have known it was all a setup. I haven't had a man chasing me since Reagan was president."

Ida Belle coughed. "Lincoln."

"I'm really sorry, ma'am," Dave said and gave her a sympathetic look. "Did you give him any money?"

Gertie shook her head. "Nothing like that, but I suppose that's where it was all going, right?"

"I'm afraid that's probably the case," he said. "I talked to a lawyer about it after Otis pulled a Houdini and Mom finally fessed up to giving him the money. The lawyer said based on what I told him, this guy Otis was a professional con man. That guys like him make a living that way. Probably has a bunch of identities and a whole book of sob stories that he uses. He said the guy we knew as Otis was probably long gone with my mom's money and using it to set up his next target."

Gertie let out a long-suffering sigh.

Dave shook his head, clearly angry. "He shouldn't have done the things he did. Taking advantage of women that way. I mean, all guys try to work an angle at times, but it's because we want to get in a woman's pants, not her wallet."

His face reddened. "Sorry. That was kinda crude."

"We're old," Ida Belle said. "We invented crude."

Gertie sniffed. "It is rather disheartening, but I can see why women would fall for it. He really has his romance routine down pat. Your attorney is probably right. I bet there's more women than just your mother with lighter purses because of him."

"Yeah, I'm sure that's the case," he said. "I suppose I should just be happy that he can't do it anymore, but I'm still too pissed that I wasn't the one who got to put him out of business."

"Your mother is much better off that it was someone else," Ida Belle said.

"I know you're right," Dave said. "But there's times when a man just needs to be a man, you know?"

"You're a good son," Ida Belle said. "That makes you a good man in my book."

Dave looked slightly embarrassed and headed back for the cabin. "I'm going to grab some chips. You guys want anything?"

We all shook our heads and he disappeared inside. I glanced over at Gertie and gave her a thumbs-up. Ida Belle gave her an approving nod.

I had to give the old girl a solid ten on her acting job. She'd played up the disenchanted senior part so well I almost bought it myself. Except that I knew Gertie. She would have never lent Otis money. And if he'd managed to take advantage of her in another way, I had no doubt she'd have made fire rain on him like something out of the Old Testament.

Dave came back out and sat on the side of the boat, eating his chips. I could see him out of the corner of my eye. His expression was somewhat morose as he stared out over the ocean. But then he turned away and for an instant, I thought I saw the flicker of a smile. I looked down at my e-reader, pretending I was into my book, but my mind was racing.

Was Dave the good ole boy he seemed to be? Or was it an act to conceal something else? He wouldn't be the first person I'd come across pretending to be something he wasn't for his own gain. My guess was the local-boy personality got him more satisfied clients than the corporate offerings that were sprinkled among the local fare. More importantly, had he really been unaware that Otis was staying at the resort? Or was he covering his butt since he had motive up the wazoo?

Maybe the smile was nothing. Or maybe he was just happy Otis was dead. Still, we only had his word for it that he hadn't known where Otis was and hadn't killed him.

His word wasn't enough.

———

THE MORNING TURNED INTO THE AFTERNOON AND stretched out quietly as everyone but me reeled in fish after fish. Finally, Dave called it quits because we'd run out of space to house any more, but the haul had definitely perked him up from his earlier mood. They reeled in their lines, packed up the gear, and then we all sat on the back deck, drinking soda and passing around a bag of chocolate chip cookies.

A pod of dolphins started surfacing near the boat and Gertie got all excited.

"Look!" she yelled, pointing as one jumped out of the water and did a twirl. "You don't see that back home."

Even Ida Belle looked pleased. "No. You certainly don't."

I watched as they poked their heads up and rolled around in the surf. "Are they eating?" I asked.

"Nah," Dave said. "They're just fooling around—probably were riding the wake of that boat over there. It pushes a pretty big one. They like to surf on the wake of the big boats."

I looked over and saw a yacht about fifty yards away. "Wow! That is some boat."

Dave nodded. "Best boat around. Looks like something that belongs in Miami, right?"

"Who does it belong to?" I asked.

Dave shrugged. "I don't know the guy. Seen him a time or two. Some suit with a two-hundred-dollar haircut. A friend of mine works over at the airport and said he flies in on a private plane. The manager at your resort is friends with him or at least knows him well enough that he gets to go out on his boat."

"Maybe it's the resort owner," Ida Belle said. "It's not part of any big conglomerate. At least not the usual names."

"That would make sense," Dave said. "Ain't no one around here with that kind of money, that's for sure. But that resort has to be making bank. I heard they charge five hundred a night in the summer."

"Yep," I said. "Which is why we're taking advantage of off-season pricing. Also fewer people."

"It's a good time to do it," Dave said. "I lower my prices when the hotels do. Got to go with the market, you know?"

"Well, we absolutely got our money's worth," Gertie said. "That's the best haul I've had fishing in a long time."

"It will take me about an hour to clean your catch," Dave said. "So we need to head back in by five if you're wanting to take those home tonight. Otherwise, you can pick 'em up tomorrow. I can package them all up for you."

"Oh, you can keep the fish," Ida Belle said. "We're not interested in cooking on our vacation."

Dave's face brightened at his good fortune. "Seriously? You don't want none of 'em?"

"I'm not putting fresh fish in that rental car," Ida Belle said. "I'd never get my deposit back."

"Thanks, guys," Dave said. "That's supercool."

"You'll be eating fish for a month," Gertie said. "That was quite a haul."

"I'll give some to my mom but I'll sell the rest," Dave said. "A lot of what we caught brings good prices down at the fish market. And I've got connections with a couple of the restaurants around. They like the fresh stuff for the daily specials. Don't get me wrong—I love me a fish fry, but selling fish pays the rent. Eating 'em doesn't."

Ida Belle nodded. "We live in a bayou town near the Gulf. Lots of professional fishermen and shrimpers. When the market's up, you sell fish and eat steak. When the market is down, you eat fish."

Dave grinned. "I like that. You ladies have been great customers. It don't always work out that way."

His marine radio went off, sending static out so loud Dave and Gertie both gave a start. He didn't seem to notice that neither Ida Belle nor I even flinched. He started cursing about the radio and hurried up the ladder to the top.

"Come in Dave," the voice on the radio said. "This is Garfish."

"Yeah, Garfish," Dave answered. "Why the hell you yelling on my radio?"

"You out today?" Garfish asked.

"Who's asking?" Dave answered.

"That deputy, Benton, was here," Garfish said. "Said he's looking for three women, two of them seniors and one young hottie. You take anyone out fitting that description?"

I grimaced. *Hottie?*

Ida Belle caught my expression and grinned.

I shot a worried look over at Gertie. This was it. Benton had tracked us down and it was too early for Byron to have arrived.

"Nope," Dave said. "Got two old men and a pit bull with bad breath. And if I had a hottie on board, I wouldn't be telling that butthole Benton about it. For that matter, you never even would have raised me on the radio."

"Roger that," Garfish said.

We all remained silent as Dave climbed down the ladder.

"I guess you heard that," he said.

We all nodded.

"Any reason I should know about that you got cops looking for you?"

CHAPTER SEVEN

WE ALL LOOKED AT DAVE AND SHOOK OUR HEADS, FEIGNING innocence.

"Oh," I said, sitting up straight. "I bet he wants to talk to Gertie—you know, since she had dinner with that scammer Otis last night."

"I bet you're right," Ida Belle said.

"What in the world do I have to tell them?" Gertie said. "We were sitting right smack in the middle of the resort restaurant, surrounded by a hundred other vacationers. Even if Otis planned on telling me all his secrets, it wouldn't have been in public. And it's not like I knew he was a scammer until today."

"That might be the case, but I wouldn't recommend talking to Benton about nothing without a lawyer," Dave said, looking a bit worried.

"That doesn't sound very encouraging," Ida Belle said.

"He's made a career out of lazy," Dave said. "I sat in jail for two days over trumped-up charges just because he didn't want to do his job. If Benton is supposed to figure out who killed

Otis, it's the killer's lucky day. Benton could have video of the whole thing and wouldn't know what to do about it."

"Maybe we *should* get an attorney before Gertie talks to the cops," I said and nodded at Dave. "Thanks for the heads-up. And for lying. You didn't have to do that. But it will give us time to run down an attorney."

"Heck, I'd hole up Jack the Ripper on my boat if Benton was looking for 'im," Dave said. "Besides, a group of Boy Scouts is more dangerous than you ladies."

I struggled not to smile. "You gotta watch those Boy Scouts. They're sneaky."

"Darn right," Dave said. "That's why I said so. I had a group of 'em on the boat once and I won't ever do it again. They cleaned me out of all my best lures and a six pack of beer."

"You're not going to get into any trouble if Benton finds out we were on your boat, are you?" Gertie asked.

Dave waved a hand in dismissal. "How's he gonna find out? He's too lazy to drive out to the dock. That's why he had Garfish radio me. Besides, all I have to do to avoid him is stay on my boat. That idiot is afraid of water."

I stared. "He works on an island."

"I know," Dave said. "Dumbest thing ever. We had a floater down at the dock a couple years back. Local drunk, so no one was really surprised, but we wasn't pulling him out of the water, either. That ain't our job. Anyway, Benton shows up and tries to fish the body over with a pole and falls off the dock. He's in maybe three feet of water and can see the bottom and was still thrashing around like he was in the middle of the ocean. We watched him and laughed for a while, but when we realized he wasn't going to get himself out, a couple guys went in and dragged him onto shore. Had to call the paramedics to get him oxygen."

I looked over at Gertie. "Well, if Benton gets sideways with you during the questioning, throw a glass of water in his face."

Dave wagged his finger at me. "I like you. You wanna grab a hot dog or something later?"

"I appreciate the offer," I said, "but I imagine we'll be busy with this Otis thing, and besides, I have a boyfriend."

"He ain't here, is he?" Dave asked.

I blinked. "Does that matter?"

"Matters to me," Dave replied.

"Well, it matters to me, too, but in a different way," I said. "So it's still a no."

Dave shrugged. "Suit yourself. If you change your mind, I'll probably be at the Shark Bar tonight. Well, and tomorrow night. Come to think of it, you can probably find me there most any night."

"I'll keep that in mind in case I lose my moral compass," I said.

"Sounds fancy," Dave said. "Hope you have it insured."

I just sighed.

———

FINALLY, THE TIME CAME WHEN WE HAD TO HEAD BACK TO the dock. We were just approaching the channel to the sound when I got a text from Byron that he was ten miles out and would meet us at a coffee shop down the street from the sheriff's department so that he and Gertie could go in together.

I passed along the information to Ida Belle and Gertie. "Guess we better pack up and get ready to deboat. Or whatever you call it."

Suddenly, the boat slowed so much that we swayed a bit. A second later, Dave peered over the rail.

"We have a problem," he said. "A buddy just phoned me. Benton is at the dock."

"How did he find out we were on the boat?" I asked.

"I thought he never came to the dock," Gertie said.

Dave shook his head. "I got no idea on either. What do you want me to do? I can take you on an overnight."

"We appreciate the offer," I said, "but Gertie's attorney is almost here and plans on meeting us in town. We were going to review things first, but I suppose we might as well get this over with."

Dave nodded. "I'm real sorry he figured it out. Kinda surprises me. Someone must have seen us going down the channel. Someone with a warrant, probably. People will give up their own mother to avoid a night in jail. Even if it means helping Benton."

"No worries," I said. "We've dealt with worse than Benton."

Dave didn't look convinced but he disappeared and the boat started moving again.

"So what's the plan?" Ida Belle asked.

I pulled out my cell phone. "First, I call Byron and tell him there's been a change in plans. He can meet us at the sheriff's department. Then we repeatedly stress to Gertie how she needs to keep her mouth shut until Byron is there."

Gertie frowned. "I know how to keep my mouth shut."

"You might know how," Ida Belle said, "but you rarely elect to."

I dialed Byron and updated him on our situation, then disconnected. We were approaching the dock and I could see Benton standing back about ten feet from the water.

"Look at that coward," Ida Belle said. "I bet he can't even take a bath."

"What coward?" Gertie asked, squinting at the dock.

Ida Belle sighed and explained Benton's choice of standing location to our nearsighted friend. Gertie smiled.

"I'm about to have some fun," she said.

"Oh no," Ida Belle said. "This isn't Sinful. You can't go having fun with law enforcement in Florida. Remember Freddy Flounder?"

Gertie waved a hand in dismissal. "Everyone knows he was sick of Freda and ran off with a cocktail waitress."

"Except said cocktail waitress is still employed at that dive bar," Ida Belle said, "but Freddy never surfaced."

"So he found another cocktail waitress to buy his line of bull," Gertie said. "There's never a shortage of foolish women."

"Who's Freddy Flounder?" I asked, unable to help myself.

"A former Sinful local," Ida Belle said. "He came to Florida on a fishing trip, had a run-in with local law enforcement over a bar fight, and we never saw him again."

"And you think law enforcement did what?" I asked. "Dumped him in the Gulf? Fed him to alligators?"

"Law enforcement didn't do anything to him," Gertie said. "If anyone bumped off Freddy, it was his wife Freda."

"Freda had an alibi," Ida Belle said. "She was at that fat camp."

"And came back even fatter," Gertie said. "Some alibi."

That familiar feeling of confusion washed over me. It was a common occurrence when Ida Belle and Gertie started discussing some of the more colorful happenings in Sinful. My mind was full of questions— Did Florida law enforcement really bump people off for being drunk? Did Freda kill her husband? And was Flounder a real last name?

But all those questions would have to wait because Dave was pulling up to the dock. I glanced over at Benton and saw him glaring at us. I grabbed my beach bag and prepared to issue the rebuttal to his accusations because I knew there was no way in hell I could keep my mouth shut. In some ways, Gertie and I had that in common.

Dave came down the ladder to tie off the boat. Even though I could have jumped off from ten feet away, I saw no reason to rush the process. Might as well irritate Benton a while longer. Apparently, everyone else had the same idea. Dave took his time with the ropes, cautioning us to wait until the boat was secure before we attempted to disembark. Benton was practically fuming before I finally stepped off onto the dock. Ida Belle followed behind, making a big production of passing me her bag first and pretending she needed help from Dave and me to make the step out. Dave stood there politely, letting her use his arm for support, struggling not to smile.

Then it was Gertie's turn.

Ida Belle and I stood by, waiting to make sure she made it onto the dock without incident, but Gertie had other plans. She stood in the back of the boat and just stared at us. Finally, she put down her bag and crossed her arms. Benton, who'd been anxiously tapping his foot, couldn't take it any longer. He stepped forward about five feet and started in on her.

"Get off that boat right now," he yelled, "or I'm placing you under arrest."

"For what exactly?" Ida Belle asked.

"For hiding from law enforcement," Benton said. "I've been looking for you all day and you intentionally fled the resort."

"Excuse me?" I said. "We're on vacation and went fishing. Are you trying to tell me that people who vacation here never go fishing? Because I don't know a judge or jury in the world that's going to buy that one."

"Back off, Benton," Dave said. "These ladies booked two

weeks ago and we've got three ice chests full of fish to show for the day. Ain't their fault some piece of crap who was scamming women finally bought it. If you guys did your job, people like Otis wouldn't be in business."

"You might want to watch your mouth," Benton said. "I'm sure I could find a reason to bring you in as well. Harboring fugitives comes to mind."

"Oh, for Christ's sake," I said. "Since no one has been arrested, much less tried and convicted, we're hardly fugitives. Unless you consider everyone on a boat with a fishing pole a fugitive."

"If she hasn't done anything, then she'll get off that boat and come with me," Benton said.

"Famous last words of every incompetent cop who railroaded a witness," Ida Belle muttered.

"Am I under arrest?" Gertie asked.

"Yes," Benton said.

"Really?" I asked him. "On what grounds? May I speak to your DA?"

A flush ran up Benton's face. "My DA is too busy to be bothered with your nonsense."

"And you're too busy to be bothered with the law," I said.

"Fine," Benton said. "I'm detaining Ms. Hebert for questioning. Just as soon as she gets off that boat."

"You're going to have to come get me," Gertie said and plopped down on the bench.

I smiled, now understanding Gertie's plan. If Benton wanted to play hardball, she was going to make him walk on water in order to take her in. It was clever and just a tiny bit evil. I loved it.

I moved over and waved Benton by. "You heard the woman," I said. "Break out the cuffs if you have to. But apparently, she's not getting off that boat unless you make her."

Gertie pulled a bag of chips out of her beach bag and started to eat. Benton's face got so red, I thought it might explode. Dave jumped back on the boat and reached for an ice chest.

"While you guys work this out, I'm just gonna unload the fish," Dave said. "I got a hot date tonight with a six-pack and these fish ain't gonna clean themselves."

I watched as he positioned the ice chest on the side of the boat, then repositioned his hands on the bottom of the chest to set it over on the dock. It was an inefficient move given that the chest had handles, but then I noticed the plug in the bottom side of the chest had been pulled loose and water was seeping out onto the dock. Dave gave me a wink, then headed to the other side of the boat for another chest.

Benton had finally decided he didn't have a choice in the matter and pulled out his handcuffs. "Since you're going to make this difficult," he said, "I'm going to have to put you in cuffs."

Gertie waved a hand in dismissal. "No matter. As bad as you're dragging butt, I'll be done with my chips by then. If I didn't know any better, I'd think you're one of those pansies who's afraid of water."

That did it. Anger and insult surpassed fear and Benton stomped toward the boat, looking mad enough to shoot her. He hesitated slightly before stepping onto the dock, but his pride was too strong to actually stop. So he barreled forward, slamming his foot down right in the slimy, fishy water that had leaked out of the ice chest.

His shoe connected with the fish water and shot right out from under him. His momentum sent him spiraling down onto the dock. He hit right on the edge and desperately clutched at the weathered wood, trying to keep himself from falling, but it was outside of his control. His hands dragged across the wood and I cringed, knowing he'd be digging splinters out of them for hours. Then he looked back at us, his eyes wide with fright, before he dropped into the sound.

He surfaced immediately, yelling like he was being attacked by sharks. Ida Belle and I strolled over and stood on the dock, looking down at him. Gertie had finished her chips and got off the bench to peer over the side of the boat. Dave simply laughed and set off to his truck with one of the ice chests.

"Help!" Benton screamed. "Please!"

"Stand up, you idiot," Ida Belle said. "You're in three feet of water."

"No!" Benton insisted, still thrashing about. "It's deep. Really deep."

"I can see your shoes," I said. "No one is getting in that water to drag your big butt out. Now put your legs underneath you and stand up."

Gertie leaned over the side of the boat with a life preserver and Benton gave her a grateful look. Then she slapped him across the face with it. Benton gasped and took in a mouthful of salt water, then he started choking. Finally, Dave ended his horror by snagging his pants with a gaff and pulling him upright.

"You better lock those knees," Dave said. "I don't hold dead weight unless I can eat it for dinner."

Benton finally managed to get control of himself and gathered his legs underneath him. Clutching the dock, he staggered up the bank. He was soaking wet from head to toe, and there was a big hole in the back of his pants where Dave had hooked him. His underwear was pink. I took that to mean Benton either had delicate taste in undergarments or had no idea how to do laundry properly.

When he was finally firmly on dry land, he turned around and shook his fist at Gertie. "I should arrest you for assault."

"You mean you should arrest the dock for assault?" Gertie asked. "Because I never touched you. But hey, go for it. I'm sure the judge and everyone in the courtroom would love to hear about you screaming like a sissy in three feet of water."

"Get off that boat or I'm calling the state police to get you off for me," Benton said.

Gertie rolled her eyes. "I'm done with my snack anyway."

She grabbed her bag and Dave assisted her onto the dock. "I don't suppose I can ride with Fortune?" she asked. "You kinda smell."

I swear, if there hadn't been so many witnesses, Benton would have throttled her with his bare hands.

"Not only are you riding in the back of my car," he said, "you're wearing cuffs."

Gertie smiled. "I usually make a man buy me dinner before he puts cuffs on me."

Dave laughed and Benton shot him a dirty look. Gertie dropped her bag and stuck out her hands. Benton snapped on the cuffs and marched her to his car where he shoved her in the back, doing that head thing that I saw on those real cop shows. Then he put the car in Drive and floored it, throwing dust and gravel all over.

I pulled a hundred out of my wallet and passed it to Dave, who looked shocked.

"I can't take this," Dave said. "You already paid me."

"Consider it a bonus," I said.

"For what?"

"For not taking us back in when you knew Benton was looking for us. For lying about when we made the reservation. And most importantly, for leaking that fishy water out on the dock. That was genius."

He grinned and slipped the hundred in his pocket. "I got him good, didn't I? That guy has had one coming from me for a long time. You best get to the sheriff's department and help out Ms. Gertie. If you want to take another trip, just let me know. You're the best customers I've had this year. And by far the most entertaining."

I smiled. "We get that a lot."

CHAPTER EIGHT

IDA BELLE AND I MET BYRON OUTSIDE THE SHERIFF'S department. I had called to update him on the situation as soon as we'd pulled away from the dock. Since Carter had probably already warned him about what he was getting into with the three of us, I saw no reason to skimp on the story and gave him the full fishy tale. He had a good laugh over all of it and promised me that he'd have Gertie back at the resort in no time.

He was sitting on a bench one building down from the sheriff's department when we pulled up. I'd never seen him before, but I knew it had to be Byron. He had that successful lawyer look. Expensive suit, perfect hair, looked like someone had just ironed him. I parked and as we headed over, I took a harder look.

Six foot two. A hundred ninety pounds. Low fat content. Probably a six-pack. No discernable flaws other than being a lawyer and agreeing to represent Gertie.

He saw us coming and rose from the bench, smiling as he extended his hand. "Carter has told me a lot about you," he said.

"I'm surprised you're not still on that phone call," I said.

He laughed. "I assume he gave me the condensed version." He gave me a once-over. "CIA operative, huh? That's hard-core."

"*Retired* CIA operative," I said.

"But just as deadly, I bet," he said. "The training never really disappears."

"I hope I don't need to find out," I said, "but you're probably right. I *am* learning to think before I react...not that the pause has changed my decision very often."

He grinned and turned to Ida Belle. "I hear you're practically sniper caliber with a rifle. Hopefully, we won't have to call you to action. So are you ready to get Gertie out of here?"

Ida Belle hesitated before answering. "I suppose we better. I mean, a day or so off sounds like a good idea, until I think about the level of trouble she can get in staying here."

"Most people don't get into more trouble when they're detained," Byron said.

"You don't know Gertie." Ida Belle and I both responded at once.

Byron nodded and looked over at me. "I figure you'd like to be in the questioning?"

I blinked, surprised. "Sure, but Benton's not going to allow that to happen. Especially sitting there fuming and dripping all at the same time."

"I can get past Benton," Byron said. "Let's do this."

I shot a look at Ida Belle that conveyed what we were both thinking, which was *I hope to God Gertie hasn't talked*, then we headed inside. An older woman with salt-and-pepper hair and a somewhat leathery face greeted us at the door. "You must be here for Ms. Hebert," she said and sighed. "Guess that means I've got to go get Deputy Benton."

"Is there a problem?" Byron asked.

"Only the personal sort," she said. "Benton's what my grandson calls a douche. I'd never really liked the word but it's rather accurate in this case. Anyway, I'll go get His Majesty."

Byron shook his head as the woman walked off down a hallway. "This Benton is one popular dude."

"Wait until you meet him," Ida Belle said. "'Douche' is polite."

The woman returned fairly quickly, Benton right on her tail, leaving a trail of water with every step. Byron stepped up and stuck out his hand. "I'm Byron Anderson, Ms. Hebert's attorney."

Benton gave Byron's hand an unenthusiastic shake as he sent an angry glance over toward Ida Belle and me. "Deputy Benton," he said. "I'm in charge of the investigation. I'd like to start the questioning right away, if possible."

Byron wrinkled his nose. "Would you like to change clothes first, or shower even?"

"I'd love to," Benton said. "But that would require going home and I'm not letting this wait another minute. Do you need to speak to your client first?"

"Depends," Byron said. "Has she said anything to you?"

"Aside from bitching nonstop about her rights to use the restroom and have a phone call, and claiming she was dehydrated and would pass out if she didn't receive water, no. She hasn't said a word. Of course, she didn't have much time in between all those things, either."

"Great," Byron said. "I'm up to speed on everything, so no need to chat privately with Ms. Hebert. Ms. Redding will be assisting me with building my defense, should it come to that. I assume you have no problem with her sitting in the questioning."

"Darn right I have a problem with it," Benton said. "That woman is a nuisance, just like her friend. I am under no obligation to allow her in the room and don't aim to accommodate such nonsense."

"You're welcome to stick to the norm, of course," Byron said. "But I would like to remind you that Ms. Redding is a former CIA operative and spent years putting her life on the line at an international level so that people like you could cruise a beach every day. I would hate to think a department like this one had such disdain for the men and women doing a job that few of us are capable of."

A flush crept up Benton's neck and I knew he wanted to tell Byron to go to hell, but the CIA thing was keeping him from jumping into that snake pit. Of all the government agencies, not one struck fear into the hearts of law enforcement like the CIA. It was the secrecy, I think. That and all the Hollywood movies. No matter how tough a person was, they still hesitated when standing their ground meant pissing off the CIA.

"Fine," Benton said. "But she better not so much as clear her throat or she's out of there."

"I'll hold my breath if necessary," I said.

Benton whirled around. "This way."

I leaned over and whispered to Ida Belle, "Talk up the dispatcher and see what you can get."

Ida Belle nodded. "On it."

Byron and I followed Benton to the back of the building and into a small room with a folding table and four chairs. Gertie was sitting in a chair on the far wall, reading a pamphlet on Florida driving laws. I noticed four empty bottles of water in front of her and a potted plant leaking water in the corner and held in a smile. Benton probably thought she was part camel.

Gertie beamed at Byron as he introduced himself. "Carter

didn't tell us you were this handsome," Gertie said. "You look like you stepped off a runway."

Byron smiled at Gertie as a young man would a favorite great-aunt and I could tell he was flattered rather than annoyed by her comments. "Such a lovely woman deserves equally attractive representation."

"You're good," Gertie said.

"Can we get on with this?" Benton said. "She's been dodging me all day. I'm past due for answers."

"For the two hundredth time," Gertie said, "I wasn't dodging. I was fishing. It's called a vacation, and it's not like you strapped an ankle bracelet on me and told me I had to stay at the condo."

"Deputy Benton," Byron said, "I'm sure we can agree that since Ms. Hebert was not under arrest, she was well within her rights to continue her vacation as planned. It's not as if she left the state."

Benton grumbled and pointed to seats. He looked even less than enthused when I took the seat next to him, which was exactly what I was going for. Agitated people tended to give things away that they wouldn't otherwise reveal. Unless charges were filed, Benton didn't have to give us detailed information on Otis's death. And I really wanted to push him into revealing some of it. Cause of death would be stellar.

Benton turned on his recorder and took down the usual basics—name, address, age, profession, etc. Then he started in on the specifics, such as why Gertie was in Florida and how she picked that resort. Finally, he got around to Otis.

"How did you meet Mr. Baker?" Benton asked.

Gertie launched into an animated and very detailed description of almost dying in the surf and lingered on flashing the beach. Benton grimaced and tried to hurry her along in her tale, but Gertie was on a roll and determined to punish Benton in any way possible.

Mission accomplished.

Finally, she concluded with Otis's dinner invitation, and Benton visibly sighed with relief.

"So you had dinner last night?" Benton asked. "Where did you eat? Did Otis meet you somewhere? Or did he come to your room?"

"We ate at the Italian restaurant at the resort," Gertie said. "I met him there at seven o'clock. He had reservations. I insisted on oysters for an appetizer. They're an aphrodisiac, you know?"

Benton looked perched on the edge of apoplexy. "And what did you do after dinner?"

Gertie launched into her romantic walk on the beach story, dwelling as much as possible on the romance part, and I could tell Benton was sorry he'd had to ask. Byron had long since leaned back in his chair, clearly enjoying the show.

"Anyway," Gertie finally concluded, "Otis walked me to my room, gave me a kiss good-night and said he'd call me today. I let myself in and went straight to bed. Too much wine and not enough oysters. Of course, if I'd had more of the appetizer, dessert might have gone an entirely different direction."

She started to giggle and Benton reached for his bottled water and took a big gulp.

"So if the date went so well," Benton said, "why did you kill him?"

It was so out of left field that even Byron looked a bit surprised, and I figured he'd heard most everything at least twice.

"I didn't kill him," Gertie said. "I had a really nice dinner. What possible motive could I have?"

"Maybe the date was more, uh, *romantic* than you're letting on," Benton said. "Maybe Otis wasn't satisfied with the performance and insulted you. What would you say to that?"

"I'd say you're as big a liar as you are a fool," Gertie said. "If Otis had experienced the privilege of my *performance*, the only thing he would have been offended by was his own lack of endurance."

Byron started choking and reached for his bottled water. I could tell he was trying not to smile. I didn't even bother trying. Gertie was on a roll.

"Maybe he owed you money," Benton said. "Word around here is that Otis has talked quite a few women into funding his lifestyle."

"I have no idea why you think dinner with a man I just met should constitute my taking him as a dependent," Gertie said, "but you're wrong. Besides, I brought two hundred dollars with me in case I spotted some silly souvenirs, and it's all still in my wallet. I have my emergency credit card, but I left my checkbook at home and I don't have jewelry worth pawning. Otis couldn't take me for more than what dinner cost him."

Benton shook his head. "You expect me to believe you came for a weeklong vacation with only two hundred dollars?"

"Fortune is treating Ida Belle and me to this vacation," Gertie said. "She insisted."

Benton glanced over at me and I nodded. Nodding wasn't the same as speaking.

Apparently, Byron had grown tired of the exchange. It was clear Benton was on a fishing expedition. "Look," Byron said, "my client has answered all your questions. She didn't know the deceased prior to yesterday, and there's no reason to think she plotted and executed his demise. Speaking of which, what exactly killed Mr. Baker?"

"That's confidential," Benton said.

"Have it your way," Byron said and rose. "Unless you're

arresting my client, which would be extraordinary since you can't offer up motive or opportunity, I think we're done here."

"I want to search her condo," Benton said.

"Not without a warrant, and good luck getting one," Byron said. "The next time you want to speak to my client, you'll make an appointment with me and you'll wait on my availability. And I better not hear about you placing an elderly woman in handcuffs again unless you're making an arrest. Are we clear?"

Benton looked past Byron and gave him a single nod before slamming his hand down on the recorder. He knew he was beat. No matter how much he'd love to pin this on Gertie and go around crowing about being a hero, he had nothing. And he wasn't going to get anything because the bottom line was that Gertie hadn't killed Otis.

But someone had.

CHAPTER NINE

Dave's story about being held on trumped-up charges lingered in the back of my mind. Just how bad was Benton at his job? And how far would he go to close the case? I'd known from the moment he told us Otis was dead that I was jumping into the middle of the mess with both feet, but his behavior had only strengthened my resolve.

We made our way back to the sheriff's department lobby where Ida Belle was waiting for us. I'd seen her talking to the dispatcher from down the hallway but as we got closer, they both went silent and pretended they weren't even aware the other was in the room. I hoped she'd gotten the dirt on Benton. I needed to know exactly what we were up against.

We were all quiet until we exited, then everyone started speaking at once. I put up a hand and whistled. "There's a café across the street," I said. "I suggest we grab a soda and have an information exchange."

We headed into the café, which was quiet at that time of day, and found an empty table at the back. We waited until the server had delivered our drinks before I took control of the conversation. I gave Ida Belle a quick rundown of our conversation with Benton, then Gertie told us about harassing Benton while she waited on us. Finally, we got to Ida Belle.

"Please tell me the angry dispatcher gave you something," I said.

"It's what we expected but worse," Ida Belle said. "Benton isn't just lazy and incompetent. He's shady. She says he's trumped up charges on people just to get arrests on his record. The current sheriff isn't healthy, and word is he might retire soon. I mean like maybe days soon. Benton thinks he's going to slide right into the job."

"So he's building his résumé," I said.

Ida Belle nodded. "And nabbing a murderer would put a big feather in his cap."

"He better rethink his cap, then," Byron said. "Because that's not going to happen. He has no evidence."

"He has no evidence yet," I said.

"You really think he'd manufacture evidence and send an innocent woman to jail for murder just to get a sheriff's job in Podunk, Florida?" Byron asked, then frowned. "Never mind. I've seen stranger."

"So have we," Ida Belle said. "I'm not saying it will happen, but I am saying we can't expect Benton to play fair. The dispatcher thinks the sheriff will announce his retirement next week. They're mid-election, so the position will be filled by appointment. If this murder is still unsolved, it won't look good for Benton."

I sighed. "The only thing worse than incompetent law enforcement is incompetent law enforcement with political ambitions."

"You said it, sister," Ida Belle said.

"Did she give you any details on the investigation?" I asked.

Ida Belle shook her head. "She said Benton was playing

everything close to the vest. He's not even letting the other deputies in on the investigation."

"Wants all the credit," Gertie said.

"That," I agreed, "and by controlling all the information, he can add to or subtract from it as needed to fit his narrative."

Even Byron looked a little less confident than before. "I know you're not licensed in Florida, so you can't do anything official," he said, "but anything you can dig up on Otis will help me launch a defense. Assuming it comes to that. If he was scamming women, some names would be a great start."

I nodded. "Just don't tell Carter you implied I should play PI out of state. I don't need the encouragement and you don't need the grief."

He grinned. "I can imagine. I'll see what I can find out on Benton and the DA. I really wish we had cause of death, but Benton wasn't parting with anything."

"No," I agreed. "Sounds like he's trying to keep everything a secret."

Ida Belle nodded. "But given the dispatcher's reputation for gossiping and her utter dislike for Benton, I have no doubt she'll try to find out something, if for no other reason than to get one up on him. As soon as she knows something, it will get around. And my guess is she went to work on it as soon as Benton left to shower. We'll work the resort staff and other locals and see what we come up with."

"And if no one knows anything," Gertie said, "we have other ways to acquire information."

Byron looked interested but not brave enough to ask. It was probably a good thing as I was certain Gertie was implying that we could break into the sheriff's department and read Benton's case files. It was one thing to break into the Sinful sheriff's department, where we knew the sheriff and the deputies and I was positive they didn't have security cameras, but it was another thing altogether to consider doing it in a strange town.

Ida Belle gave her a disapproving frown. "I'm sure we'll find out what we need from the resort staff. That's usually where all the good gossip is."

"Great," Byron said, and rose from the table. "I'm going to head out. If you run into any trouble with Benton, call me immediately. And it goes without saying that you don't speak to him without me present. None of you."

"What if he gets a search warrant?" I asked.

"I'd be shocked if he can manage it, but there's nothing we can do about it," Byron said. "Just call me if he presents with one."

I nodded. "Thanks for coming out so quickly."

"No problem," Byron said. "I owe Carter one. This is a much easier way to pay him back than taking a bullet like he did for me." He gave us a wave and headed out of the café.

Gertie stared. "Carter took a bullet for him?"

I shrugged. "Beats me. I mean, he's got a couple wounds that are definitely bullet holes, but Carter doesn't talk about his service."

"And you don't ask." Gertie sighed. "I honestly don't know how you sleep at night knowing all that fascinating information is right there in front of you and you're refusing to access it."

"It's not like I can punch in a pass code and Google on his chest," I said. "If Carter wants me to know something, he'll tell me. Probably most of it's classified anyway. It's not like I spend dinners telling him about my missions."

"I can't imagine talking about either would be pleasant," Ida Belle said. "You and Carter are decent people. Regardless of how necessary and important your roles were, I don't have any doubt of the difficulty it took to fulfill them. It's not something I would want to dwell on in the past, especially if I was trying to move forward with my new life."

"I suppose you're right," Gertie said. "But man, I bet the stories would be something."

"There's no disagreement there," Ida Belle said. "So back to our current problem...where do we start?"

"I think the suspect angle is most important," I said. "If Otis was really a full-time scammer of women, then my guess is this all comes back to an angry woman."

"Or son or brother of an angry woman," Ida Belle said.

"Yep," I agreed. "So we develop a list of potential victims of scamming, then we investigate them and those close to them. Hopefully, we'll be able to eliminate some based on opportunity, as they'll all have the same motive. Then we can get a list to Byron."

Ida Belle nodded. "So we chat up the resort staff and visit some of the local haunts and see if anyone's talkative."

"And we might want to chat up any of the older female vacationers," I said. "Otis probably targeted someone before Gertie. If one of the resort staff took notice and knew Otis's reputation, they might have warned someone off."

"That's a lot of people to cover," Gertie said. "Probably a couple hundred between staff, guests, and locals."

"I know," I agreed. "It's a lot of ground. All we can do is start talking and hope some names shake out."

"Well, I have no problem with the talking part," Gertie said.

"Don't we know it," Ida Belle grumbled.

Gertie shot her a dirty look.

"This is one of those times when being a nosy old lady comes in handy," Ida Belle said. "It's not like Fortune can go around chatting up perfect strangers with intrusive questions

—assuming she was even capable of chatting up perfect strangers. But everyone expects old ladies to do it."

"Where are we going to get some old ladies to help?" Gertie asked.

Ida Belle stared.

"I mean," Gertie continued, "I'm sure a middle-aged woman like myself can handle the gossip as well. This is the South."

Ida Belle looked over at me. "Apparently, Gertie is planning on living to two hundred."

"I must be a child then," I said.

"You'll just have to settle for having the 'lady' part covered," Gertie said.

"I'm settling for nothing," Ida Belle said. "Ladies don't get accused of murder."

"Ladies are boring," Gertie said. "I'm a woman of the world."

"So while you two young ladies of mystery are running around hitting up people who are far more elder for clues, what should I do?" I asked. "Nap in my stroller? Eat dirt?"

I didn't know that much about kids, but those were the two things I'd consistently seen the little ones in Sinful do.

"You'll hit up the old men, of course," Gertie said.

I grimaced. "Yuck. Why would I want to do that?"

"Because old men are even worse gossips than old women," Ida Belle said. "They go fishing all day and come back with nothing. What do you think they're doing out there?"

I thought about what I was doing when I was supposed to be fishing. "Drinking beer? Reading a book? Sleeping?"

Ida Belle nodded. "You go alone. Men always go in pairs. When they go alone, they're up to no good or only have a six-pack of beer and don't want to share."

"They also might owe everyone money and don't want to pay," Gertie said.

"You two should really write a book on requirements for Southern living," I said. "It would help all us Yankees to integrate."

"No one would believe us," Ida Belle said. "Except old Southern women, and we already know everything."

"Probably true," I said. "So I'm supposed to say what to these men, exactly? Chatting up men is not my forte. You know I only landed Carter because I never killed him."

"You came close a time or two," Ida Belle said, "but I see your point. Maybe you could eat a Popsicle or something. I saw a commercial with a woman doing that last week. All the men seemed to be entranced."

Gertie shook her head. "Ida Belle is hopeless when it comes to entertaining men, so don't listen to her. If you ate a Popsicle like that commercial, you'd give half the men here heart attacks. Dead people don't give up clues. All you have to do is sit down and talk. Trust me, any man over the age of forty will tell you everything he knows in a matter of minutes."

"Just like that?" I asked, still not convinced.

"I've been on the beach," Gertie said. "I've seen your competition and I'm the nearest you've got. I'm hot but I've got a few years on you."

Ida Belle snorted and Gertie shot her a dirty look.

"She's probably right," Ida Belle said. "Most men are fools when it comes to a young, beautiful woman."

"Exactly," Gertie agreed. "Just sit next to them and say how you're thinking about leaving because there was a murder and you're worried for your safety. They'll jump all over themselves trying to reassure you, and if they know any negative thing about Otis, it will come right out."

I thought about it for a couple seconds, then it clicked. "Oh, it's that whole white-knight thing you talk about."

Ida Belle grinned. "Hard to wrap your mind around being rescued by a man, right?"

"It's hard to wrap my mind around needing to be rescued at all," I said. "Even though I do owe my life to several people and their well-placed shots. I suppose this means I have to act like a normal girl."

Gertie laughed. "I'd love to see you try. First up is a mani-pedi. Your polish is chipped and men like pretty pink."

I stared at her in dismay. "I have to paint my nails again for this?"

"It *is* a murder rap," Ida Belle said.

"Says the woman who doesn't have to have a mani-pedi," I said.

"Touché," Ida Belle said.

"You'll never get an appointment this late," Gertie said. "I'll pick up something in the gift shop downstairs and do them myself."

I was still mentally squirming over having to sit still long enough to have pink splashed on my toes and hands again when my cell phone rang. It was Carter.

"I heard from Byron," Carter said. "You made quite an impression."

"Really?"

"Yes. He wanted to know if you had a sister. I told him the world could barely handle one of you. If there was another, it would mean the apocalypse."

"Probably."

"Anyway, he filled me in on Gertie's situation. Sounds like she's making friends with the local deputy."

"Benton's a douche."

"Byron said that as well. But unfortunately, he's a douche

with a badge and jurisdiction, so try not to agitate him by doing things that could get you tossed into jail."

"What kind of things?" I asked innocently.

"Things like making a man with a water phobia fall in the water."

"That totally wasn't us. Fishy water leaked out of one of the ice chests and he slipped. We never touched him."

"You rarely do and yet..."

"Trust me, we're doing everything we can to stay away from Benton, which is why we went fishing to begin with. Now that we know he's afraid of the water, we might just move onto the boat. The boat captain offered to take us on an overnight."

"I just bet he did. That boat captain has a bit of a record, so don't be making friends with him."

"What kind of record?"

"The usual stuff that guys like that get up to—bar fights, illegal gambling, drunk and disorderly—"

"So he'd fit right in with the Sinful locals."

"Pretty much, although he might lean toward the Swamp Bar crowd."

"I don't think we'll be hanging with Dave any time soon," I said. "He was a big help today, but my guess is he'd like to put some distance between us, especially once Benton narrows in on him as a suspect."

"What do you mean?"

"He told us Otis took his mother for money. If that bit of gossip has made the local rounds, then Benton might shift from Gertie to him. They've got history and Dave would be an easy target. Easier than Gertie. Benton doesn't seem concerned with launching a real investigation. Apparently, he's waiting for the sheriff to retire so he can get the position by appointment. An open murder case would cramp his style."

"That's not good."

I frowned.

"You went silent," Carter said. "Silent women are rarely a good thing."

"Most of my career was spent in silence."

"Because you were aiming."

"I was just thinking that if Dave had killed Otis, why would he tell us about his mother? Seems like that would be the sort of thing he'd want to keep secret."

"It does, but you know the rule—never underestimate the stupidity of a criminal."

"Is that the first rule of law enforcement?"

"No. The first rule of law enforcement is to keep civilians out of the investigation."

"Kinda hard to do when one of my best friends is a murder suspect and the deputy in charge of the investigation is looking to railroad her to fulfill his own political ambitions."

He sighed. "Look, I harbor no illusions that the three of you will sit quietly and wait for this to resolve itself, but can you please keep your nose-poking to random gossip and other completely benign and legal things?"

"Probably. I mean, it will be easier since Gertie's purse isn't as lethal as usual."

"Meaning it's still partially lethal?"

"I don't know. I figure she probably pocketed a dinner knife at some point, but I'm pretty sure she hasn't found an explosives connection here yet."

"Yet?" His dismay was clear.

"Blame it on the internet. Makes that kind of thing too easy."

"This entire conversation gets more frightening the longer we talk, so I'm going to let you go. Besides, I have deputy business to attend to myself."

"Anything interesting?"

"Yes. Your crazy neighbor Ronald has accused you of ringing his doorbell all night."

"I'm in another state."

"Which is why I'm on my way to his house to show him the picture of you, Gertie, and Ida Belle on the beach that you sent me yesterday. If the location and time stamp don't get him to back off, seeing Gertie in a bikini will do it."

"You sure? He might want to borrow it."

Carter groaned and I knew I'd put a mental picture in his mind that he really didn't want. He already had the real image of Gertie in a bikini up there. It was a lot to take in.

"I'll call you tonight when we're back in the condo," I said. "We're starving so we're going to go grab some food now."

I set my phone back on the table.

"We're eating now?" Gertie said.

I shook my head. "Should I have told him that we're going to leave here and start investigating?"

"So you're okay with lying to him?" Gertie asked. "I figured once you two were a serious item, you might develop a conscience in that arena."

"My conscience is clear," I said. "He told me to lie."

Ida Belle stared. "Carter asked you to lie to him."

I nodded. "A while back. He said if we were up to things that he was better off not knowing, then lie."

"Huh." Ida Belle looked impressed. "A man there might be hope for."

I nodded. "It's pretty smart of him. I don't know how good I'll be at it. If I want to say something, it has a tendency to come out, but at least I have the option. So what's the plan for tonight? All the old gossips will abandon the beach soon, if they haven't already, so no enticing old men to talk with my bathing suit until tomorrow."

"Gertie and I will head to the restaurant," Ida Belle said.

"It's easy enough to find an empty seat with a table of old biddies who are dying to gossip with someone new. We can split up and see what we can find out."

"What about me?" I asked. "Do old men not eat dinner?"

Gertie shook her head. "They do, but you're not going to like this..."

I sighed. "You're going to make me go to the bar, aren't you?"

"I'm afraid that's where the kind of men you're looking for will be," Ida Belle said. "Some of the women might move in later on for a drink before retiring, but the men will eat their dinner in the bar, working out their come-on lines for later."

"Gross," I said. "I can't believe you're going to make me listen to old men come-on lines. I hate that crap from young men. And since they never learn, it's not like they get any better with age."

"Just hum in your mind until you get a chance to put on your scared woman act," Ida Belle said.

"And be smart about your seat selection," Gertie said. "Your natural inclination will be to find a spot away from everyone and let them come to you, but that only allows for one at a time. If you pick a spot in the middle of the room then you can strike up a conversation with a few at once. Others will gravitate over, trying to get in on the action, and if they have anything to offer, you'll get it a lot faster that way."

"Nice!" I said, appreciating her strategy. "I like the sound of faster."

Gertie patted my arm. "Don't worry. Most of those fools will be asleep in their beer by nine o'clock."

"And the women will be ready to take off their bras," Ida Belle said, "so they won't be lingering much either. Lunch is for lingering. Dinner is for storing up food for overnight hibernation."

"So you're saying we'll be back in our room in plenty of time for room service dessert and a movie rental," I said.

"Count on it," Ida Belle said.

I thought about my immediate future—pretending to need protection and reassurance from a bunch of men old enough to be my grandfather—and started counting.

CHAPTER TEN

"PULL YOUR BOOBS UP MORE," GERTIE SAID AS SHE GAVE ME A critical eye. "You want to make sure you get their attention first thing."

"Having a pulse will get their attention," Ida Belle said. "Her boobs are fine. The whole bar will probably be a high-blood-pressure fest as soon as she walks in the door. We don't need another death on our watch. Even by natural causes."

I looked at myself in the living room mirror. Since it was a beach vacation resort, I'd stuck with casual. Shorts, tank top, and sandals. I figured that was risqué enough for the intended audience. After all, my shorts were well above my knees. My boobs were shoved into a bra with the straps too tight—Gertie's idea—and had created a line of cleavage in the middle of my tank. I would probably have marks on my body for a day and breathing wasn't the most comfortable thing, but I should be able to manage it for a couple hours.

"If I pull any more, I'll have stretch marks," I said. "I'm not exactly working with oversize equipment here."

"It's a good thing," Ida Belle said. "A large chest would have been a real hindrance when you worked for the CIA. Hard to crawl with double-Ds."

"But now that you're retired from that line of work, you should look into implants," Gertie said.

"Why on earth would she do something like that?" Ida Belle asked. "Her boobs are good enough for Carter. Who else matters?"

"I suppose you're right," Gertie said. "But a nice big set would look good during sweater season."

"You mean all two days of it," Ida Belle said. "Sure. They'll look really good in a sweater under a raincoat. You know how winter in Sinful is."

"I'm not getting implants," I said. "Not even if it cured cancer. I clicked on the wrong link the other day and saw pictures of that surgery. They cut very important parts entirely off and reposition them. If I wanted my parts repositioned, I would have stayed with the CIA. It happens to everyone if they keep the job long enough and at least medical insurance would cover it."

Ida Belle cringed. "I think I've seen those same pictures. I went around clutching my chest for two days."

"Look, I'm sure with Gertie's hard work my boobs will be the focus of all attention for the next couple hours, so can we get this over with? I think one of these bra hooks is going to break skin."

"No bleeding on your shirt until you've gotten the goods," Gertie said as we headed out of the room and down the hall.

"I'll let my skin know," I said.

When we got to the lobby, Ida Belle and Gertie headed toward the restaurant, with Ida Belle trailing behind Gertie at a much slower pace, giving her room to enter the restaurant alone and look for a group she could blend into. I let out a long-suffering sigh, then walked in the opposite direction for the bar.

It was a typical hotel bar—low light, tacky cloth-covered chairs around ten tiny tables, and musty-smelling carpet. A bar stood along the back of the room. A couple of men sat at the bar, but most were sitting one or two to a four-top. Right smack in the middle was an empty table. Perfect.

The sound level dropped to absolutely nothing as soon as I stepped into the bar. It was so quiet, it was as if someone had hit Pause. Every set of eyes turned to me and I forced myself to keep moving into the room rather than turning around and fleeing, which is exactly what I felt like doing.

This is for Gertie.

I scanned the patrons as I headed for the center table.

All old as Christ. Biggest threat is being grossed out when they hit on me. No need for individual ratings.

I slipped into the chair and looked up at the server who'd stepped up to the table almost as soon as I'd sat. He was younger and smiling, and I could only assume he figured that my presence meant everyone would stay longer, drink more, and tip better. I didn't hold out much hope for any of them, but I didn't want to rain on his parade. At least he'd get a good tip from mc.

"My name is Chance and I'll be your server," he said. "Can I get you something to drink?"

"Beer, please," I said. "Whatever light beer you have on tap."

I know I probably could have played the helpless damsel better with a fruity drink or a glass of wine in front of me, but I had to draw the line somewhere.

"Of course," he said. "Are you interested in seeing a menu?"

"That would be great," I said.

He perked up a bit more and practically bounced back to

the bar to retrieve a menu. The patrons surrounding me were shifting in their seats, and I could tell they were just waiting for Chance to finish up so they could pounce. Chance returned with the menu and my beer, and I ordered a burger and fries. He flashed me a hundred-watt smile and headed for the computer to put in my order.

He hadn't made it two steps before the first guy made his move.

"Are you vacationing here?" he asked.

I turned to my right and saw a man wearing blue shorts, a white short-sleeve dress shirt, and a pink bow tie.

"Yes," I said. "I'm really enjoying the beach."

"The weather's been nice," a man to my left said.

I looked over and found a giant set of eyes staring at me through glasses so thick I wondered how he managed to walk without running into things.

"It has been," I said. "I was a little worried that it might be rainy this time of year."

A bald man sitting at the table in front of me turned his entire chair around to face me. "We're on the back end of hurricane season," he said. "I always come this time of year. Not so many families. It's a lot quieter."

"I can definitely see the advantage of that," I agreed.

"You don't have kids?" Pink Tie asked, inching closer.

"No kids," I said.

"Doesn't your husband want any?" Thick Glasses asked, shifting his chair for a better angle.

His fishing was so apparent that I had to work hard not to roll my eyes but at least he was verifying before moving forward. Most didn't bother. Or didn't care. I was guessing more the latter.

"No husband either," I said and smiled. "I'm not really looking for anything permanent at the moment."

"You've got plenty of time for all that," Bald Man said. "Best not to rush into such important things."

"So are you all vacationing as well?" I asked.

Bald Man nodded. "I come every year around this time. Usually for a couple weeks, maybe more if the weather stays good."

The other two shook their heads.

"I live across the bridge," Pink Tie said. "There's only a couple bars over there though, and at one of them you're more likely to get shot than served a drink."

Thick Glasses nodded. "I have a condo on the island but the bar there is tiny and they water down the drinks."

"I thought all resorts watered down the drinks," I said.

"They do," Thick Glasses said, "but this place is better than most. And they don't play the music so loud you can't hear yourself think."

Pink Tie nodded. "I hate that. Who wants to listen to that rap music when you can have an intelligent conversation with a beautiful woman?"

The other two held up their glasses as if toasting his comment. I looked up at the ceiling. *Gertie, you owe me big time.*

"This seems like a really nice place," I said. "Except...well, that whole thing with the man being murdered."

I gave them what I hoped was a worried look and picked at my napkin. "I was thinking I might leave early. Maybe check out tomorrow. I mean, I just got here, but I don't want to stay somewhere that isn't safe."

The two locals frowned and glanced at each other, and I was certain they knew exactly who Otis was. And it didn't look like they were fans.

"That was all the talk over lunch today," Bald Man said. "I don't recall meeting the guy but I think I might know who he was based on a description I got from my waiter. Did the cops say it was murder? I figured it was a heart attack or something, but you know these resorts. They run from a potential lawsuit like a greyhound chasing a rabbit. I figured they called the cops in to cover their butts."

Pink Tie shook his head. "My sister is friends with the dispatcher down at the sheriff's department. She said he was poisoned. Didn't know what with. I think they try to keep things from the dispatcher. She loves to gossip, but she's never been wrong about police stuff and she says they're investigating."

I tried to control my excitement. We had a cause of death! Or at least a start on it. Poison was broad, but if the dispatcher had gotten that much, then there was a good chance she might get more.

"Gonna have to cast a wide net when it comes to suspects," Thick Glasses said. "I know you're not supposed to speak ill of the dead, but Otis Baker was an...uh, creep."

I was certain he was about to say something much more colorful. It was cute how he had altered his thought to account for not cursing in front of a lady. Of course, that lady was me so that also made it hilarious.

I frowned. "What kind of creep? I mean, there's all sorts."

"A womanizer for one," Pink Tie said. "He ran through the local widows across the bridge pretty fast. Finally, enough of them started talking among themselves and they got his number. Then he moved his show over here."

"Did he attack them?" I asked. "I mean, surely the police would arrest him for that."

"Nothing like that," Thick Glasses said. "If I had to guess, he hit them up for money. I heard some whispering among the womenfolk, but they don't like to admit to being taken by a smooth-talking stranger."

Pink Tie nodded. "I heard the same grumblings, but when

women close ranks, it's hard to find out much. I saw Otis at dinner a couple times with different women and he never reached for his wallet. I figure if he's got a woman paying for dinner, he wouldn't hesitate to ask her for some money for whatever made-up excuse he has. Probably some sob story about a sick grandchild or a screwup in his retirement payout. This isn't the first time a guy like Otis landed here."

"It's an unfortunate part of living in an area with so many widows and retirees," Thick Glasses said. "It cuts both ways, of course, but usually it's more of a woman's game than a man's. Still, we get a new Otis every year or two. They make the rounds, collect what's there for the taking, then head out before the resorts blacklist them or the local cops get tired of the complaints and come knocking."

"I'm surprised they get away with it," I said.

Bald Man shrugged. "Happened to my sister back in Idaho. They don't want to report it. Feel stupid and all and don't want people to know. Heck, I didn't find out until after she passed."

Thick Glasses nodded. "And that goes double for men. No man worth his salt is going to run to the cops and admit to being taken by a pretty face."

"I guess I can understand that," I said. "But by not reporting it, the scammers get to keep working their scam."

"That's unfortunately true," Pink Tie said.

"So do you think this Otis was killed by one of the women he scammed money off of? It would make me feel a lot better about staying if I knew it was something personal like that. But with me thinking it's random, I'm still planning on checking out tomorrow. A woman can't be too careful these days."

"No!" They all protested at once.

"I'm sure it was personal," Pink Tie said. "I overheard some talk in the diner over where I live. Apparently, he scammed one of the local widows out of a good bit of money, and word was her son was looking to get his hands on Otis. Can't say that I blame him. If it had been my mother, I'd have been out for blood as well."

"And you think this woman's son might have done it?" I said. "I mean, plenty of people say they would but when it comes down to the actual act..."

"Of course, of course," Pink Tie agreed. "There's a big difference in words said in anger and actually following through with such a thing, but the guys talking made it sound like the son was capable. He sounded like a rough sort, if you know what I mean."

"I do," I said. "And I guess it's possible he was the one, but I'm still not sure."

I wondered if he was referring to Dave, who I absolutely thought was capable. But when I pictured Dave killing Otis, I saw him strangling the life out of the scammer. I just didn't make him for a poison kind of guy.

"There's been whispering around the resort," Bald Man said. "I overheard the maids a couple days ago, talking about one of the staff falling for a scammer and giving him money. They said she was too embarrassed to tell the cops. One of them suggested putting hair remover in his shampoo bottle. They never said a name, but it sounds like they could have been talking about this Otis character."

"Hair remover in his shampoo wouldn't have done much damage," Pink Tie said. "Otis wasn't exactly sporting a full head of hair, but I suppose they felt they needed to do something for their friend."

"Did they say who the coworker was?" I asked.

Bald Man shook his head. "And I'm afraid I don't know the staff well enough to speculate."

"There's a few that might fit the bill," Thick Glasses said.

"There's a recently widowed woman in the front office. Probably in her sixties."

Pink Tie let out a guffaw. "Her husband probably died just to get away from her. Have you spent five minutes talking to the woman? She's a royal pain in the butt. Besides, she's notoriously cheap. All the servers here complain about her. I can't imagine her giving someone like Otis money."

"She isn't the most pleasant of people," Thick Glasses agreed, "but the ones who never get any attention from men are usually the best ones for scammers like Otis to target."

"I suppose so," Pink Tie admitted. "Still, the woman running housekeeping is probably a better pick. I bet she was a looker in her day and seems nice enough."

"Never been married though," Thick Glasses said. "A woman her age who's never been married is always suspect."

I held in a smile. Ida Belle and Gertie were definitely suspect.

"Probably one of those feminists," Bald Man said. "My cousin took up that nonsense. Burned all her bras on the front lawn and shaved her head. Her husband went fishing. Been on that fishing trip going on twenty-two years now."

"Wise man," Thick Glasses said.

"I don't suppose the housekeeping supervisor has an angry son to follow up for her though," I said.

"I know a lady like you would have some trouble believing it," Pink Tie said, "but it's possible a woman could have done it."

The smile I'd been holding in finally broke loose and I scrambled to explain myself to the three men who were staring at me with varying degrees of uncertainly.

"How very progressive of you," I said brightly. "I don't run into that manner of thinking very often."

Pink Tie blushed but was obviously pleased with the

compliment. If he knew I could kill him with the umbrella in his fruity drink, he would be turning white instead of red.

"He's absolutely right," Bald Man jumped in, trying to get on the progressive bandwagon. "It's not like Otis was strangled, so strength wouldn't have been a factor."

"Well, I suppose you gentlemen are right," I said. "It does sound like this Otis was a bad sort. If it was personal and not some sort of robbing-the-tourist thing then I guess I'm safe."

"Definitely safe," Thick Glasses said. "Don't even worry about it a second more. Just enjoy your vacation. The cops will sort it out."

"Ha!" Pink Tie said. "If you think Deputy Dawg is going to sort anything out, you haven't lived here long enough or needed the cops. The guy makes idiots look like Einstein and has completely rebranded lazy. Yet somehow, he thinks he's going to get elected sheriff when the current one retires."

Thick Glasses frowned. "Benton is in charge of the investigation?"

Pink Tie nodded.

Thick Glasses sighed. "That man couldn't catch a criminal even if he witnessed the crime himself. Well, I guess whoever did the deed lucked out."

"That's the thing," Pink Tie said. "The mayor won't stand for no arrest at all. He wants to be reelected, and guests being murdered at resorts doesn't look so good when it happens on his watch. So he'll be pressuring Benton. And there's rumblings that the sheriff is going to retire, and you know Benton has been angling for that job since the cradle. *Someone* will get arrested. It's just the likelihood of it being the right person is low."

"What a mess," Thick Glasses said. "Glad I never had any interaction with Otis. But if Benton's looking for a scapegoat,

I don't suppose he has any shortage of angry women, assuming he works hard enough to find them."

"Okay, guys," the server stepped up to the table, carrying my tray of food. "Give the lady some room so she can have her dinner."

All of them looked disappointed but were raised in an era when it was bad manners to stare at someone while they ate—particularly bad manners if you weren't actually their date. So they shuffled their chairs back into position and I dived into the burger like I hadn't eaten in a year. For bar food, it was pretty good. At least the meat was real, thick, and not overcooked.

As I ate, I thought about everything I'd learned. It was pretty much exactly what we'd figured, but I did glean a couple of potential suspects from the conversation as well as a cause of death. Unfortunately, I didn't have the poison used, which could help narrow things down even more, but I figured that information would eventually surface.

I polished off the burger and fries in record time. I'd barely washed down the last bite when I saw the men fidgeting, clearly trying to gauge how soon they could launch back at me. But I was done with all that riveting fun. I'd gotten everything I could from them and had no intention of sitting there and being bored by whatever conversation was next. Likely fishing prospects, the weather, and someone's bad back or sciatica.

I popped up from my seat and gave them a wave as I headed for the bar. "Thank you, gentlemen, for the reassurances. Maybe I'll see you again."

None of their knees could compete with my launch away from the table, and they had the good sense to forgo attempting to follow me to the bar. The bartender handed me a bill and I added a tip and my room information.

"Those guys bothering you?" he asked.

"No. They're harmless," I said. "In fact, they were a big help. I was worried about the murder that happened here and was considering cutting my vacation short. But they assured me that the deceased had no shortage of people who would celebrate his demise."

"That's true enough," the bartender said. "I didn't know him but the staff talks."

"Really? I'm surprised. I figured since he was scamming women, the bar would be like a second home."

The bartender shook his head. "He was smarter about it. Look at those three you just talked to. One of them haunts this bar twice a year on his vacation. The two locals are here probably four nights a week. You know how many times I've seen them leave with a woman? None. But Otis was different. He approached women in a way that didn't seem like he was hitting on them."

"I heard he rescued a woman from the surf yesterday."

"That's not exactly the way I heard it, but yeah, I'm sure Otis jumped in pretending to save the day. And these older broads eat that up. Most of them have been widowed or divorced and they're easy targets for someone like Otis, who has the moves down."

"I don't know how some people sleep at night."

"Well, Otis slept in a bed that he never had to make, in a resort that average people can't afford all too well."

"Point taken. I suppose those of us with a conscience will never quite get it."

"Nope."

"The guys said they thought Otis took a couple of staff members for some money."

The bartender frowned. "I heard some talking along those lines among the girls in housekeeping, but when I asked about it, they clammed up. I think the woman in question was their boss, so that would explain their desire to keep their gossip to a minimum."

"What a shame. Being taken by a scammer is bad enough but then for everyone to know about it..."

"Yeah. Can't be all that pleasant."

"Well, thanks for the chat. I'm going to head up to bed. It's been a long day."

"Enjoy your stay."

I gave the guys a wave and headed out of the bar. I glanced back as I exited, and they were all staring at me, wistful looks on their faces. A better person might have been a tiny bit empathetic, but since I was young enough to be their grand-daughter, I just found them delusional. Clearly, Otis had honed his skills for getting women on the line. Of course, he was going for an entirely different end game than those guys and picked his targets very well.

I headed for the lobby and sent Ida Belle a text, letting her know the mission was accomplished and I was headed back to the room. For all I knew, they might have beaten me back there. Ida Belle claimed men were worse gossips than women, and the three tonight hadn't disappointed. But women had a way of taking ten minutes to tell a story when twenty seconds would have done just fine, so Ida Belle and Gertie might be a bit behind me. I reached over to press the button for the elevator and that's when I heard a commotion coming from the direction of the restaurant. My radar immediately went off.

Gertie!

CHAPTER ELEVEN

I STARTED SPRINTING FOR THE RESTAURANT, DODGING BOTH vacationers and staff as I went. There was no doubt in my mind that something unfortunate was going down and that Gertie was right in the middle of it. In fact, I would have bet Ida Belle's SUV on it.

I slid to a stop at the entry for the restaurant, almost knocking over the young hostess, who was staring into the restaurant, a frightened look on her face. I scanned the room and had to say, I didn't blame her.

Gertie was running down a row between tables, a giant clod of something white dripping from her head and onto her face and body. Another woman ran behind her, screaming unintelligibly and trying to hit Gertie with a pink plastic flamingo that I assumed she'd taken from the buffet centerpiece since the remnants of the centerpiece were scattered on the floor. I gave the woman with the flamingo a solid look.

A hundred and sixty-two years old, give or take a day. Five foot four. Maybe ninety pounds including the flamingo. Only dangerous if she tripped and bludgeoned someone with the bright pink bird.

I spotted Ida Belle in the crowd of panicked onlookers, her

cell phone held up in the air. I assumed she was recording everything, which made me feel a little better. Clearly, she didn't feel the situation was going to escalate beyond the flamingo as a weapon. That was a safer bet here since Gertie didn't have her usual handbag of tricks.

As the two rounded the front of the restaurant, I could finally make out what Flamingo Lady was saying.

"You two-bit floozy! He was mine!"

They ran past and I looked over at the hostess. "Is this normal?" I asked.

The young woman sucked in a breath, clearly at the point of breakdown. "Oh. My. God. No."

She flapped her hands up and down, and I wasn't sure whether that helped her think or she was attempting to take flight.

"I don't know what to do," she said. "I'm going to be fired and I need this job. I mean, it's a crappy job—look at this mess —but there's not a lot of work for college students that has decent hours and doesn't involve showing your boobs."

I cringed. "Yeah, that sucks. Let me see if I can help."

"Would you? Oh. My. God. That would be awesome."

I nodded. It would be worth the hassle just to get her to stop flapping and saying Oh. My. God.

I pulled a chair from a nearby table and hopped on it to get an aerial view of the situation and consider my options. Gertie and Flamingo Lady had run up the middle row of the restaurant tables again and had turned around and were headed back my direction. Simple, I thought. When they passed, I'd simply nab Flamingo Lady.

I frowned. Or maybe I wouldn't. As sure as I did, she'd have grounds to press charges against me for assault. I no longer had the CIA to back me up on my actions. Everything I did would be viewed with me as an average citizen and I would be held to the same behavioral standards. Tackling old ladies—even if it was done carefully and even if they were sporting a weapon, of sorts—would probably not be taken well.

I heard yelling down the hall and figured someone had alerted management to the crisis. If I was going to save the hostess and her boobs from an awful future, I had to act fast. I jumped off the chair, reached for the tablecloth on an empty table, and yanked it off. Then I gripped opposite ends of it and flipped it over a bit to make it smaller in width and jumped back onto the chair. I'd barely gotten set up when Gertie ran past me.

"Do something!" she yelled. "Before I really do kill someone!"

Flamingo Lady was starting to lag, but I didn't think for a minute she was ready to give up. And Gertie had already run longer than I'd figured she could. Her face was red from the effort.

As Flamingo Lady passed, I jumped off the chair, draping the tablecloth around her, effectively roping her with linens. I got in a secure stance and heard an "oof" as Flamingo Lady ran into the last bit of slack in the tablecloth. Before she could attempt to wrangle out, I crossed the cloth and tightened it, wrapping her up as though she were wearing a straitjacket.

Unfortunately, she'd managed to get the arm with the flamingo free before I tightened, and the combination of her forward momentum and her sudden stop caused her to lose her grip on the plastic decoration.

The pink bird went tumbling through the air and hit Gertie right in the back of the head. Given her general lack of physical conditioning and the fact that she'd just spent several minutes being chased by a crazy woman wielding a plastic bird, it wasn't a surprise when she lost control. She lurched forward at impact and her already-tired legs buckled. She threw her arms out in front of her, trying to regain her balance, but there was no stopping that moving train.

She slid right onto the buffet table like a drunken college kid at a frat party, her outstretched arms flinging containers of food in all directions. Women started screaming as shrimp, fish, cocktail sauce, rice, and a host of other dishes became part of their dinner wear. I pulled Flamingo Lady into the chair I'd used for my roping event and deftly tied her in place. Gertie finally slid to a stop in the middle of the buffet line and rolled off the table with a groan. Her legs were wobbling, but at least she was standing.

A second later, a harried-looking man wearing black slacks and a button-up shirt skidded to a stop beside me. His expression was a combination of "What the hell happened here?" and "How can I be sued for it?" I figured he must be the resort manager.

He looked over at the distraught hostess. "What in the world is going on?" he asked.

The hostess lifted a menu in front of her chest—probably a subconscious move—and paled. "I don't know," she managed. "There was yelling and when I looked, that woman," she pointed at Flamingo Lady, "was chasing another one, trying to hit her with the flamingo from the table decoration."

The manager stared at her for a second, clearly trying to process what must have been a fairly absurd explanation, even for a vacation resort. Then he looked over at Flamingo Lady and froze when he realized she was tied to a chair with table linen. She was attempting to free herself but couldn't reach the back knot.

I figured that was my cue so I stepped forward. "I arrived at the restaurant right after the commotion started. It's just as the young lady stated. This woman was chasing another with the apparent thought of using the flamingo as a weapon."

"And how did she manage to tie herself to the chair?" he asked.

"Oh, I did that," I said. "I didn't figure it was a good idea to tackle an old lady, but I was afraid other people were going to be hurt if she kept running like a crazy person. So I lassoed her with the tablecloth and tied her up so she couldn't go for round two."

"Who are you calling old?" Flamingo Lady yelled.

"I think age is the least of your problems," I said.

The manager still looked slightly confused but was clearly moving past surprised to angry. "Someone is going to pay for this damage," he said.

"Well, it's not going to be me," Flamingo Lady argued. "It's all her fault." She pointed at Gertie, who was limping in our direction, wearing the remnants of most of the buffet. The manager glanced over and did a double take.

"Are you all right, ma'am?" he asked. "Do you need medical attention?"

"No," Gertie said. "But I'll probably need to shower in bleach or I'll smell like shrimp for the next fifty years."

"I'm not footing the bill for that floozy," Flamingo Lady ranted. "She's lucky I'm tied up or I'd finish giving her what she has coming."

"What did this woman do to you?" the manager asked.

"She stole my man!" Flamingo Lady screamed, and she wriggled in the tablecloth.

And finally, it all clicked. Pink Plastic Weapon Woman must have been one of Otis's targets, and she'd seen him with Gertie the night before. I shook my head. For someone who made a living scamming, Otis should have been smart enough to target women in different resorts. Or at least avoid taking a second target to dinner *at* the resort when he already had a first target on the line. But then, greed was often the downfall of the criminal sort.

"He was *not* your man," Gertie said. "I don't see a ring on your finger and there sure as heck wasn't one on his. If you had a problem with Otis, you should have taken it up with him...or maybe you did."

Gertie narrowed her eyes at Flamingo Lady, who began to gasp and sputter.

"Are you insinuating that I had something to do with Otis's death?" the enraged woman asked. "I could never kill someone."

"You could have tonight," I said. "All it would have taken was for someone to fall on a steak knife or break their neck or crash into one of those vacationers with an oxygen tank. You're certainly mad enough to kill someone. And you're clearly delusional enough to think it would improve your situation."

Flamingo Lady turned beet red and thrashed in the table-cloth so hard that the chair started to rock. She was yelling so loud and fast that most of what she said was unintelligible, except for the occasional curse word. Finally, the chair reached tipping point and flipped on its side, slamming her into the ground.

"I want that woman arrested for assault," Flamingo Lady yelled from the floor. "And I'm suing this resort."

The manager froze. The hostess dropped the menu and slunk back behind a plant.

Ida Belle stepped up to the manager and waved her phone. "Please do call the police. I filmed the entire thing. The only person who needs some jail time is the crazy woman in the tablecloth. And I'm happy to provide a copy for the resort's attorney for when you sue for damages."

The manager stared at Ida Belle, completely silent, and I

could tell he was attempting to process the odds of the lawsuit lottery. Finally, he nodded. "I'll call the police now," he said. "They're going to want to talk to all of you, so if you could just make yourselves comfortable."

"Do I look like comfort is achievable?" Gertie asked as a glob of cocktail sauce slid off the top of her head and down her nose.

The manager whirled around and spotted the hostess behind the plant. "Get this woman some warm, wet towels and some dry ones."

The hostess made a sound like baby birds do when they're hungry, then scurried off in the direction of the kitchen.

"What about me?" Flamingo Lady asked, a bit more subdued now that the police were being called. "Are you just going to leave me down here?"

I looked over at the manager and shrugged. "I'm okay with it, but I suppose that's your call."

He gave me a pained look. "I suppose we should upright her, but I'm inclined to leave her...um, incapacitated, until the police arrive."

"Good call," I said as I reached over and pulled the chair upright.

The manager blinked, apparently surprised that I'd so easily lifted the chair and woman, and he gave me a hard look, probably trying to figure out exactly what kind of woman had tablecloth wrangling skills and the ability to lift close to her own body weight without straining. I had a feeling he came up short on the answer.

The manager waved me over to the restaurant entry and extended his hand. "I'm Fletcher Sampson, the resort manager."

"Fortune Redding," I said as I clasped his hand.

His eyes widened and I knew he recognized the name.

"Yep," I said. "The same Fortune Redding rooming with the woman Deputy Benton was hunting for today. She's the one wearing your buffet." I pointed at Gertie, who was dripping on the carpet.

Ida Belle stepped up beside me and I nodded my head toward her. "The lady with the video is my other roomie."

"I...oh my." He looked slightly ill. "I've only been here three months and until now, no trouble. But this week, the wheels seem to have come off. The owner flew in today and I met with him this afternoon. He's already very upset over the, er, situation we currently have. When he hears the police had to come out again, I don't know what he's going to do."

"Are you afraid you'll lose your job?" I asked.

"What?" He jerked a bit, then stared at me, as if trying to catch up to the conversation. "Yes. It's definitely a concern."

"One of the locals told me you guys were friends. That you get to take his yacht out. Surely he wouldn't fire you over this or the other situation? Neither is your fault."

"I...we know each other from another resort he has in the Keys where I was an assistant manager. He recruited me from there to work for him here. I'd say we're friendly but not friends. I don't have the economic status to call someone of his caliber a friend."

"I saw the boat today when we were fishing," I said. "That's a heck of a loaner for someone just being friendly."

He gave me a small smile. "I'm afraid that's simply more work, although it's not much of a hardship. He needs someone to look after his boat. My father was a harbormaster at a marina, so I grew up around boats and know how to handle them properly. I do him the favor of making sure his boat is always ready for him to use and in return, I get to spend time on an excellent vessel."

"That's a good deal," Ida Belle said. "I wonder if I can make friends with a rich guy who owns a Formula 1 team. I'd give my right foot to drive one of those cars. Well, maybe not my right one as I'd need it, but you know what I mean."

"My dream is flying an F-16," I said.

"Do you even know how to fly a plane?" Ida Belle asked.

I shook my head. "That's why it's a dream."

The hostess returned with a stack of towels, dry and wet, and Gertie began going about the business of attempting to remove the food from her face and head.

"I don't suppose you have any cheesecake left?" I asked. "All this security work has made me hungry."

Fletcher stared at me a moment, attempting to process my out-of-left-field request.

"I, uh, sure," he said as he waved at a server. "Please get this woman a slice of cheesecake and whatever else her party needs."

The silence that had eclipsed the restaurant while we'd been arguing had disappeared and was slowly being replaced by grumbling. Fletcher jolted out of his stupor and stepped back into the restaurant, waving his hands in the air.

"Everyone," he announced to the curious dining patrons, "I am so sorry for the disruption to your dinner. It will be comped, of course, and your servers will be happy to assist you with anything you need to complete your meal." He glanced over at the mangled buffet. "Assuming what you want is still available."

A few of the women sat back down, clearly not about to let a free meal go to waste, even though there wasn't much left of it. The rest mumbled among themselves and started moving toward the exit.

Ida Belle elbowed the manager. "You should get a list of names for the police and for your attorney."

"Yes, of course!" He spun around and hurried off in an attempt to get ahead of the vacating crowd.

Gertie had finally finished getting what food she could off of her body and clothes, and I motioned toward the coffee bar. She gave me a nod and limped off. I headed over to a table near Flamingo Lady and took a seat, Ida Belle in tow.

"This is not going to play out well with Benton," Ida Belle said.

I shrugged. "Can't do anything about it now. Besides, you have video and Gertie has an attorney."

Ida Belle nodded and sat back in her chair, looking at her phone. I could tell by her grin that she was watching the Great Flamingo Chase all over again.

I pulled my chair closer to Flamingo Lady, who was still glaring at me. "So," I said. "You did all this damage over a man? That's foolish. If he was stepping out on you already, doesn't seem like he'd be worth the trouble."

Flamingo Lady stiffened. "He was *not* stepping out on me. That floozy propositioned him. You know how weak men are."

I nodded. "So you're saying that despite the fact that he was all in for you, he was easily swayed by the wiles of another woman. Yeah, I'm still not getting why he's worth assault and property damage charges, but I guess we all have different standards."

"I didn't assault anyone," Flamingo Lady said.

"That table decoration might beg to differ," Ida Belle said.

"So here's the deal," I said. "If this guy is the center of all this trouble, why not just call him down here to face the music? Make him explain himself. Seems like the simple, nonviolent way to settle this."

The anger faded from Flamingo Lady's face and was replaced with sadness and regret. "I can't. He died this morning. You probably heard about it."

"*That* guy?" I asked. "Wow. Yeah, I guess getting a straight answer out of him now isn't going to happen."

"Wasn't going to happen when he was alive," Ida Belle said.

"What do you know?" Flamingo Lady asked. "You didn't know Otis. He was the kindest, sweetest man. He was always trying to take care of people. That must have been why he took that floozy to dinner. He felt sorry for her."

Ida Belle rolled her eyes. "Yeah. I'm sure that's it."

I leaned toward the woman. "Look. I'm not trying to crap on your memories or anything, but word around the resort was that guy liked to borrow money from women, then never got around to repaying it. Maybe that's why he was out with the floozy. He'd tapped you out and needed to find another target."

Her face flushed as she dropped her eyes to the floor, and I knew I'd nailed it.

"How much did you give him?" I asked.

"I didn't *give* him anything," she said. "I made an investment in a business venture. It was going to pay big dividends. I saw all the paperwork."

"Maybe he didn't include the page where he was looking for more investors," I said.

Uncertainty wavered in her eyes and finally she sighed. "You really think it was all a lie?"

I nodded. "According to the local bar gossip, you're not the first woman he's gotten money from."

"But you'll be the last," Ida Belle said.

Flamingo Lady didn't look remotely placated.

"Do you think the cops can get my money back?" she asked.

I frowned. "I doubt it, but you can ask. You realize that this stunt you pulled is also going to get you placed on the suspect list, right?"

"What?" Her eyes widened and she paled. "I didn't...I couldn't...I would have hit the floozy with the flamingo, I'll admit that. And I *did* hit her in the head with half a sheet cake, but there's no way I could kill someone."

"That might be the case," I said. "But given the circumstances, you see where the police might feel differently, right?"

Suddenly everything I was saying clicked and she started to sway.

"She's going to pass out," I said.

"Let her," Ida Belle said. "I was tired of hearing her yap anyway. This murder thing is really putting a cramp in our relaxation. We should be sitting on the balcony, drinking ourselves into a stupor, and eating a pile of sugary goodness right now."

Flamingo Lady's head made a big circle before her chin came to rest on her chest.

I looked over at Ida Belle. "There's probably still some sheet cake left in Gertie's hair."

CHAPTER TWELVE

WHEN BENTON WALKED INTO THE RESTAURANT AND CAUGHT sight of Gertie, he scowled. "I should have known you'd be in trouble before nightfall," he said. "You're one of those people. A chronic problem. You may have some people fooled with that silver hair and nice old lady face, but I know what you are."

"Old lady face?" Gertie looked outraged. "Says the deputy who's so afraid of water he almost drowned in three feet of it. You probably have a urinal in your house because the toilet gives you the vapors."

"You're afraid of water?" Fletcher asked. "You work on an island."

"I'm not afraid of water!" Benton yelled. "Now, if you'll just move aside and let me arrest this woman, we can all get on with our lives."

"I'm afraid I can't allow that," Fletcher said. "This woman is the victim, not the perpetrator. The woman passed out in the tablecloth attempted to assault her with a flamingo and during that event, most of my buffet was destroyed."

Benton glanced around the room, taking in the cleaning

staff working diligently to pick strewn food off the tables, chairs, floor, and one chandelier. Then he gave the woman in the tablecloth a good once-over.

"Let me get this straight," Benton said. "That woman attempted to assault another with a flamingo? How is that even possible?"

"A plastic flamingo," I clarified. "From the centerpiece on the buffet."

Benton looked from me to the manager, his disbelief clear. Ida Belle stepped forward.

"I have the incident on video," Ida Belle said and held up her phone.

Benton stretched out his hand. "I'm going to have to take that."

"No," Ida Belle said. "You're not. I will send you the file and you can do whatever you'd like with it. But I highly suggest you take this woman to a cell to sleep off her mad because the resort will likely be pursuing a damage lawsuit. It wouldn't look good if the local police failed to do anything about such an occurrence, especially as it happened at the most exclusive resort on the island."

Benton scowled but Ida Belle's point was clear. The resort paid a ton of taxes, which paid a chunk of Benton's salary. Tourism was what kept their area of the state alive. If vacationers were allowed to run around assaulting others and trashing dining rooms, then people might not want to come to the resort. That wasn't even taking into account the dead tourist.

Resigned to his duties, Benton's shoulders slumped. "How the heck am I supposed to get her to jail if she's passed out?"

Gertie grabbed a pitcher of water from a nearby serving cart and tossed the entire container full in Flamingo Lady's face. Her eyes flew open and she started sputtering, spitting water everywhere. She looked wildly around the room, finally locking her gaze on Gertie, who was still holding the pitcher.

"I want that woman arrested," Flamingo Lady demanded.

"There you go," I said. "All awake and able to walk. I bet she entertains you all night with completely inaccurate stories of how she's the victim."

Ida Belle nodded and waved her phone. "But oh, the wonders of the digital age."

I looked over at Benton. "Since you've got your hands full, can I assume we're free to leave? It's been a long day and I'd like to get some rest."

"I'm going to need statements from all of you," Benton said.

"We'll be happy to provide them tomorrow," I said.

"When tomorrow?" Benton pushed.

"When we get good and ready," Ida Belle said. "We're on vacation and the last person I want to spend time with is you."

Fletcher covered his mouth with his hand and inched backward, perhaps wondering if he could disappear into the drapes. He was probably trying to figure out how to explain this level of absurdity to the owner. I had a feeling that if he couldn't come up with something good, he might be chartering with Deep Sea Dave like the rest of us. Or managing a storage facility in Idaho.

Ida Belle motioned to me and Gertie and we headed off, leaving Benton still glaring at us. As we reached the exit, Gertie spotted the offending pink flamingo on the floor and kicked it.

Then promptly fell into a fake hibiscus bush.

———

BY THE TIME WE GOT SHOWERED AND ONTO THE BALCONY, it was close to 10:00 p.m. and we were all already yawning. Instead of beer, we'd all opted for a round of coffee. After all, we had work to do before we could turn in. I filled Ida Belle and Gertie in on what I'd discovered from the men in the bar and made notes on my laptop as I went.

"That's all I got," I said. "It's not a lot, but we have a couple leads on suspects to check out."

Ida Belle shook her head. "I disagree. You got a whole lot. You got cause of death."

"Sort of," I said. "But it's going to be hard to narrow things down without knowing what kind of poison was used. And poison also presents other problems."

"Like what?" Gertie asked.

"Like barrier to entry," I said. "If Otis had been shot or strangled or stabbed to death, then we would have known where and exactly when the delivery of death occurred, so to speak."

Ida Belle sighed. "But with poison, someone could have slipped it into a bottle of water on the beach or injected a candy bar...things he might not have consumed immediately after the poison was administered."

I nodded. "Which explains why Gertie was Benton's first stop. She was the last to share a meal with the deceased."

"Well, crap," Gertie said. "I figured the room access issue was going to be the thing that wrapped this up. Check the cameras and the room entry cards and you've got a list of potentials. Even if Otis made a booty call after he dropped me off, cameras still would have caught her walking down the hallway."

I cringed a little at the words "booty call" but her point was accurate, if not unnecessary.

"That also means everyone is back on the suspect list," I said. "At least as far as opportunity goes."

"Our list, anyway," Ida Belle said. "But if we could find out what poison was used and how it was administered, we might be back to a narrower list."

"Sure," I agreed, "but how do we get that information? You bonded well with the dispatcher, but I still don't think she'll give you case information."

"Especially when my friend is one of the suspects," Ida Belle said.

"This would be so much easier if we were in Sinful," Gertie said.

It was an unfortunate truth. Of course, "easier" referred to our ability to break into the sheriff's department and lift information from the case files, so not on the legal side of things. But since Sinful was too cheap to spring for the security cameras Carter kept asking for, breaking and entering remained an option.

"Maybe—" Gertie started.

Ida Belle held up her hand. "Don't even go there. We cannot break into the sheriff's department. They have cameras and Benton is just looking for a reason to lock us all up and throw away the key. No sense in giving him ammunition."

"I wasn't going to suggest a break-in," Gertie said. "I'm not stupid. Reckless, perhaps, but even I know where the line is."

I raised one eyebrow but remained silent.

"I see that look," Gertie said to me. "Okay, here's the thing. There are cameras on the exterior of the sheriff's department building, so we can't break in. But there aren't any cameras inside."

"Are you suggesting we teleport into the building then?" Ida Belle asked. "Because that would be very cool, but *Star Trek* is not real."

Gertie rolled her eyes. "Your sarcasm is both unappreciated and inappropriate. I'm suggesting we walk in the front door. We have to give statements, right? There were only a couple of people in the department last time we were there. All we need is for one or two of us to create a distraction and then the other can look for the case file."

"Just like that?" Ida Belle said. "You ask for a tissue or something and in that span of time, we're supposed to not only locate the case file, but the specific document detailing the cause and manner of death."

"Why not?" Gertie asked.

Ida Belle shook her head. "We'd do better waiting on that teleporting thing to be invented."

I stared out into the darkness.

"Fortune?" Gertie asked. "Are you still with us?"

"What?" I asked. "Yes. Sorry. I was just thinking."

"Please tell me you weren't actually considering Gertie's harebrained idea," Ida Belle said.

"Maybe," I said. "It's not the worst idea."

"It's not even *Gertie's* worst idea," Ida Belle said. "But that doesn't mean we should try it."

"I'm not saying we could successfully execute it, because the big unknown is whether or not we could find the case file in the time allotted," I said. "But I think we could easily create enough distraction to give someone a chance to look. At least we can if it's only Benton and the dispatcher in the office."

Ida Belle sighed. "And what kind of distraction do you suggest? Please don't say fire."

During a recent unauthorized investigation, we'd attempted to clear out an office by setting off the fire alarms with a smoke bomb. Unfortunately, we'd ended up starting an actual fire. I'd put it out before it progressed beyond a treadmill, but it definitely wasn't our finest hour for mission execution.

"As much as I wouldn't mind setting Benton's desk on fire," I said, "I don't think that's the best option in this case. With so few people and a small space, anyone lagging behind on the evacuation would be obvious."

"What then?" Ida Belle asked.

I thought about it for a minute, then an idea slowly began to form. "Let's start with the basis that it's only Benton and the dispatcher. If there are more people in the building, then it's a no-go. Too risky."

"Okay," Ida Belle said. "I'm listening."

"So we have someone call in an emergency that requires Benton to respond. That leaves only the dispatcher. Gertie fakes a heart attack or some other malady, you and the dispatcher assist, and that gives me time to see if I can locate the case file."

"Won't the dispatcher notice if Gertie is in the throes of death and you go wandering off?" Ida Belle asked.

I frowned. "You're probably right. So I'll have to go back to give my statement first. That way, I'm in the back of the building. When Benton is paged to leave, I'll ask to use the ladies' room. Then Gertie does her thing and I show up after the fact, faking surprise and worry."

"It would be worth doing just to see you fake surprise and worry," Gertie said.

Ida Belle was silent for several seconds, then nodded. "I suppose it could work, but only if a million things fall in line like dominoes. Something else to be considered is that if another deputy is already on patrol, the dispatcher will send them on a call rather than Benton."

"Oh, but not if the caller is specifically requesting Benton," I said.

"Who in the world would request him?" Gertie said.

I smiled. "Our friend Fletcher, maybe? Benton's the one who took the call here tonight. My guess is Flamingo Lady will be out first thing in the morning. So if someone were to call saying she was causing problems again, and that the manager needed Benton specifically as he was already versed in the situation, then he'd have to go."

"Since we're all going to be in the sheriff's department building," Gertie asked, "who's going to make that call?"

"Marie could do it," I said. "She can use a prepaid cell and we can reimburse her when we get back. She can say she's an employee calling for Fletcher."

"They can still trace the call to the nearest tower," Ida Belle said.

"And that proves what?" I asked. "If we were springing someone out of jail, then it would be a problem. But since nothing is actually going to happen as far as the sheriff's department employees are concerned, then it's just a crank call. The fact that it comes from our hometown is definitely suspicious but doesn't give away motive."

"It's convoluted," Ida Belle said. "But it just might work."

Gertie clapped her hands and bounced once, then grabbed her head. "Jesus, that flamingo really packed a wallop."

Ida Belle nodded. "Ole girl was still carrying a bit of speed when Fortune nabbed her. Nice move there, by the way."

"Thanks," I said.

"Speaking of moves," Gertie said, narrowing her eyes at Ida Belle. "Why didn't you do anything?"

"I was filming," Ida Belle said. "And it's a good thing I was because without that indisputable proof, you'd probably be sitting in a jail cell tonight instead of that crazy woman."

"I guess," Gertie said. "But it still seems kind of mean,

letting that woman assault me with bad centerpiece art and destroy a perfectly good buffet."

"You would have done the same," Ida Belle said.

Gertie grinned. "Yeah, I would have. Let's watch the video again. The faces of the other diners are priceless."

"Later," I said. "You guys haven't told me what you found out. Or was inciting an assault charge the only thing you managed?"

"I don't know what Gertie did before the Great Flamingo Chase," Ida Belle said, "but I did get some information. Of course, it's not nearly as interesting now that we know Otis was poisoned."

"What is it?" I asked.

"One of the ladies I was sitting with has a great-niece with a friend who works in housekeeping. The friend overheard a couple of the security guards talking, and they said no one entered Otis's room last night after he did and he was alone when he went in. Of course, now that we know it was poison, it could have been someone who entered earlier that day or someone who was very clever and never entered at all."

"I told you he didn't make a booty call," Gertie said. "He was probably too stung by my rejection."

Ida Belle rolled her eyes. "The only thing he might have been stung by—sometime in the future—was your failure to write him a check."

"Even scammers can get the hots for someone," Gertie said. "You saw that dining room of options. I'm the obvious choice if he was going to have a romantic fling."

"Anyway," Ida Belle said, "this woman's niece also said that the security guys spotted several copies of checks on the kitchen counter when they went to secure the room after the maintenance reported finding Otis. The checks were made out to Otis from different women."

"Did they mention any names?" I asked.

"If they did, the friend didn't hear," Ida Belle said. "The security guys finally noticed her cleaning nearby and left."

I nodded and frowned, a new thought occurring to me. "You know," I said, "given that information, I'm more inclined to believe someone did enter Otis's room with the poison rather than spiking something while he was out and about."

"Why is that?" Gertie asked. "It's a far bigger risk to do it in his room."

"Yes," I agreed, "but there was also a big risk of poisoning the wrong person if they did it while he was on the beach or at the pool or whatever. Think about it. Otis's inroad with Gertie was coming to her rescue. It's probably a well-used ploy. So he'd be just as likely to give a woman who was coughing his bottle of water, say, than drink it himself. It sounds like he was a consummate opportunist and probably had a play for every situation."

"But if they put the poison in something in his room, couldn't the same thing happen?" Gertie asked. "If Otis brought a woman back to his room, he could just as easily have given her the poisoned whatever rather than consuming it himself."

"I don't think he brought women back to his room," I said. "Those checks from other women were sitting out on the table. He wouldn't have them sitting out like that if he was bringing marks to his room."

"She's right," Ida Belle said. "Besides, it sounds like Otis was working several women at one time and all passed through the same resort property, either as vacationers or staff. It would be beyond foolish to have them in his room. What would prevent one from showing up unannounced when he already had one inside? He had less chance of being caught if he always went to the woman's room or house or whatever."

"Then why did he take me to dinner at the resort?" Gertie asked. "He outed himself to Flamingo Lady that way."

"Based on her cheap bleach job and discount clothes," Ida Belle said, "I'm going to guess that Otis figured he'd gotten everything he could out of her. Besides, he could always say it wasn't a romance. It was a business loan."

"So *she* says," I said. "I believe that about as much as I believe that bleach job. I have no doubt he pitched her a business deal, but he definitely did it with a romantic bent."

"Absolutely," Ida Belle agreed. "But if there was nothing left on that vine, then Otis would have insisted she misconstrued their relationship. Of course, the money would already be invested, and he'd assure her that everything was legit. Whatever got rid of her."

"Oohhhh," Gertie said. "The fastest way to get rid of her was to be seen with another woman. I bet that's why he booked dinner at the onsite restaurant."

Ida Belle nodded. "It's certainly possible. He would have been killing two birds with one stone. He could get rid of Flamingo Lady and put a new target in his sights."

"But what about the women who worked at the resort?" Gertie asked.

"My guess is he'd either already collected or knew he wasn't going to," Ida Belle said.

"I think Ida Belle's right," I said. "Plus, if Otis has been pitching his plea for cash as an investment, then he could have told the others that you were a potential investor and it was strictly business."

"You think they would have bought that?" Gertie asked.

"If they wanted the attention bad enough, yeah," Ida Belle said. "You heard Flamingo Lady. She already had you painted as a combination of the Pied Piper and the Scarlet Letter. She had convinced herself that any romantic inclinations were all your doing. That Otis was the innocent in all of it."

Gertie sighed. "I'm not going to lie—it's been a long time since I've enjoyed romantic company. But even if it's another decade, I just don't see giving up my dignity and self-respect for a lie."

"Me either," Ida Belle said. "But there's a lot of lonely old people out there. And they're easy prey for the unscrupulous."

Gertie shook her head. "I hope Otis enjoyed his time on earth, because I have a feeling he's toasting somewhere a lot hotter than the beach about now."

"He's got a lot of company," I said.

"I'm sure," Ida Belle agreed, then sighed. "You know, if the poison was in something in Otis's room, we still can't narrow down when. It could have been in a bottle of whiskey that he didn't drink for a week."

"That's unfortunately true," I said. "Opportunity is a wide-open field at the moment. If Otis was scamming employees, then they would have had opportunity to do something any time if they had room access."

"Security footage would narrow things down, but if we had two weeks' worth to go through, how many people would that be? With different housekeeping staff, maintenance, security, management, room service...and who knows who else, any number of people could have been in his room in the course of the two weeks he was here."

"Yeah. I think working on the list of those with motive is going to be the most productive route for now. If this long shot at the sheriff's department works, then maybe we can narrow things down more by the type of poison used."

"I hope so, because it's looking like Otis might have offended a long list of people," Ida Belle said.

"What about you?" I asked Gertie. "Did you glean any nuggets of wisdom before you had to start sprinting?"

"Just one small thing," Gertie said. "One of the women said when she went to the front desk a couple days ago to pick up a package, she heard our friend Fletcher complaining to someone in the office behind the desk. She couldn't make out everything but got the impression that he was trying to figure out a way to boot Otis from the resort. She gathered he was hoping Otis had an outstanding bill he could call him on, but apparently, Otis prepaid a week at a time and never charged anything to his room. He was already paid through this weekend."

"I can see why Fletcher wouldn't want a predator wandering among his guests," Ida Belle said. "It could be a big problem for the resort. These days, all it takes is one social media post to go viral and everything can go straight into the toilet. And it seems like the owner keeps his thumb on everything. Probably best for Fletcher to get rid of potential problems before they can even arise."

"Assuming Fletcher was onto Otis's game, I'm sure he didn't like it," I said. "But there's a bit of a chasm between trying to boot him out of the resort and killing him."

"Yes," Ida Belle agreed. "But people aren't always rational. Especially when it comes to money. I imagine he makes a decent living for a resort town, this being the most expensive resort on the island. If he lost his job here, his prospects probably don't compare, assuming he could get another management job at all. And his boat privileges are definitely a perk that doesn't come along often."

I made some notes. "I agree he had plenty to lose, but surely he could have trumped up some reason to get Otis out of the resort if he thought things were getting too hot. One of the guys at the bar mentioned something about the resorts blacklisting scammers, so they must have ways of handling the situation. It might have taken a bit longer than Fletcher would have wanted, but I'm sure he had ways of getting Otis off the premises aside from in a body bag."

"Good point," Ida Belle said. "And poison *is* traditionally a woman's game."

"Okay," I said. "Anyone else for the list?"

Gertie shook her head. "Flamingo Lady was the only one of the vacationers I found that Otis had on the hook."

"The only one who admitted it," Ida Belle said.

I nodded. "The women he scammed wouldn't have spoken out before because of embarrassment. Now that it's a murder investigation, they definitely aren't going to be offering themselves up. Gossip and rumor will be the only way to ferret them out."

"Unless we could get a look at those check copies," Gertie said. "Maybe they'll be in the case file as well."

"Maybe, but we can't depend on it," I said. "We can't even depend on seeing the case file. It's a long shot, at best. And while I'm willing to give a long shot a whirl, I still think our best bet is working people based on the information we got tonight."

Ida Belle nodded. "I agree. I think Gertie should start tomorrow morning with housekeeping. They usually start on this floor early. I imagine she can coax some information out of one of them at least, even if it takes a little cash to do it, but it's probably better if she hits them up alone. Too many people and they won't be as willing to talk. Plus, I think the fewer people who see us together, the better off we'll be getting information down the line."

I nodded. "The Otis and Gertie connection is going to come out sooner rather than later, especially with Benton pushing everyone around. If the rest of the staff connects the three of us, then none of us will be able to get information out of them. Fortunately, housekeeping wouldn't have been around to see the Great Flamingo Chase, so Gertie is probably in the clear talking to them for now."

Ida Belle nodded. "We should probably try to stay separated when we're out and about in the resort, at least until we've gotten all we can out of the staff. We don't have much time until everyone links us, though, so we should get everything we can tomorrow."

"What about the front office person that Fortune got a line on?" Gertie asked.

"I think it's better if I work that angle," Ida Belle said. "If the woman bought into Otis's bull, then she might feel the same way about you as Flamingo Lady does. Housekeeping is different as none of them were the victims, at least that we know of."

"What about me?" I asked.

CHAPTER THIRTEEN

IDA BELLE HESITATED BEFORE ANSWERING AND I STIFFENED, already worried about what might come.

"I know it's a convoluted avenue, but I think you should talk to the security guys," Ida Belle said. "See if you can get some information out of them about the camera footage or key cards used to enter Otis's room."

I sighed. "You want me to flirt with security so I can pump them for information."

"You're sorta the only one qualified for the job," Ida Belle said.

"Hello," Gertie said. "I could flirt with security."

"I want them to flap their gums," Ida Belle said. "Not take a sick day."

"Fine," Gertie said. "Security at resorts like this are a bunch of techies anyway. Geeks aren't my thing."

I stared at Gertie in dismay, then looked over at Ida Belle. "Geeks? I scare geeks. Every time I had to go down to the IT department at the CIA, it was like I'd brought a funeral procession with me. All the guys froze and no one would look me in the eye. Apparently my sneakers were far more interesting. Speaking was at an all-time premium and usually only happened if their boss yelled at them to answer a direct question."

Ida Belle patted my arm. "Your looks will put most geeks off-kilter but the geeks at the CIA also knew what you did for a living."

"Ah! So you're saying I shouldn't tell security that I'm retired CIA," I said. "Got it. Guess I'll just play the random vacationer like I did in the bar. It seemed to work for the old guys. Do the young ones go for that whole white-knight thing?"

"If they have a pulse, they'll go for it," Gertie said.

"It will help if you compliment them on how smart they are," Ida Belle said. "Geeks value their intelligence higher than anything else."

"Because they don't have the muscle strength to open a jar of pickles," Gertie said. "Give me a set of muscles any day."

"Otis didn't have muscles," I pointed out.

"No guys our age have muscles," Ida Belle said. "Lifting the TV remote doesn't exactly keep the biceps bulging. Remember to make up a fake name when you talk to them."

I nodded. I was sure they could locate me easily enough if they wanted, but there was no point spelling it out for them.

Gertie clapped her hands. "Oooohhh, I have a name! Candy."

I shook my head. "No stripper names."

"Sapphire is a stripper name," Gertie said. "Candy is a high school cheerleader name."

"I don't even think I can say 'Hi, I'm Candy' without shooting myself," I said.

"You managed 'Hi, I'm Sandy-Sue,'" Ida Belle said.

"Yeah, but my life was on the line, and I was getting paid."

"Candy is perfect," Gertie said. "Makes them think of

young, hot cheerleaders who wear strawberry-flavored lip gloss. They taste sweet."

"Gross," I said. "I don't care if you have to go to jail. No one is tasting me."

"There will be no tasting during this investigation," Ida Belle said. "Not of or by suspects, anyway. But I still want to hit that frozen drink tasting party Friday night."

"I think we're going to need it," I said.

"So, do we have our assignments for tomorrow?" Ida Belle asked.

Gertie and I nodded, then Gertie rose from her chair. "I'm going to head to bed," she said. "Running from that crazy woman wore me out."

She shuffled back into the condo, closing the sliding glass door behind her. I looked over at Ida Belle, who was staring out at the ocean, frowning.

"You worried?" I asked.

"About Gertie? Not really. It might be more of a hassle than we'd like it to be and definitely money that no one wanted to spend, but Gertie has a way of always coming out on top."

"Or without a top."

"Ha! Yeah, well, clothes and Gertie don't always agree on how long they should grace her body."

"Clothes don't always agree that they *should* grace her body."

She laughed but I could tell her mind was somewhere else. If Gertie wasn't her concern, what was? Ida Belle was never a chatterbox, but her silence felt ominous. I was new to this close friendship thing so I wasn't sure what my role was here. Did I sit in silence with her or did I press her to see if there was something on her mind she wanted to share? Finally, nosiness won out.

"Anything else bothering you?" I asked.

She looked over at me. "Is it that obvious?"

"You were a different kind of quiet. My mom did it sometimes when my dad was away. I realized later on that he'd probably missed a check-in and she was wondering if it was ever going to come."

Ida Belle nodded, her expression sympathetic. "But she didn't want you to think something was wrong."

"No. But I still knew. I just didn't understand the severity of the possibilities. You're okay, right? I mean, physically?"

"Oh yes. It's nothing like that. Nothing at all, really. Just the musings of an old lady."

I started to reply but decided to wait. If Ida Belle had something she wanted me to know, she'd offer it up to fill the silence. If not, then I'd head on to bed myself and leave her to her thoughts.

"Do you ever think about the road you didn't travel?" Ida Belle asked.

"Are you kidding? All the time. Hell, since I arrived in Sinful, I've called into question every choice I've ever made. Not to mention everything I thought I knew about myself and everyone else."

She gave me a small smile. "You've definitely had a lot to process. But you're doing a fine job of it."

"If I am, it's because I've had some fine support."

"You're worth it. You're a good woman, Fortune. A good friend."

My chest tightened just a bit. I had finally gotten used to the idea that these two women were the family I'd always needed, but sometimes it still made me clench with gratitude. When I'd been forced to hide out in Sinful, I'd thought it was the end of world. And in a way it was. The end of the world I used to know. A world that was full of professional accomplishment but little personal joy.

I was hell-bent on tipping the scales in the other direction in my second life stage.

"You thinking about the Walter road?" I asked, taking a stab at what I thought she might be dwelling on.

She gave me a single nod. "You think it's silly, right? I mean, I made my choice long ago. You know my reasons, and they're sound."

I hesitated before replying. I knew Ida Belle felt that even though he had carried a torch for her his entire life, Walter would have been miserable being in a relationship with her. I understood her logic. Walter was the kind of man who loved with all his heart and wanted to protect the people he cared about. Ida Belle was the kind of woman who did what she pleased, even if it meant putting herself at risk. She thought Walter would have grown resentful that she put her desires ahead of his feelings. I knew her reasons, and they sounded good on paper. But I still wondered.

Apparently, so did she.

"Your reasons are sound," I said. "I was so young when my mother died that I didn't see things then like I do looking back. I think being married to my father was hard on her. Not just because he was a hard man but because there was so much uncertainty."

"The uncertainty is definitely the culprit."

I nodded. "Even Carter had a problem with me because of it—probably still does but he's smart enough not to say it. And he's the last person who should be worrying about someone taking risks."

"Maybe. Maybe not. Carter knows better than most exactly what those risks are. He's been on that line between life and death. Most haven't. They can only imagine what it's like, but I guarantee you their imagination comes up way short."

Having straddled that line more than a few times, I agreed with her.

"But still..." I said.

"Yes. Still..."

"It's not too late, you know," I said. "If you wanted to retrace your steps...take a walk down that road now."

"I'm still the same woman now that I was back then. That hasn't changed."

"You're not jumping out of planes into a war zone. You're not a US military spy pretending to be an average enlisted."

Ida Belle smiled. "I don't know. I jumped out of a plane last month. Gertie ensured it was a war zone before I landed."

I laughed. Gertie's insistence that we go skydiving with her had ended with a landing that had spawned a call for the police, the paramedics, two attorneys, and a priest.

"So you're saying as long as Gertie's alive, you're still at risk," I said. "I don't suppose being friends with me is doing much to improve your odds."

"Are you kidding? Being friends with you has probably already saved my life a time or two. It wasn't like Gertie and I were sitting around knitting before you showed up. We were still smack in the middle of everything we could be smack in the middle of. Stuff just wasn't as critical as the things that've cropped up since you arrived."

"Which is exactly why some of the citizens of Sinful think I brought it with me."

"They're wrong. Sinful is a pot of slow-boiling water, but once that first bubble surfaced, the rest followed. Things don't stay hidden forever, but you didn't set that pot to boil. You just happened to appear when it was showtime."

"Lucky me."

"Lucky Sinful. Some very bad people might have gotten away if you hadn't been involved."

"Hmm. Maybe." I took in a deep breath of the salt air, listening to the crash of the waves on the beach. "So...back to Walter. You don't think after all this time, he's learned anything?"

"I don't know that you can learn enough to change your nature."

"Seems like Carter did in order to be with me."

"I think the hardest thing for Carter was to learn to live in the moment. His training and natural inclination are to assess risk and mitigate it, not to sit back while people he cares about rush headlong into danger. If you spend too much time thinking about what might happen, you lose the joy of what's happening right now."

"And you don't think Walter can do that? Learn to be in the moment and not count on the next day or the next?"

Ida Belle sighed. "Walter is an old-fashioned man. Mind you, he loves to see women get an education and have a profession and all. But at his roots, he still believes a man should protect and take care of his lady, even if she's capable of taking care of herself. He's an honorable man. And an honest one. The last thing I want to do is put him in the position of having to lie to himself in order to be in a relationship with me."

"You think asking Walter to live in the moment is the same as asking him to lie to himself?"

"Yes."

Maybe she was right. Maybe it was too late for Walter to change. I frowned.

What if Carter hadn't really changed? What if he was still waiting for me to become a different person? One he didn't have to stress over every day? Could he pretend so well that he'd fooled me into believing he'd come to terms with who I was? Had he fooled himself?

"You're worried that maybe Carter hasn't changed," Ida Belle said quietly. "That one day he'll simply walk out, claiming he can't do it anymore."

Her ability to home in on my thoughts was somewhat eerie. Also annoying.

"It might have crossed my mind," I said.

She nodded. "I can see why it would. But I don't think you have anything to worry about. Carter never was able to hide the way he felt. I'm not going to say he's thrilled that he fell in love with a woman who won't back down from a gunfight. But I'll also say that he would have never been happy with one who baked cookies and knitted. And don't think he doesn't know that. There's no shortage of cookie-baking, knitting single women in Sinful—all of whom have had an unsuccessful run at Carter."

I knew she was right. Carter had admitted as much to me. He wouldn't have been able to settle down with the baking and knitting type any more than I could have been happy with an accountant. We were simply made different. We craved the excitement, the energy that came from the unknown. Ida Belle was made the same way. But Walter. Walter wasn't like that at all.

"What about Gertie?" I asked. "You think she ever has any doubts?"

"That woman hasn't had a second guess in her life. No matter how poor the choice might turn out to be, she just barrels right through it, making notes for the next time. Her optimism about life could empower entire nations of people."

"If the contents of her purse didn't blow them up first."

"There is that."

"But I meant on the man side of things. I know the Sinful

Ladies have their motto and all, but Gertie hasn't lost her eye for a good-looking man. I just wondered if maybe she wishes she'd taken the commitment route."

"Lord help us all. A man wouldn't have lasted a week with that woman." Ida Belle laughed and shook her head. "Gertie never came across a man who made her think twice about changing things. Maybe if she had...maybe. But I don't think so. I think Gertie is happiest being her own woman with no one to answer to. She's always had, as you say, the eye for a good-looking man, but it's never progressed beyond a fling. I think she likes the idea of romance but not the practicality of a day-to-day relationship."

I nodded. It made perfect sense. Gertie had always talked a good game when it came to men but I'd never heard her lament anything lasting. "The day-to-day is definitely not like what the movies portray."

"A little fling here and there gives Gertie energy. Makes her feel young and vital again."

"I thought hanging out with me did that," I joked.

She smiled. "I think the men are offering up something a little different."

"I don't know. Otis offered up crime and a murder."

"Yes, but when you offer it up, you're neither the criminal nor the victim."

"Oh, yeah. I'm a much safer bet. Such a bore. I don't know how you two stand me."

"I'm not sure how we stood life without you."

CHAPTER FOURTEEN

I WAS HURRYING TO GRAB MY PHONE OFF THE NIGHTSTAND when I heard the knock on the door. Crap! Housekeeping was early. Ida Belle had left in her usual casual stroll ten minutes earlier, hot on her mission to find an inroad to gossip with the resort staff. I had actually overslept and then couldn't seem to get everything together for my own morning assignment. First, Gertie had sent me back to my room to change out of the T-shirt and hiking shorts I'd put on to switch to a tank and shorter shorts. I was afraid it might be too much for the geeks to handle—after all, I wanted them talking, not stunned into silence—but Gertie assured me the partial paralysis I'd induce would only work in my favor.

After I'd changed, I'd grabbed my bag and started to run out when I remembered I'd left my phone. No means of communication wasn't an option, so I had to reverse once more and jog back for the phone. Unfortunately, my tardiness and housekeeping's efficiency had conspired to put me on the scene when I was supposed to be downstairs. We knew that eventually the staff would connect the three of us, but we were really trying to push that out as long as possible.

I froze, and Gertie and I stared at each other for several seconds. Finally, she waved at the coat closet.

"Get inside," she said. "I'll see if I can get them to start in the bedrooms. As soon as the coast is clear, you can run out."

I dashed into the closet, leaving a tiny crack in the door so I could see when my window of opportunity appeared. Gertie waved the housekeeping crew inside and I frowned. Four women. Three bedrooms. Unless they tag-teamed the other rooms, my chances of making an escape just went downhill. Gertie shot a look in my direction and frowned.

They hurried in with their cart and three of them grabbed supplies and headed off for the bedrooms. The remaining housekeeper, a smiling young woman, stepped into the kitchen and sprayed the sink with cleaner.

Gertie grabbed a croissant and took a seat at the kitchen counter. "I'm just going to have a bite of breakfast before heading out. I won't be in your way, will I?"

"Of course not, ma'am," the housekeeper said. "Take all the time you need. I'll clean the counter last. Not that it needs much. You keep everything pretty neat."

"I am convinced that people who make a filthy mess where they're vacationing have dirty homes," Gertie said.

"My momma says the same thing, but you wouldn't believe the damage some people can do in a single night. I'd be embarrassed, but they don't seem to care."

Gertie nodded. "People aren't being raised right anymore. Sounds like you are and that's a credit to your mother."

"I'll tell her you said so. I'm Monica, by the way."

"I'm Gertie. It's a pleasure to meet you, Monica. Hopefully my words will get you a little credit with your mother."

Monica rolled her eyes. "She's always on me—get your education, never depend on a man for money. She's biased, of course, because my dad took off on us when I was five. But I get what she's saying."

"It's hard for a woman, especially one with a young child. A good career helps. Not worrying about how to make rent is a lot off one's shoulders."

Monica nodded as she scrubbed. "That's exactly what momma says. She never likes anyone I go out with. Says none of them have enough ambition."

"Finding a quality man is no easy task," Gertie said. "I've never managed it myself."

Monica stopped scrubbing and stared at her. "You never married?"

"Nope. And my life has been just fine. Don't get me wrong, I'm not opposed to marriage. I just never found anyone I was willing to put the work in with."

"That's interesting. Most women of your generation were married with children so young. It's refreshing to meet someone who took a different direction and isn't unhappy about it."

"No point in being unhappy, is there? It was my choice, after all." She took a sip of coffee. "I heard that man who got killed here at the resort was hitting up women for money."

Monica froze for a minute, then nodded. "I think he got money from my boss."

"Oh no," Gertie said. "That's horrible. Your boss is an older lady?"

"In her sixties, I would guess. And like you, she's never been married, but I don't think it's necessarily from a lack of desire. She's just...I don't know, odd. I've seen her around men and she kinda sends mixed signals. And since she's not exactly the kind of woman men flock to, she really should work on her technique. That and she really should get rid of some of those cats. I think she's up to five."

Gertie nodded. "A hazard I've managed to avoid. I guess your boss heard about the scamming after he was killed. How did she take it all?"

Monica frowned. "She seemed shocked but not really surprised, if that makes sense. But I think she might have known about the scamming before he died. I heard her on the phone a couple days ago trying to get her bank to stop payment on a check, but apparently it had already cleared. She sounded really angry and started crying when she hung up the phone. I was waiting to speak with her but I just left before she saw me standing there."

"I imagine he ran straight to the bank with any checks before women could change their minds. What a horrible man. I'm not surprised someone killed him."

"Monica!" One of the other housekeepers hurried into the living room, a disapproving look on her face. "You shouldn't be talking about Ms. Rawlins to guests. You shouldn't be talking about her to anyone. It's her private business and I don't think she'd like it spread around."

Monica looked chagrined. "I'm sorry, Penny. I didn't mean to gossip. I guess I'm still a little uncomfortable with the whole thing and talking it out makes me feel better."

Some of the irritation left Penny's face. "We're all still upset. It's not every day you find yourself in the middle of things you usually see on the news. But we have to be careful. The police are investigating, and we don't want to say things that might put Ms. Rawlins in a bad light. She's already got enough to deal with. We don't want that idiot deputy that questioned us accusing her of things she didn't do."

Monica glanced over at Gertie, and I could tell she wasn't completely convinced of her boss's innocence. But she nodded at Penny.

"You're right," Monica said. "It won't happen again."

"No harm done," Gertie said. "Your boss's secret is safe with me."

Penny gave her a grateful look, then turned and headed straight for the closet. "I'm going to take a couple hangers out of the coat closet," she said. "I need them in the bedroom."

"You don't have to—" Gertie started to protest, but it was too late. Penny had already grabbed the closet door, so I did the only thing that seemed plausible.

I dropped onto the ground and pretended to be asleep.

Penny yanked open the door and let out a strangled cry when she saw me slumped against the back wall of the closet. I bolted up as a startled person was likely to do and Penny jumped backward, falling into a recliner.

Penny motioned to Monica as the other two housekeepers ran into the room. "Call security!"

Gertie hurried over as I stood up. "That's not necessary. She's supposed to be here. Well, not in the closet exactly, although I suppose as long as you pay your bill management doesn't really care where you sleep."

"This woman is staying in the room?" Penny asked, pushing herself up from the chair.

Gertie nodded. "This is Fortune. The vacation was actually her idea. She's treating me and our other friend."

Gertie looked over at the other two housekeepers. "It's okay. She didn't mean to startle anyone."

They didn't look convinced but went back to the bedrooms.

Penny gave me a suspicious look. "Why were you sleeping in the closet?"

I was intending to go with a "too many margaritas" defense, but Gertie started in before I could even get the words out.

"She's been doing that some," Gertie said. "Although I

hoped she wouldn't feel inclined to do so here. There was a burglary at her house. The burglar startled her in bed and if her cousin hadn't been visiting and scared him away, we're not sure what would have happened."

Monica gave me a sympathetic look. "How frightening! You poor thing. I'd sleep in closets too if that happened to me."

"I'm sure you're safe in the condo, ma'am," Penny said. She appeared to accept the explanation but still gave me the side-eye as if she was clearly certain I was unstable.

"I bet that's what the dead guy thought," I said. "Someone got into his room. *You* got into this room."

Monica and Penny gave each other wary glances as if they'd just realized the implications of the access their job provided.

"I assure you," Penny said, "housekeeping only enters the room to do our jobs. We're never alone and we always knock. We're done with our job by three p.m. and we have to turn in the access card. They keep a log and everything."

"Sure, but you're not the only ones with access," I said. "What about maintenance or security or the front desk? They can just stick a card in that machine thingy and get a room key to anything."

"Yes, but all of that is tracked," Penny assured me. "Management can see every card made and where and when it was used. I promise you that no one can just come into your room without someone knowing."

"Then security must know who went into that man's room, or at least what key accessed it, right?" I asked.

Both their eyes widened.

"They would," Monica said. "But if they knew, wouldn't they tell the police?" She looked at Penny.

"I...I guess so," Penny said. "I mean, I'm sure they would."

"But no one has been arrested," Monica said.

"Maybe they didn't use a card," Penny said. "Maybe it was someone he brought back to his room. Or someone he let in."

Monica relaxed a bit. "I didn't think about that." She reached over and squeezed my arm. "I don't think you have anything to worry about. You're safe here. But would you like me to put an extra pillow and blanket in the closet?"

"That's nice," Gertie said, "but let's not encourage her." She gave me a once-over. "Looks like you showered and dressed last night. You'd better get downstairs before Ida Belle sends out the troops to find you. She left some time ago to meet up for breakfast."

I nodded and said a quick thanks to Penny and Monica before hurrying out of the room. If I stayed much longer, God only knew what kind of stories Gertie would make up. Penny was probably ready to call a shrink for me as it was.

I made my way downstairs and headed for a hallway just past the front desk. Ida Belle had done a bit of recon on her way to breakfast and had texted me the location of the business offices. Since this wasn't the CIA, I figured the door would prominently display the department and I wasn't disappointed. The last door had a big brass sign on it that read Security.

Without even thinking, I made a note of the length of the hall and the fact that the fire exit was located next to the security department. I caught myself when I was mentally calculating the amount of time it would take me to sprint down the hallway versus around the building via the fire exit and shook my head.

This wasn't a terrorist cell in the sandbox where I use to work. It was a vacation resort. And the targets inside probably had IQs higher than their body weight. I tugged my tank top down just a bit and knocked on the door. A couple seconds later, it opened.

Probably midtwenties but he looks thirteen. Five feet ten. One hundred forty pounds including the iPhone in his hand and giant radio attached to the belt. Probably a huge threat in cyberspace. Not so much in the hallway.

I gave him a second to speak, but he didn't seem capable, so I pushed forward.

"Hi, I'm Candy. I'm having this problem with my phone and I know it's not your job or anything, but one of the maids said you guys might be able to help..."

I almost choked on the "Candy" part, but I had to give Gertie credit when his eyes widened. I suppose all those years teaching sexually charged teens had given her an insight or two.

"I, uh...yeah, I can probably help you," he finally managed, looking at the floor the entire time.

"Can I come in?" I asked.

He looked pained and I figured it was against the rules and he was about to refuse, so I laid it on thick.

"I kinda hurt my foot yesterday," I said. "If you could offer me a chair, that would be great. I can't believe some guy left his radio right there in the middle of the beach. It was so embarrassing. I tripped over it and fell right into a sand castle. Broke the string on my bikini top on the way down. Showed my goodies to half of Florida. I thought I was going to die."

The color drained from his face, and I thought the resort was about to have a second death on its hands.

"In...come," he sputtered and stepped back to allow me to enter. He leaned over to look down the hallway before closing the door behind us.

I popped over to an office chair behind a set of monitors and took a seat. "So what's your name?" I asked.

"Uh, me?" He pointed to himself.

"Of course, you. Wait, let me guess. You look like a Liam, like that actor."

His white face shifted to red and he looked a little frightened. Maybe I'd pushed too hard. He might think I was on drugs.

"I, uh, most people think I look like Sheldon," he said.

I pursed my lips, then smiled. "You mean like on *Big Bang Theory*? I love that show."

He gave me a shy smile, finally managing to look at my face. Well, my chin. But hey, at least he wasn't staring at my chest, so I considered it a win.

"So you're not a Liam," I said.

"Nothing that cool. I'm Stewart." He sighed. "Named after my dad. You'd think he would have known better."

"You don't look like a Stewart, so I'm going to call you Stu. Is that okay?"

"Sure. That would be great." He looked both pleased that I'd hit on something reasonably cool and somewhat upset that the thought hadn't occurred to him before.

"So what's wrong with your phone?" he asked as he sat in the chair next to me.

"I'm not sure. I just got it, so it's probably me, but I took a picture and tried to text it to my friend, but it wouldn't go." I unlocked the phone and handed it to him.

"It's probably something in your settings. Let me just check a few things."

It was definitely something in my settings. I knew because I'd changed them this morning. I figured it wouldn't take Stewart two seconds to figure it out, but I also figured my compliments and bubbly former cheerleader routine had him roped in. At this point, he'd probably give me his Social Security number and birth date.

"Here's the problem," he said. "There's a couple of settings that are wrong. I'm not sure how they got this way...this isn't how the phone comes."

"I probably did it. I was trying to fix it myself from a YouTube video and I bet I made it worse. I don't know why these things have to be so hard. You have to be a genius to do anything with them."

He blushed again and handed me back my phone. "Not really, but it helps if you know a couple things."

"It's fixed? Just like that? Oh wow, thank you so much." I gave him a huge smile and he finally managed to look me in the eye for a second. I felt a tiny twinge of regret for playing him, as he seemed like a genuinely nice guy, but there was a murderer on the loose and I needed to keep Gertie out of jail. Guilt had no place in a mission. All this living as a regular person was making me soft. It was time to get on to the real reason for my visit.

I waved my hand at all the monitors. "This is something else. Do you really watch these all day? I mean, how do you keep up?"

"Two people work each shift, so it's not like I have to watch them alone."

I glanced around and frowned. "But you're the only one here."

"My coworker is up fixing the cameras on the tenth floor right now."

I perked up. The tenth floor was where Otis's room was.

"What's wrong with them?" I asked. "I mean, I don't have to worry about security on my floor, do I? You guys can fix stuff like you did my phone, right?"

"It depends on what the problem is. Right now, he's just making an adjustment to the direction of the cameras so the coverage area is wider. There was a problem with the wiring on that floor recently and we just got it fixed night before last.

The cameras were moved some in the process and need to be tweaked."

"This is all so interesting. How do you know when there's a problem with wiring and stuff?"

"In this case, it was easy—the cameras on that floor stopped working completely about a week ago, so we went looking for the problem."

Which meant that there was no footage of the ins and outs of Otis's room prior to the day he was killed. Which meant Benton couldn't easily latch onto another suspect. I held in a sigh. Back to square one. Next up was the key card angle.

I opened my eyes wide and attempted to feign concern. "So there was like, no security at all while they were broken? That's scary."

"We had to order some parts so it took longer than usual, but there's nothing to worry about. The resort is really secure."

"But...I mean, didn't some guy get killed here? On that floor?"

Stewart stiffened a bit and I knew he'd probably already taken an earful from Benton about the lack of footage.

"Yeah," he said finally, "but I'm not supposed to talk about it."

I gave him a sympathetic look. "I heard that cop—Benton, right—talking to the resort manager the other day. He doesn't seem like a very nice person. Benton, I mean, not the manager."

"Benton's a douche." He blurted it out, then his ears reddened. "Sorry. I didn't mean to be crass."

"That's all right. I keep hearing that word in regard to him. It seems particularly fitting based on what I overheard."

I could tell he was trying to keep from asking me anything but his built-in drive to know everything won out. "What did you hear?" he asked. "I mean, if you don't mind saying."

"I don't mind at all. That Benton was complaining about video, which made no sense to me then, but I guess it does now that I know about the camera problem. Then he started complaining about the key cards." I paused and stared at him. "Those aren't broken too, are they? Do I need to get a new card? Or have them redo the lock thingy on my door?"

He shook his head and sighed. "You don't need to do anything. The key card system is working fine. Benton just doesn't want to believe it because the only people who ever used a key card to access that particular room were housekeeping, maintenance, and the man who was staying there."

I frowned. "What difference does that make? The man could have let someone in himself."

"That's the problem. The cameras were working again that night and no one went in his room but him."

A thought occurred to me—a potential chink in the armor, so to speak. And I was pretty sure Stewart had the answer I needed. It was just a matter of getting it out of him.

"Oh, wow," I said. "That's interesting. It's a real mystery, right? Just like *Veronica Mars*. I used to love that show." Which was partly true. I hadn't hated it when Gertie had made me watch it last week. I grabbed his arm and he jumped, looking a bit frightened.

"You should totally be an investigator," I said. "You're really smart...so much smarter than Benton. I bet you could figure out who killed that man. Then you'd be a hero. I bet you'd get a big promotion and a raise. Maybe even be interviewed on the evening news. That would be really cool."

His eyes widened. "No. I can't...I don't know anything about cop stuff."

"But you know everything that goes on at the resort. You're like the Wizard of Oz, running everything behind the curtain."

"Well, I'm not really running anything. Maybe recording things."

I waved my hand in dismissal. "That's beside the point. You know stuff. Like the key cards."

"But that information doesn't provide any clues. It's very straightforward. Housekeeping uses the same master key cards they have to check out each day. All the cards have been checked in and out as required and that room was accessed as recorded on the housekeeping log. I had to do a comparison. Maintenance keeps a log as well. Everything matched the log. No one was in his room without a valid reason."

"And the dead guy was the only other one to use a card to open the door, right?" I scrunched my brow, pretending that thinking required effort. "How do you know it's the same card? Do they have numbers or something?"

"Yes. Although technically, it wasn't just one card he used. It was two different ones."

"Is that normal? I only got one card when I checked in."

"Some people request two and both the cards used were assigned to the man staying in the room."

"Would you be able to tell when the man got the cards? I mean, if there were two, maybe someone else got one some-how. Maybe he *wasn't* the only one who went into his room."

"I suppose that's possible. I didn't think about it really." He turned his chair around and tapped on the computer, looked at a screen of numbers, then accessed something else. When the next screen came up, he ran his finger down the monitor, then looked over at me.

"He didn't get both cards at check-in," Stewart said. "He reported his first card lost and got another one."

"When did he get the new card?"

"The day he was killed. That evening, to be exact."

"And was the old one ever used again?"

"It was used four times that morning, but not again after he requested the new one. The old cards are deactivated in the system when they're reported lost."

"Of course. Safety and all."

He frowned and I wondered if he was realizing what all that meant.

"What's wrong?" I asked.

"Nothing. I mean, probably nothing. It's just that I have no way of knowing what time during the day he actually lost his card."

"So someone else could have stolen his card and you wouldn't be able to see them because the cameras weren't working. You solved the mystery!" I clapped my hands. "I told you that you could do it."

He blushed. "I didn't solve it. I've just proven that there was a chance someone else could have gotten into his room."

His shoulders slumped a bit. "But I don't see why it matters. Even if someone went in his room with the old card, they didn't use it the night he was killed. It's not on the log and no one is on video. And even if someone was crazy enough to access the room during the day and wait for him until night, we still would have seen them on the video footage leaving the room."

Everything Stewart said was accurate, and since he didn't know the cause of death was poison, he was working with the idea that someone had killed Otis in person. I'm not sure how he thought that had happened unless they were a ghost or a vampire. Or could you see vampires on camera? I couldn't remember the lore.

"Well, I still think you've done a great job," I said.

Stewart was still frowning and I could tell he was working through the facts of the situation and they didn't add up. He probably hadn't spent much time dwelling on it before because murder wasn't exactly the sort of thing that regular folk liked to think too hard on.

"There's no way someone could have killed this guy," Stewart said finally.

"What about a connecting room?" I asked, figuring I might as well keep playing along.

"The connecting room was empty but it wasn't accessed either, and the video doesn't show anyone entering or exiting."

"I don't suppose someone could scale those balconies, could they?" I asked, hating myself for asking such a stupid question.

"If they did, there would have been a rope or something tied to it."

"Oh yeah." I shrugged. "Then I guess that stupid cop is wrong. The man must have killed himself."

Stewart gave me a hopeful look. "Given the facts, that's really the only thing that makes sense."

"Well, then, you need to call and put that horrible deputy in his place. And I suppose you should tell him about the replacement card, right? I mean, in case it matters."

"Except Benton won't feel like I put him in his place at all. He'll just blame me for not knowing the card was lost."

"Did Benton even ask any detailed questions? Did he come back here and learn about your job before he ran off half-cocked, thinking he knew everything?"

Stewart slowly shook his head. "No. I gave him exactly what he asked for, and he cussed some, then stomped off. I never would have thought about it more if you hadn't come by. Maybe *you* should think about doing the Veronica Mars thing."

"Oh, that's way too dangerous for me."

Stewart sucked in a breath. "Crap. Oh man. I shouldn't have done this. What if the killer comes after me next? That's always what happens in the movies. The guy who figures out something is always the next to go. I live with my mom and three cats. What if he comes after them?"

He'd moved past upset and straight for outright panic. I was afraid he might start hyperventilating, so I placed my hand on his arm and squeezed.

"Calm down," I said. "We already figured out he must have killed himself. Besides, you don't know anything that implicates someone. And even if you did, no one would know about it but me and you. All you have to do is tell Benton what you do know, then you're off the hook."

He stared at me for a couple seconds, processing what I'd said. Logic must have finally trumped emotion, because he eventually let out the breath he'd been holding and nodded.

"Okay. You're right," he said. "As soon as Benton knows, I'm good. I should call him. Right now."

I jumped up from my chair. "Definitely. That way we're both safe. I mean, no one knows I'm in here but you can't be too careful, right? I'm going to leave before someone sees me. Thanks so much for fixing my phone."

"Sure. Just come back if you have any more problems."

He gave the phone a hopeful look, as if willing it to break. I gave him a quick hug, which probably sent his pulse rate into the stratosphere, and hurried out before he could ask me for my phone number or for anything else that I had to say no to.

As I hurried down the hall, I smiled. Things weren't progressing quickly but at least we were moving forward. I seriously doubted Otis had lost his card. More likely, whoever had killed him had lifted it and he'd had to request a new one. But before he'd noticed, the killer had entered his room and poisoned something. It was a ballsy move.

I came to a lurching stop.

It wasn't just ballsy. It was incredibly stupid.

Unless the killer knew the cameras were broken.

CHAPTER FIFTEEN

I FOLLOWED THE SMELL OF THE BREAKFAST BUFFET AND located Ida Belle and Gertie at a table in the back, a giant fake palm partially blocking them from view.

"I take it we've given up on the separation theory?" I asked as I sat.

Ida Belle nodded. "We probably got everything out of the employees that we're going to this morning. And besides, housekeeping has already put you and Gertie together. I give it until this afternoon before everyone is up to speed on the major players."

I waved the server over. "I'll have sweet tea and the buffet, please."

The server nodded and hurried off.

"I'm starving," I said. "So give me a minute and I'll fill you in."

I hurried off to the buffet and loaded up a plate with an omelet, bacon, toast, pancakes, strawberries, and two dough-nuts. When I returned to the table, Gertie looked at my plate and nodded her approval.

"Calories don't count on vacation," she said.

Ida Belle snorted. "You better pass that information to your rear. Your plate made Fortune's look empty."

"Some of us don't spend our vacation dining on egg whites and dry toast," Gertie said. "Who does that?"

"Someone who's saving their calories for alcohol and dessert night," Ida Belle said.

"Good point," I said. "Maybe I should cut out one of the doughnuts."

Ida Belle waved her hand. "I wouldn't worry about it. After all, we're on an investigation. At some point, we'll end up running."

Gertie looked disappointed. "If you change your mind, I'll take it."

Ida Belle shook her head. "There's an entire tray of doughnuts twenty feet from you. If you hadn't eaten so many of those cream cheese crepes, you'd be able to walk over there and get your own."

"There's cream cheese crepes?" I asked.

"You two are impossible," Ida Belle said. "Can you at least tell us in between bites what you found out?"

I managed to consume the omelet, toast, and one of the doughnuts while I filled them in, then hurried off to grab some crepes before they were gone.

"The missing room key and broken cameras explain a lot about why Benton is flinging mud at the wall and hoping it sticks," Ida Belle said. "It also brings up the interesting angle you presented about who knew the cameras were broken."

"Seems like an employee of the resort is the best bet," Gertie said.

"Or someone connected to one," I said. "Although it's not the sort of information that's juicy enough to spur random gossip. Did Gertie fill you in on the housekeeper info?"

Ida Belle grinned. "I know all about you sleeping in closets because you're emotionally scarred. I wish I'd been a fly on the wall. It's a wonder you kept a straight face."

"You should have seen me playing Candy the Wonder Idiot with security," I said. "I think I'm getting good at this."

"It probably helps that you've finally been exposed to the rest of society," Gertie said. "It's hard to play a role when you've only known the one for most of your life."

"True," I said. "All those movies and television shows you've had me watch have definitely helped. And I have something to throw out there that other people connect with. But the home invasion PTSD was definitely a stretch."

"I had to think fast," Gertie said. "What was I supposed to say?"

"That I was drunk?" I suggested.

"Oh, yeah," Gertie said. "That probably would have worked."

"The simplest explanation is usually the most likely," Ida Belle said.

"In addition to my apparent emotional problems," I said, "I assume Gertie filled you in on the housekeeping boss being taken by Otis?"

Ida Belle nodded.

"So what about you?" I asked Ida Belle. "Did you run down anything?"

"Yep. I got a fix on the other suspect. One of the front desk clerks was having breakfast before her shift. I played the lonely old lady routine and invited myself to sit with her."

I smiled. Ida Belle playing the lonely old lady was almost as big a stretch as me playing the bubbly former cheerleader.

She noticed my smile. "Two can do the research game. I've been watching those Hallmark movies. They're ridiculous, of course, but since people seem to buy into all that mess, I figured I should work on my cast of characters.

Although I wasn't expecting to be called into duty on vacation."

She glanced over at Gertie, who was busy sneaking the last doughnut off my plate.

"I know, I know," Gertie said. "It's all my fault. Blah, blah, blah. It's like a broken record."

"Maybe because it keeps repeating," Ida Belle said. "Anyway, the front desk clerk said Otis put the moves on one of the older ladies who works the night shift. Name is Betty Palmer and the clerk guesses she's in her fifties. She's widowed but the clerk said she didn't think her husband had left her with much. This is the first job she's ever held, and I'm sure she's not raking in big pay."

"No," I agreed. "And she's probably not working for the fun of it. Night shift at a resort has got to be a horrible job."

"If you don't like people," Gertie said.

"Who likes people?" I asked. "Seriously? I'm not talking about people you know. I'm talking about the random public."

"They make it pretty hard," Ida Belle agreed. "The clerk said she overheard Betty on the phone one day with someone —she assumed a friend—saying she'd met this great guy who was going to open a restaurant on the island in a space for rent a couple blocks over. He was looking for investors and she was wanting to know what the friend thought about it."

"Sounds like he's been working the business angle with more than just Flamingo Lady," I said.

Ida Belle nodded. "Well, whatever the person on the other end of the phone said made Betty mad. The clerk said she turned red and practically yelled, 'I don't believe you. Otis wouldn't lie to me. You're just jealous that I found someone.' Then she saw the clerk at the copier and hung up, then stormed out of the office. The clerk said she was in tears."

"I wonder what the friend told her," Gertie said.

"Me too," Ida Belle said. "Especially if it was specific rather than general, which is what it sounds like."

"Yeah," I agreed. "It would be completely normal for a friend to warn a woman off of giving money to a relative stranger, especially when he's offering romance as part of the deal. But if the clerk is remembering correctly, Betty's first response was 'I don't believe you,' which makes it seem like the friend told her something specific."

"That's true," Gertie said. "If it had been the general warning like 'be careful that he's not scamming you' then a more likely response would have been something like 'you always think the worst' or 'I'm not stupid.'"

"Exactly," I said. "I don't suppose the clerk knew who she was talking to, did she?"

Ida Belle shook her head. "I managed to work in the question but the clerk said she didn't know. But if we're going with the theory that this person offered up specific cautions, then that says local to me. Betty doesn't have any family here, so the friend angle is the most likely. The clerk said she sees Betty having lunch sometimes with an older woman with big blond hair, lots of jewelry, and bright red lipstick, but she doesn't know who the woman is."

I tapped my finger on the table. "I wonder if Betty gave him the money."

"The clerk didn't know," Ida Belle said. "Betty never mentioned anything and in fact, seemed to avoid her after the phone call. Probably embarrassed."

"Probably," I agreed. "It's possible that even though Betty was upset, she listened to her friend and did some poking around. If she found out Otis was playing her, what would she do about it?"

"You mean would she be mad enough to kill him over it?"

Gertie said. "That's the question with all of them, isn't it? Where that line is."

"The answer is going to be different for everyone," Ida Belle said. "And we have no way of knowing."

"It's also possible Betty had already given Otis money and didn't want to admit it to her friend," Gertie said.

Ida Belle nodded. "That's very likely. Betty might have called her friend, fishing for support, but instead, she got an earful of something she didn't want to hear."

"Either way," Gertie said, "we have to assume that all the women scammed or potentially scammed had motive."

"I agree," I said. "Which puts us back to opportunity."

"Any one of them could have created a situation where they could have lifted that key card," Ida Belle said. "When we were at the beach, I noticed everyone just walked off to swim and left their bags in or near their chairs. It might be a bit forward to go digging through someone's items, but it wouldn't be impossible to find a window of opportunity where people weren't paying much attention."

"It would have been really easy with Otis," Gertie said. "He carried his room key in one of those lanyards with a pocket. I bet it was just sitting in his chair while he was in the water. Easy to lean over and pretend to fix a shoe and swipe the lanyard."

"There you go," Ida Belle said.

Gertie sighed. "This sucks. Everyone had motive. Everyone had opportunity. At least as far as we can tell. So what are we left with?"

"Method," I said. "We really need the name of that poison."

"Then we better pull off this three-ring circus at the sheriff's department," Ida Belle said.

"We've pulled off harder," Gertie said.

"And botched easier," Ida Belle reminded her.

"No matter the outcome," I said, "at least we have some names for Byron. So even if Benton fluffs up his file enough to get the go-ahead to arrest Gertie, there's no way the DA will pursue charges without more evidence against Gertie and those other people completely cleared."

"True," Ida Belle said. "But how long will Gertie have to sit in jail waiting for the DA to review the file and make a decision? Given Benton's lack of popularity, he might drag his feet as long as he can, just to avoid dealing with him."

"I refuse to let that waste of air ruin my vacation," Gertie said. "And I'm not spending even one night in that crap building of theirs. I heard Benton complaining because the AC doesn't work half the time. Might as well be in jail in Mexico."

"I think Mexico might be a little worse," I said. "But our main goal is keeping you out of any jail cell, even if only for a day."

Ida Belle nodded. "Then we might as well get this over with. Let's head upstairs and get changed for our visit to the sheriff's department. We can call Marie then, too, and let her know to get ready. I called her last night to explain the situation and told her to grab a prepaid phone from my stash this morning."

I stared. "I'm not sure what it says about a person when they keep a stash of prepaid phones."

"Drug dealer, usually," Gertie said. "But in this case, it says 'optimistic.'"

"How is that?" Ida Belle asked.

"Because if we need one of the phones," Gertie said, "then that means we're neck-deep in an investigation. And there's nothing more fun than our investigations."

I grinned. "God help me, but I might agree with you."

———

WHEN WE ENTERED THE SHERIFF'S DEPARTMENT, THE dispatcher gave us a big smile. "I see you ladies just can't stay away," she said.

"Can't stay away from trouble, anyway," Ida Belle said. "It follows this one like a stray dog." She pointed at Gertie.

"You try to work a little romance into your vacation and everything falls apart," Gertie said. "What is the world coming to?"

The dispatcher shook her head. "Wasn't no romance coming from a date with that guy. At least, not after you parted with some cash. He was a bad lot."

"If everyone knows that, then why is Benton so focused on Gertie for killing him?" I asked. "Given the general gossip we've heard, seems like there should be no shortage of suspects. Some who actually lost money in the deal."

The dispatcher glanced back down the hallway, then turned around and leaned forward, lowering her voice. "But most of the other women are locals. If the sheriff retires as we suspect, that appointment will happen soon. Putting a local in jail for murder upsets people and could affect the decision on a replacement."

"So Benton thinks trying to pin a murder on the wrong person is okay because if he arrests a local he might not get appointed?" Ida Belle asked. "What the hell is wrong with him?"

"He's lazy and stupid," the dispatcher said.

"But poor taste in dinner partners isn't evidence of murder, especially when there are a ton of better suspects," I said. "His plan doesn't make sense. Even if he's the laziest and stupidest person on the planet."

"He doesn't have to make it work forever," the dispatcher

said. "Just until after the appointment. Popularity among the voters is everything down here."

And suddenly, Benton's fixation on Gertie made perfect sense. He didn't care if a completely innocent woman spent time in jail or thousands of dollars on a lawyer. As long as he arrested someone who wasn't a local, then he wasn't in the hot seat with the local politicians and judges.

"Unbelievable," Ida Belle said. "And I thought Louisiana politics were corrupt."

"Oh, I could tell you some stories," the dispatcher said.

"I'm sure you could," I said. "But I guess we should give our statements and get out of here while we're all still able. I don't suppose there's another deputy who could take them?"

"I'm afraid not," the dispatcher said. "We run full staff in the summer because the resorts are full, so as soon as season is over, everyone takes vacation or medical leave for things they put off for months. At the moment, I'm it for office staff. We've only got one other deputy working today and he just left to break up some drunks fighting at the beach. You could wait, but it will probably take him an hour or better to get things sorted."

I sighed and hoped my excitement was disguised by the disappointed look I was aiming for. "Then I guess we best get this over with. Call Benton and let him know we're here." I looked over at Ida Belle and Gertie. "Do you guys mind if I go first? I need to run to the drugstore and figured I could get that done while you guys finish up."

They both nodded and the dispatcher picked up her phone and let Benton know we were there. A minute later, he walked down the hall, already glaring at us. I tamped down the urge to do a flying kick to his head. Just looking at him put me in the red. Benton was everything that was wrong with a certain type of law enforcement officers.

"I'd like to go first," I said as he approached. "I have some errands to run."

He said something that came out as a grunt, turned around and trudged back down the hall.

"I guess that's my cue to follow?" I asked.

"Knowing Benton, it's all you're going to get," the dispatcher said.

"Okay, well, I'll make this as quick as possible," I said, and headed after him.

Ida Belle knew that as soon as the door closed behind me, she was to text Marie and let her know to make the phone call. I hoped to God she wasn't in the restroom or if she was, took her phone with her, because I didn't want to spend a single second longer with Benton than I had to.

As I walked, I scanned the offices and spotted Benton's nameplate on the messiest one. It figured. He probably had every case file he'd ever worked on his desk. But at least it was the last one on the hallway, right before the room they used for questioning. And while you could see all the way down the hallway from the seats Ida Belle and Gertie had taken in the lobby, the dispatcher's desk was offset so that she couldn't see past the first two rooms.

Benton was already seated and ready with the recorder when I stepped into the room. He didn't even bother to look up at me. Just waved at the chair and readied his fingers on the Record button. Apparently, he was just as anxious to get me out of the department as I was.

He gave the usual particulars for the recording—his name and mine, date, situation—then looked at me. "Please describe the scene when you entered the restaurant and continue until the point where I arrived."

I started talking, not bothering to put in extraneous description. Even though I wasn't going to finish my statement now, I would have to at some point. No sense dragging it out with adjectives, especially as Ida Belle was already recording when I arrived. If Benton noticed my sparse sentences, he didn't care to comment.

I was about two minutes into my statement when the dispatcher poked her head into the room.

"Got a situation at the resort," she said.

Benton clicked off the recorder. "Send McGill," he said.

"Can't," the dispatcher said. "McGill's still working the drunks at the beach. Besides, the resort manager asked specifically for you. Said you were already dealing with a related issue."

Benton cursed and rose from his chair as the dispatcher hurried off. He started out of the room and I cleared my throat.

"Uh, so I guess we'll do this later?" I asked.

"Don't have a choice," he mumbled.

"Okay. Can I use the ladies' before I leave?"

"Across the hall," he said as he walked off. I waited until he was at the front desk and Ida Belle asked where I was. He barked out something about the ladies' room and then left the building, slamming the door behind him.

I stepped out into the hall and watched as Gertie started coughing, then fell out of her chair and onto the floor.

CHAPTER SIXTEEN

I DASHED INTO BENTON'S OFFICE AS IDA BELLE YELLED AT the dispatcher for help. I scanned the top of the desk, hoping the file would be clearly labeled and stand out, but I was out of luck. Piles of unlabeled folders were strewn in every direction, as if someone had opened the filing cabinet and thrown them onto the desk.

I started opening folders and scanning the documents as quickly as possible, closing them and moving on to the next as soon as I could zero in on a name. I heard excited voices coming from the lobby and the dispatcher saying she'd call the paramedics. I grabbed the next file, then the next, hoping I could find what I was looking for before the paramedics showed up and the dispatcher had calmed down enough to realize I still hadn't appeared.

After four more unsuccessful attempts, I finally hit pay dirt. I flipped through the completely unorganized papers in the file and finally located the medical examiner's report. Without even bothering to read it, I simply snapped a pic of the two pages with my phone. As I flipped over the last, I saw a copy of a check, then another, then another. I took pics of them and by the time I finished, I heard a man's voice in the lobby.

I checked the images to make sure they were all clear, then hauled butt up front, feigning shock and alarm when I arrived.

"Oh my God," I cried as a paramedic dropped onto the floor next to Gertie. "What happened?"

"I don't know," Ida Belle said. "She just collapsed."

"I hope it's not a heart attack," the dispatcher said as she clasped her hands together. "That happened last year. Guy just keeled over right there in that same chair."

"Maybe you should get rid of that chair," I said.

The dispatcher nodded. "As soon as I get off work, I'll shoot it into pieces with my Desert Eagle then burn it."

I gave her an approving nod. "I like your style."

The paramedic looked up at us. "Her vitals are strong. I think she just passed out."

I glanced over at Ida Belle, who barely shook her head then inched forward and poked Gertie in the ribs with her shoe. Gertie bolted upright, smacking the paramedic in the face with her head, sending him reeling sideways into the entry and straight into Benton, who'd just opened the door.

He must have forgotten something, because no way he should have been back so soon. And he couldn't have picked a worse moment to show up. He clutched the doorframe, trying to maintain his balance. But the paramedic was built more like a linebacker than a wide receiver, and Benton's complete lack of muscle tone was no match for two hundred twenty pounds of falling mass. He lost his grip and fell backward into a woman carrying a huge pink cake.

The woman screamed and the cake went straight up into the air and came crashing down right in Benton's face. Benton scrambled up and looked wildly around, trying to figure out who to arrest for this most recent embarrassment. The woman who'd lost her cake stared in dismay at the pink icing dripping onto Benton's shirt and started yelling like a crazy woman about the most important baby shower of the decade.

I saw Benton reach for his gun and was afraid he was actually going to shoot her when another woman hurried up next to the screaming lady and grabbed her around the shoulders. She leaned in and said something that I couldn't hear, then tugged on the distraught cake lady and led her across the street. The paramedic stepped in front of Benton and held up his hands.

"Sir," the paramedic said. "You need to calm down."

"Don't tell me to calm down," Benton yelled. "I ought to arrest you."

"For falling?" Ida Belle asked. "How does that work?"

Benton glared at us, then it must have dawned on him that the guy who'd knocked him down was a medical professional. He looked down at Gertie, who was still sitting on the floor, and scowled. I was fairly certain he was mad enough to flush but with all the pink icing on him, I couldn't really tell.

"I should have known you'd be the cause of this," Benton said. "Everything bad that's happened this week has had you at the center of it. I'm done playing nice."

"That was you playing nice?" Gertie asked. "Let me ask you something—if you died tomorrow, would anyone come to the funeral?"

"Not likely," the dispatcher grumbled.

"Get up off that floor!" Benton yelled.

"Sir, this woman has had a medical incident," the paramedic said. "She's not doing anything without my okay."

"Then you better okay her to get out of my sight before I lock her up," Benton said.

The paramedic was completely confused but apparently

saw the futility of arguing with an idiot. He leaned over and extended a hand to Gertie. "Are you okay to stand?" he asked.

Gertie nodded and he pulled her up, then clutched her shoulders and took a good look at her eyes.

"Are you dizzy?" he asked.

"A little," Gertie said.

"I think I should take you to the hospital," he said. "Get you checked out."

"That's not necessary," Gertie said. "I'm sure it's just my blood sugar. I skipped breakfast. I know I shouldn't, but I just wasn't hungry."

"Then at least let me check and give you a shot of glucagon if you need it," he said.

"No need to go to all that trouble," Gertie said. She reached out and swiped a hunk of icing off Benton's shirt and popped it in her mouth.

Benton's jaw dropped and he threw his hands up in the air, sending icing flying everywhere. "All of you get out!"

"What about our statements?" Ida Belle asked.

"I don't care," Benton said.

"You don't care that a woman assaulted someone and destroyed the resort's buffet?" Ida Belle asked.

Benton glared at her. "The only thing I wish is that the woman with the flamingo had been a faster runner."

He stomped off down the hall.

"What about the call at the resort?" the dispatcher called after him.

"I don't care if the whole thing falls into the sea," Benton yelled.

We all looked at one another for a couple seconds, no one sure how to react. Then the dispatcher started laughing.

"I haven't seen Benton this mad in forever," she said, wiping tears from her face. "You ladies have made my week."

I looked over at Gertie. "We better get out of here before Benton decides to arrest you for not eating breakfast."

The paramedic shook his head. "That guy needs therapy."

"He needs more than that," Gertie said. "My mother would have recommended a good old-fashioned butt-whooping."

The paramedic grinned. "Are you sure you're all right?"

Gertie nodded. "Thanks for your help. I'll try to be more careful about my meals."

He gave us a nod and headed out. We thanked the dispatcher for her assistance and followed behind him.

"Well?" Ida Belle asked as soon as the door closed behind us. "Did you get it?"

"Yep," I said. "The ME report and the check copies."

"Then let's head over to that café and get something to eat while you fill us in," Gertie said.

Ida Belle stared. "You ate half the breakfast buffet. How can you possibly be hungry?"

"Acting is hard work," Gertie said. "I got a complete core workout just trying not to laugh. I'll be able to skip sit-ups for a week."

"You've skipped sit-ups since 1952," Ida Belle said. "The only sit-ups you do is when you get out of bed in the morning."

"Not true," Gertie said. "I sit up when I'm out back reading in my lawn chair."

"I wouldn't mind a root beer float," I said. "There's an advertisement for them in the café window."

"I could probably do a float," Ida Belle said.

We headed across the street and I slowed as we were passing the building that I saw the woman take the cake lady into. I knew from the sign on the building that it was a real estate office. On the front window was a picture of the woman, indicating she was the owner of the agency. Her name was Janet Barlow.

"Something there caught your attention?" Ida Belle asked, noticing my pause.

"Ooooohhhhh," Gertie said. "You should totally buy a vacation home."

"Even if I had that kind of money, no way would I buy a house in a place that employed Benton," I said.

"Then what's up?" Ida Belle asked. "You have that look."

"Did you see the woman who pulled Cake Lady away?" I asked.

They both shook their heads.

"We didn't have a clear view from the floor," Ida Belle said. "I could only see part of Cake Lady. Why?"

"She was midfifties," I said. "With big blond hair, bright red lipstick, and rings on six fingers. Sound like someone?"

Ida Belle's eyes widened. "The night clerk's friend. I bet you're right. And her being a real estate agent makes perfect sense in context."

I nodded. "What do you want to bet this Janet Barlow knew good and well Otis wasn't leasing a building for a restaurant and *that's* what she told Betty Palmer."

"If that's the case, then Betty definitely knew Otis was a scammer before he was killed," Gertie said. "I wonder if she confronted him."

"No way to know unless she admits to it," I said as I opened the door to the café.

"I wouldn't hold my breath on that one," Ida Belle said.

We strolled inside and took a table away from the other patrons. We stopped talking until the server came over and took our order—three root beer floats and a piece of key lime pie for Gertie. When the server left, I pulled out my phone and accessed the photos.

"I only checked to see that the images were clear," I said. "I didn't have time to read anything."

"Well, don't keep us in suspense," Gertie said. "Read."

I enlarged the medical examiner's document and scanned it for the cause of death, then frowned.

"Cause of death is tetrodotoxin poisoning," I said.

"What is that?" Gertie asked.

"Puffer fish," I said.

"You've got to be kidding me," Ida Belle said.

"I'm afraid not," I said. "You don't have to consume much to cause respiratory failure."

Ida Belle sighed. "So we have a poison that anyone with a fishing rod can acquire. That's not going to narrow things down."

"It's worse than that," I said. "Did you read the events list they gave us when we checked in? There's a guest chef who comes to the resort once a month. Guess what he prepares."

"I don't suppose it could have been an accident then," Gertie said.

"No," I said. "The guest chef isn't due until this Friday. Besides, if Otis ate poorly prepared puffer fish, then he would have had side effects right there in the restaurant. That stuff is deadly and fast."

"Then how did someone poison him?" Ida Belle asked. "Can it be liquefied and put into a drink?"

"I honestly don't know," I said. "But you're right. That's definitely a snag. The killer could have lifted the card and had access to his room, but if a random container of fish showed up, that would look odd."

"Maybe not," Gertie said. "I mean, yes, if a random container appeared it would look odd. But when we had dinner, Otis wasn't crazy about his lasagna. He probably only ate three or four bites. I tried to get him to order something else, but he said he had leftover seafood étouffée in his room."

"That's it," Ida Belle said. "The killer stole the card and

added the poisoned fish to Otis's leftover étouffée. You could hide a flip-flop in leftover étouffée."

"But how did they know Otis had the étouffée to poison?" Gertie asked. "Seems risky to walk around with poisonous fish, hoping to find something to put it in."

"There are two possible answers," I said. "The first is that the killer stole the card and accessed Otis's room, saw the étouffée, then came back with the fish."

"And the second?" Gertie asked.

"Simple," I said. "The killer saw Otis take the étouffée to go or was the one eating with him."

Ida Belle nodded. "The first is risky. Even with the broken cameras, accessing the room twice doubles the opportunity for someone to see them."

"I agree," I said. "I prefer the second option for that reason, and because if we can figure out where Otis ate the day before he died—and even better, who with—then we might be able to narrow the field of suspects."

"So," Gertie said. "All we have to do is find a restaurant that serves seafood étouffée ...in coastal Florida."

"There's probably no shortage," Ida Belle said. "But we can start a list and maybe we'll get lucky."

"First up is the restaurant at the resort," I said. "They have seafood étouffée."

"It couldn't be that easy, right?" Gertie asked.

"Easy, perhaps, but not simple," I said. "If he ate at the restaurant on site, that also means that anyone staying or working there could have seen his dinner and to-go box, not just the person he was eating with. That means everyone is in play until we can put them somewhere else during that time frame."

Ida Belle shook her head. "And given the way this case is

going, that's probably going to be harder than we want it to be. What about the checks? Maybe we can narrow things down that way."

Gertie snorted. "More likely, we'll just add more people on the pile."

"Let's hope not," I said, and accessed the first pic. "No surprise here. A check from Cynthia Rawlins for five thousand. Second one is Rita Walker for two thousand."

Gertie sighed. "Another person to investigate."

"That's Flamingo Lady," Ida Belle said. "I asked around this morning."

"Good," I said. "Last one up is Betty Palmer." I whistled. "Ten thousand."

"I thought Betty was supposed to be the cheap one," Gertie said.

Ida Belle frowned. "She is. Quite frankly, given the general gossip about her situation and the fact that she's working a night shift here, I'm surprised she had ten thousand to give."

"I wonder if that ten thousand was *all* she had to give," I said.

"If so, that's ten thousand reasons to kill Otis," Ida Belle said.

"Ten thousand good ones as far as I'm concerned," Gertie grumbled.

"I don't think either of us disagrees with the sentiment," I said. "But unfortunately, whoever decided to take that very big step put you in the middle of it."

"Benton put me in the middle of it," Gertie said. "No cop worth his salt would have given me more than a glance. Good Lord, he has people practically lining up to be suspects, and he's wasting valuable time on me."

"Yeah, but the only one that isn't local, besides you, is

Flamingo Lady," I said. "And since he's already started his case against you—and you've caused him more than a few embarrassing incidents—I don't look for him to shift gears."

"Flamingo Lady has family in the area, so there's no way Benton is giving up Gertie," Ida Belle said. "And he's not going to do any real investigating until that appointment happens."

"So the three of us are my only hope," Gertie said and grinned. "Usually when people say that, they're afraid things will go south. I have the luxury of knowing that with Swamp Team 3 on the job, everything will be fine."

Ida Belle stared at her, clearly unconvinced. She probably wasn't doubting our ability to get Gertie off the hook. I was going to hazard a guess that her difference of opinion came with the definition of the word "fine."

"So what now?" Gertie asked.

"I want to stop by the Realtor's office on the way back and see if I can get anything out of her," I said. "Betty is out the most money, and I'd like to find out what the Realtor told her."

Ida Belle nodded. "In addition to the money, we also need to consider the emotional component and not just the financial. Cynthia never married and given her age, that's not the norm. Otis might have been the first man she let her guard down for."

"Or the second," Gertie said. "She might have been burned so bad years ago that she didn't pursue another relationship. If she broke her self-imposed rule after all these years, only to get taken again, no telling how angry she'd be."

I knew more than anyone how emotion could drive someone to lose everything. The arms dealer, Ahmad, had made it his personal mission to hunt me down and kill me. It cost him his business, the respect of the people who worked for him, and ultimately his life. But if someone was in that red zone, it was sometimes impossible to shake them out of it, regardless of cost.

"So how do you want to play the Realtor?" Ida Belle asked.

"I think I'm going to approach it as looking for a vacation home—something I can also rent," I said. "Then I can broach the subject of commercial real estate and the situation at the resort and see if she's worked up enough to talk."

Ida Belle nodded. "You should take me with you and introduce me as your mother. Two generations of women with no men in tow might appeal to her on a talking level."

"Why can't I play Fortune's mother?" Gertie asked.

"Because there's no telling how many people got a picture or video of you running from Flamingo Lady," Ida Belle said. "You know how that sort of thing circulates. We only have one shot at this and can't risk her recognizing you."

"Fine," Gertie said. "I look way too young to play Fortune's mother anyway."

"You look old enough to play Jesus's mother," Ida Belle said.

"I don't know why we have remained friends this long," Gertie said.

"At least she didn't say Moses," I pointed out. "You made it into the New Testament."

"So what am I supposed to do while you two are having fun gossiping with the Realtor?" Gertie asked.

"Maybe check out some of the shops," I said. "You wanted to buy some stuff to take home anyway. And if any of the clerks are looking to chat, you might be able to clue in on some local gossip."

"Please," Ida Belle said, "for the love of God, don't get into any trouble. If Benton gets one more call that involves you, he's going to arrest you for disturbing his peace."

"You say that like I cause trouble everywhere I go," Gertie said.

Ida Belle stared. "I am amazed, sometimes, how you can say certain things with a straight face."

"Years of practice," Gertie said.

I grinned. "But New Testament years."

CHAPTER SEVENTEEN

I PUSHED OPEN THE DOOR TO THE REAL ESTATE OFFICE AND stepped inside, glancing around. It was small, but neat, with three desks in a large open area and an office with glass walls behind them. None of the front desks were occupied, but Janet was seated in her office and looked up when we walked in. A couple seconds later, she rose from her desk and made her way over to us, wearing a huge smile.

"Welcome, ladies," she said, extending her hand to Ida Belle first. "My name is Janet Barlow. How can I help you today?"

I shook her hand and smiled back. "I'm Patricia and this is my mother, Margaret. We're here on vacation but I've been so impressed with the landscape and the climate that it got me considering a vacation home."

The smile widened. "Well, you've come to the right place. Come on back."

We followed her into her office and sat in the two chairs in front of her desk.

"No one knows Quiet Key like me," Janet said. "I still live in the same beach cottage I was born in. My momma, God rest her soul, was one of those that didn't believe in going to the hospital to have a baby."

"Sounds like a tough woman," I said.

"She was a fool," Janet said. "As soon as the first contraction hit me, I went straight to the ER and told them to give me something or just shoot me on the spot. And my son came out just fine, despite that evil epidural."

"I've always seen progress in a favorable light," Ida Belle said. "Especially the medical kind."

Janet nodded. "I'm pretty sure having me changed her mind on the whole process, but my daddy ran off shortly after and momma swore off men, so she never had to revisit the issue."

"So not as big a fool as one might think," I said.

Janet laughed. "I guess you got me there. I didn't have any better luck in that department than momma did. Guess that whole psychological thing about marrying your father is true to some extent. Mine didn't even stick around for the birth, but I have some cousins who were happy to provide the manly side of things for me. My son's a surgeon, so I guess it all turned out all right."

"That's great," Ida Belle said. "You must be very proud."

"I am," Janet said. "What about you two? Any grandkids that I need to factor into this vacation home search?"

Ida Belle shook her head. "This one has gone the route of no men before they can cause her any trouble. Her father died young and I decided that road was too much for me to attempt again. It's been just the two of us for quite a while now."

Janet gave me an approving nod. "You're still young enough to change your mind if you come across the right one."

"It seems the wrong ones are way more plentiful," I said. "Plus, I've had some success in my business—security systems—and I'm always afraid they see the money first and not me."

Janet's expression shifted to a flash of anger and she shook her head. "I don't know what's wrong with our society that men are preying on women for their living these days."

Ida Belle nodded. "It happened to my cousin. She was widowed and an easy target. He took her for quite a bit of the insurance money she got when her husband died. I would give my eyeteeth to get my hands on him, but he disappeared before I knew about it."

"That's just awful," Janet said. "A friend of mine got taken recently for a good chunk of her savings. She's barely getting by, so the loss was a big one."

"Did he pull the dying of cancer routine?" Ida Belle asked. "That's how my friend lost her shirt."

"No," Janet said. "He told her he was opening a business on the island and her money was an investment. He promised to double her money in a year. When she called me about it, I told her he was lying. I know every commercial property deal on this island. There's only one building zoned for the restaurant nonsense he told her about, and it was leased a week ago to the shop next door for an expansion."

I glanced over at Ida Belle. Bingo. Janet was Betty Palmer's friend.

"I take it she didn't listen to you?" I asked.

Janet sighed. "More like it was too late. I'm sure she'd already given him the money. I think she told me thinking I'd be excited about the potential for her to double her savings. She didn't expect to hear that it was a scam."

"If only she'd called you sooner," Ida Belle said.

"The worst part is," Janet said, "this business deal was all wrapped up in romantic promises so he didn't just take her money. He broke her heart. She's never been the same after losing her husband. I guess I didn't realize how desperate she was for that sort of connection."

"That sucks," I said. "Did she report him to the police? Maybe they can get her money back."

A flicker of uncertainty crossed Janet's face as she realized how much of what she'd said implicated her friend in Otis's murder.

"Unfortunately, he's long gone," Janet said.

"That's too bad," Ida Belle said. "I know some would say it's a lesson learned, but it seems particularly harsh to me."

"Me too," Janet said, then put on her big smile again. "So what kind of vacation home are you looking for?"

We spent another thirty minutes going over listings and I took a sheet with me to "think about it." Janet assured me that the price was a bit negotiable on all of them, but they were priced well and all in great condition, not needing any repair. One of them was a two-bedroom condo with a view of the beach that was so pretty I almost forgot I wasn't really there to shop. Then, on the other hand, I did have quite a bit of money saved, and Janet assured me the condo would almost pay for itself if I rented it during the summer. Heck, maybe I'd think about it.

As we headed out, Ida Belle sent a text to Gertie, telling her to meet us at the car.

"Well," Ida Belle said. "We confirmed your suspicions. Sounds like Otis pitched this restaurant thing to Betty and Flamingo Lady."

"Probably to Cynthia as well," I said. "Why change things up if it was working? And based on Flamingo Lady's behavior, we already suspected Otis was wrapping romance up in the package, but Janet confirmed that as well."

"So still three that are the best possibilities."

"I'm not liking Flamingo Lady for it," I said. "She attacked

Gertie because she saw him at dinner with her the night he was killed. If that was the first chink in Otis's white-knight armor, then Flamingo Lady wouldn't have been plotting to kill him earlier that day. And if she had killed him, the last thing she would have done was draw attention to herself by attacking Gertie in a public place."

"You're right," Ida Belle said. "Plus, she'd be less likely to know about the broken cameras. I think we should move her to the end of the list. Which leaves Betty and Cynthia."

"So the question is, which one of them was heartbroken enough to kill?"

"Given what we know, it could go either way. I think it's time we talk to the suspects. You'll know if they're lying."

"And if they both are?"

"We'll figure it out. We always do."

———

I HAD JUST PULLED INTO THE PARKING LOT AT THE RESORT when my cell phone rang. It was Carter. I answered as I parked and could tell from the sound of his voice that this wasn't a social call.

"What's wrong?" I asked.

"I talked to Byron a couple minutes ago," Carter said. "The DA gave Benton the go-ahead to arrest Gertie."

"Crap! Should we clear out? We can book the fishing charter again. Dave will turn off the radio if we ask. He hates Benton."

"If you're off on a fishing boat, you can't go poking around into things like I know you've been doing."

"What would give you that impression?"

"I don't know, maybe Gertie faking a heart attack down at the sheriff's department."

"How in the world do you know that?" I asked.

"I got a phone call from the angry deputy, trying to track a mysterious cell phone call that came from Sinful. He's convinced you did it. He just thinks it's to aggravate him. I know better. I finally managed to get the entire garbled story out of him, complete with him being assaulted by a cake, and I figured Gertie for the medical victim."

"You know Gertie."

"Yeah. I know all three of you, which is why I'm certain you put someone here up to making that call. I'm praying it was Marie because I'm really hoping my dispatcher would be smart enough to opt out of that request. I'm equally certain that Gertie didn't have a real medical malady."

"It could have been a blood sugar thing," I said.

"Only if it was high as a kite. That's a vacation resort, which means breakfast buffet. Gertie probably ate half her weight in pastries."

"Maybe not quite half."

"I guess I should just be happy you didn't do it in the middle of the night and get all your butts thrown in the clink. So did you find anything when you searched Benton's office?"

He didn't have proof of what we did, but Carter knew us so well I saw no point in denying it. It would only waste time and I wanted to get back to the arresting-Gertie thing.

"We got cause of death and check copies," I said, and then I filled him in on the details of what we'd found and the restaurant business scam Otis had been running.

"Puffer fish?" he asked, sounding a bit surprised.

"It's different, right? Of course, we're on an island in the Gulf of Mexico so that doesn't do much to narrow our list of suspects down."

"No. But it's a hell of a lot more interesting than arsenic."

"I'll tell the killer you said so when we figure out who it is."

He was silent for several seconds and I knew he was mentally calculating all the things that could go wrong with a civilian pursuing a murderer. Then he was adjusting those calculations for the civilian being me.

The killer must have come out on the short end of the math stick because finally he said, "I know this is pointless to say, but will you please be careful? The killer is likely to be one of the women who were scammed, not a professional hit man. If she thinks you're zeroing in on her, she's going to feel trapped and desperate. Desperate people are capable of things they never would be otherwise."

"Well, given that Benton is about to outfit Gertie with a set of handcuffs, do you think it's best if we become scarce?"

"No. It's probably not a good idea to go running from Benton. All you'd do is delay the inevitable and if you book that boat, you're only going to get the captain in trouble as well. Besides, Benton's not going to arrest Gertie. Not yet."

"What? I thought you said...I'm so confused."

"The DA gave him the okay to arrest her but then he changed his mind."

"Why?"

"That's what Byron wanted to know, but neither Benton nor the DA is talking. Benton just told him that things were delayed for a small administrative issue they needed to clear up but that he better make sure Gertie stayed put and was available for further questioning."

"What kind of administrative issue could there be?"

"Byron wondered that himself, so he made a few phone calls. A friend of a friend of a former military buddy has a nephew who works in the ME office down there. And it's no small administrative problem. Otis Baker isn't Otis Baker."

CHAPTER EIGHTEEN

I STRAIGHTENED IN MY SEAT, CLENCHING MY PHONE. "What? No way. We looked Otis up online. He was a real person."

"Yes. And the real Otis Baker died six months ago of a heart attack on an island off Key West. Just fell out in a bar and died. The place is called Barefoot Key. He'd rented a beach house there."

"So who the hell was the dead guy here?"

"His real name is Martin Hughes. He's a petty criminal with an arrest record as long as a CVS receipt. Fraud, extortion, forgery, theft...but the most interesting thing is that Martin buried three wives and disappeared on a fourth."

"Holy crap! You think he killed them?"

"He collected a hundred thousand apiece on the three of them."

"But not the fourth. I wonder why he disappeared."

"My guess—someone was onto him. The cops or insurance investigators, probably."

"Wow," I said. "If you're right then they probably saved the fourth wife's life."

"That's a very strong possibility."

"But he hasn't married anyone as Otis Baker."

"Not that I've been able to find. My guess is he was afraid he'd get caught when it was time for insurance to pay up."

"He thought someone would connect the dots."

"And someone probably would have," Carter said. "Everything's electronic these days. It's a lot easier to match up crimes. Don't get me wrong, people can get away with things for a long time if they're smart about it, and some manage to right up till the grave, but it's not as easy as it used to be."

"So he shifted to the business scam like he was running here."

"Sounds like the perfect setup. Mix a little romance with business and you've got the perfect combination. And the business thing allowed him to target several women in one location without them going after each other as he could pass them off to each other as potential investors."

"Tell that to Flamingo Lady. I'm afraid to think what she might have done with that flamingo if she'd caught up with Gertie. She wasn't buying the investor angle for a second."

"There's always the possibility of a loose cannon, but it's a calculated risk. It was easy money if he could sell his story and his only investment was dinner and some time."

"Not as much money as an insurance payout, though."

"But not nearly the amount of time invested. How many women has he gotten money out of just in that one location? He's been on the island a couple weeks. And not exactly slumming it while he was working his scam."

I sighed. "You're right. Even a couple thousand per mark would add up if he hit five to ten over a span of a month or two."

"And all the while living with full-time housekeeping, a great view, and a never-ending supply of lonely older women."

"It's practically a revolving door, but I suppose it's harder to talk women out of money over the course of a vacation. That must be why he was working the locals."

"Yep, and my guess is he was probably about to max out his luck there. Then he would have picked up and moved to the next location. He's probably been working his way around the Florida coast."

"He said as much to Gertie, although his reason was a lot different. What do you want to bet one of his stops was Barefoot Key and that's how he grabbed the Otis Baker identity? He heard about his death or maybe he was even in the bar when it happened. Heck, he might have even known him casually."

"I'd say any of that is highly likely."

"I wonder how the ME's office figured out something was off. I mean, they must have run prints to get his real identity, but what prompted them to do it?"

"This is just speculation, but I'm going to guess that they tried to notify next of kin on Otis and found out he was already deceased. Given that the identity was stolen, and the victim's 'profession' was scamming women out of money, they probably figured he had a record."

"So they ran him. That makes sense. You know, if anyone ever deserved to be taken out, it was this guy."

"All the older women in Florida are definitely safer, but I wish people would let the law handle things."

"Handle them how? If the cops couldn't pin Martin for killing three wives, then how were they going to put him away for scamming some money? He'd have just said the money was a gift or whatever. Their word against his. I mean, I know a pattern of behavior could be proven, but in order to do so, the women would have to be willing to come forward."

He sighed. "Yeah, that's always a problem with this sort of crime."

"Look, I respect your work. You know that. But you and I both know that there are gaps between crime and punishment. I'm not saying I endorse vigilante justice, but I understand why it happens."

"The problem is, the vigilante is usually the one who ends up in prison. People like Martin aren't worth good people going to prison."

"Yeah, and if we don't figure out who killed him, then Gertie is going to be sent up the river. Or at least on an extended stay at the sheriff's department accompanied by a hefty legal bill."

"Then I guess you guys best get around to doing what you do best—making local law enforcement type up resignation letters."

"You never typed up a resignation letter because of me."

"That's because I felt too guilty for whoever would have to come behind me and deal with you. And since I take partial responsibility for you relocating to Sinful, I guess I have to stay on the job. Penance, you know?"

I laughed. "Your ego is only eclipsed by your massive barbecue grill."

"Of course. I'm a red-blooded Southern man."

"Well, I'm going to get off of here before the testosterone reaches all the way to Florida."

"Too late."

I disconnected and Ida Belle and Gertie both started talking at once.

"I can't believe Otis wasn't Otis!"

"I knew he was scum before but wow!"

"Do you think he killed his wives?" Gertie asked. "I mean, scamming is one thing but killing people...I spent an entire evening with the guy. Shouldn't I have seen something off?"

"Sociopaths can be very convincing," Ida Belle said. "If one isn't burdened with guilt, I suppose it's easy to go about each day completely normal."

I nodded. "And Otis has had years to perfect his technique. Or Martin, I mean."

"So what now?" Gertie asked.

Ida Belle looked at me. "You still want to make a run at Betty and Cynthia?"

I nodded, a plan forming. "Yes. But with a different angle. I want to talk to them alone and present myself as a detective, hired by a woman who was scammed in the Keys. I think they're more likely to talk one-on-one. I'll tell them I've been tracking Otis, trying to collect enough information to build a fraud case against him."

"The direct approach," Ida Belle said. "That's interesting, and it just might work."

"I figured attempting to get either of them to gossip about Otis would be a waste of time," I said. "Especially since they're both trying to keep their involvement a secret."

"But Benton has the check copies," Gertie said.

"And is probably sitting on them until he gets the sheriff appointment," I said. "And they had no way of knowing Otis kept copies of the checks, so they might think they're in the clear as long as they keep their mouths shut."

Ida Belle nodded. "I'm sure they know people are talking but people talking doesn't prove anything." She frowned. "I wonder why he kept copies of the checks."

"Probably to steal the account information," I said. "Easy enough to print up some checks and pass them off to small businesses. By the time they figured out they're not good, he would be long gone."

Gertie shook her head. "The more we learn about Otis-Martin-whoever, the more I'm glad he's dead."

"What do you want us to do?" Ida Belle asked.

"See if you can figure out where Martin got that étouffée. Bonus points if you can find out who he was eating with."

"So we're doing this now?" Gertie asked.

"I don't think we can afford to put it off," I said. "The DA was thrown off by the identity thing, but the reality is a man's dead and you're still the person Benton is focusing on."

"Okay," Ida Belle said. "We'll start poking around here and see if someone saw Martin eating at the seafood restaurant the day before he died. If not, we'll find out who else on the island has étouffée on the menu and go from there."

"Sounds good," I said. "But if you leave the resort, you're going to have to walk. I can corner Cynthia somewhere during her shift, but Betty doesn't come on until this evening and I don't want to wait. Word could get back to her that a detective was asking questions. I don't want her to have time to prepare."

Gertie grimaced. "Walking? There's at least five miles of hotels and resorts here."

"And you ate ten miles worth of breakfast," Ida Belle said. "*Plus* two root beer floats and a piece of pie. Maybe you should think about burning some of it off before dinner."

Gertie sighed. "I suppose asking about étouffée isn't likely to get us shot at, so there won't be any forced running."

Ida Belle rolled her eyes. "With you doing the questioning, there's always hope."

CHAPTER NINETEEN

I TRACKED DOWN SOME HOUSEKEEPERS IN THE LAUNDRY room and they told me Cynthia was checking on a cleaning complaint on the fifth floor. I thanked them and headed up, hoping that I could catch her by roaming the hallways. I had walked half the length of one side when I got lucky. Cynthia was coming out of a room at the end of the hall. I made my way over and she seemed surprised when I addressed her by name and told her I'd like to speak with her.

"About what?" she asked, clearly wary.

I pulled out my business card and handed it to her. "I'm a private investigator based in Louisiana, but my client is in Florida. I'd like to ask you some questions about Otis Baker."

She dropped her gaze down and shook her head. "I don't know anything about him."

"I'm afraid you know at least five thousand things about him," I said.

Her eyes widened and she glanced down the hallway behind me.

"Is there an empty room we can use to talk in private?" I

asked, figuring she didn't want to be seen talking to me, much less overheard.

She nodded and opened the room nearest us. It was a three-bedroom, like ours, and I headed for the kitchen area and motioned to a stool. She hesitated for a moment, then finally took a seat.

"I don't understand," she said. "You said you're a private investigator?"

"Yes. A friend of mine had an aunt who was taken by a scammer—Otis. Her aunt didn't tell her for a while but finally had to when she needed to borrow money. My friend was outraged and hired me to track Otis down. I finally caught up with him here."

"But you're here with that other lady—the one who had dinner with Otis the night he died."

"She's an associate of mine. So is the other lady traveling with us. I found quite a trail of victims in Otis's wake. My friend didn't hold out any hope of getting her aunt's money back, but she asked me to accumulate evidence so that she could convince the authorities to push a fraud charge against him. The lady who had dinner with him was simply trying to get his exact method so we could document it."

Her eyes widened. "She was investigating him?"

I nodded. "We needed to know exactly how Otis was getting money out of women. What promises he was making them, if any. I was trying to establish a pattern of behavior so that he couldn't use the cop-out of 'it was a gift.'"

"But I thought Benton arrested your...uh, associate?"

"Between you and me, Benton is an idiot. He'd like the easy answer so he doesn't have to actually work, but he can't pin a murder on someone who didn't do it."

"How did you know...about the money?"

"Otis made copies of the checks and I had a way of seeing them."

"Do the police know?"

"I'm pretty sure they do."

She nodded and I could tell by the frightened look on her face that she was processing all the implications. And those implications only led to Benton looking at her for murder.

"Checks?" she asked and frowned. "There was more than one person he got money from here on the island?"

"And on the mainland. He worked it before he came here. Did you know he was working other women at the resort?"

She glanced down and shook her head. "I heard rumors, but I didn't know for certain."

"Didn't know or didn't want to know?"

She sighed and looked at me, her expression sad. "Someone like you would never understand. You probably have men fighting over you just because you walked into a room."

"I'm sorry he hurt you. He hurt my friend's aunt as well. Made romantic overtures and promises that were all lies. She was recently widowed, so she was an easy target."

"I never married. There was a guy, once. He said all the right things, then he went back home to his wife."

"You didn't know?"

She gave me an indignant look. "Of course not. I'm not that kind of woman."

"And you never tried again?"

"No. Every woman I knew had problems with her relationship. They all caught their husbands or boyfriends lying about things. Sometimes big things. Sometimes small things. But it doesn't make a difference to me. If you'll lie about small things, you'll lie about the big ones as well."

"I agree."

A flash of anger crossed her face. "I can't believe I let Otis play me. I thought I had heard every ploy in the book. And yet he still managed to convince me that what he promised me was real when it was all a lie from the beginning. How can that happen? How could I be so stupid again?"

"Men like Otis have a way of choosing the right people at the right time. I don't know you, so I can't speak to your personal situation, but I'm guessing Otis clued in on some weakness in your wall."

"So they take your emotional crisis and turn it into their way in. How can they do that? How can they fool people so easily?"

"Because they aren't just smooth talkers," I said. "They're sociopaths. And sociopaths are believable because they have no conscience. They can say or do anything without even a twitch."

"So they can lie right to your face and never think twice about it."

"Even worse. They often consider it a game."

"Well, I guess he turned out to be the big loser this time, didn't he?"

She seemed almost pleased as she delivered that statement.

"Given all that I know, it's hard for me to mourn his death," I said. "Although I would have loved to have seen him on trial and known that he was languishing behind bars."

She nodded. "Death is harsh but at least it's final." She gave me a curious look. "So now that Otis is dead, why are you still investigating?"

"Because my client wants the full story and I want to give it to her."

"Well, I don't know what I can tell you that you don't already know. He pursued me romantically, lied to me about investing in a business he was planning on opening on the island, but once he got the money, he became less available. I'd been trying to pin him down for days before he was killed but he always had some excuse about why we couldn't get together. Looking back, I don't understand why it took me so long to clue in on the fact that he was cutting me loose."

"Because you didn't want that to be the case."

"No. I didn't." She rubbed her nose and sniffed. "A good friend of mine passed away earlier this year. She was my age and like me, never married. She'd been ill for some time and the worst part about it was how alone she was. Being house-bound, she couldn't get out and do things like she used to, and I saw her as much as possible but with my job and my own life to manage, I know it wasn't enough. As time passed, her other friends faded away, and after she died, I couldn't stop thinking about her sitting alone in that house, drawing her last breath."

I placed my hand on her arm. "You don't have anything to be embarrassed about. No one wants to think about being alone at the end. Otis took advantage of you. You were seriously questioning your choices about relationships and then he appeared like magic, offering you the opportunity to test the waters of the other side."

She sniffed again and nodded. "Well, it's all over now and I need to just move on. Do you have any more questions? I've got to get back downstairs before the staff meeting."

"Did you ever take a look through Otis's room?"

"No. I...that's against the rules. I can only enter a unit to address a complaint."

"I get what the rules say, but if the guy who'd promised me the moon had backed off and I had access, I definitely would have gone through his things looking for answers. I understand the security cameras were down for several days, right? That would have been the perfect time to do it."

She looked down.

"Cynthia? I'm not going to tell anyone. This is only for my

friend. So that she can convince her aunt that what happened wasn't her fault. I'm afraid her health has been failing ever since she realized Otis wasn't coming back."

"That's awful." She sighed. "Okay, when he didn't return my calls, I went into his room. I saw him go into the breakfast buffet and knew he'd be there a while. He always read the newspaper while he ate breakfast."

Probably looking at the obituaries for a new identity to nab, I thought.

"And what did you find?" I asked.

"Nothing. I mean, nothing that meant anything."

"What do you mean?"

"I mean his room looked like any other person's who was on vacation. He had a couple of cheap souvenirs, a few of those collector drink glasses, and pictures of fish and boats."

"Pictures of fish?" I asked.

She nodded. "Otis loved fishing. He did a charter a couple times a week."

"I guess he had a freezer full then. The fishing's really good here."

"He never brought any back. Said he liked the sport of fishing but didn't want to deal with cleaning it and packaging it up. Said he'd rather eat his fish in the restaurant."

"Seems like a waste to never eat something he caught."

"I tried to get him to bring some back to me. I told him he didn't have to clean them or anything. I'd even supply him with a cooler, but he still wouldn't do it. Hell, he could have been giving them to some other woman for all I know."

"I suppose anything's possible. I don't suppose you know who he used for the charter, do you?"

"Some guy over on the mainland. He said he didn't like the charters on the island. Their boats were too old. He was always saying he was going to buy his own boat. I guess I know how he planned on paying for it."

"And there wasn't anything else you can think of?"

She shook her head. "Like I said. There wasn't really much of anything. I suppose he could have had some super-secret stuff locked in the safe, but I don't have access to that, so I have no way of knowing."

"What about his personal items? Did he have clothes hanging in the closet? Or were they in his suitcase?"

"They were packed. He'd told me a few days before that he was going to have to leave for a couple days for business."

"Did he say what kind of business?"

She shook her head. "Just that he had a line on a big investor and if he landed him, then he'd never have to worry about funding again."

I studied her face as she spoke. She wasn't lying, exactly. I was sure that's what Otis told her. But I didn't believe for a moment that she bought it. Cynthia had taken one look at that packed suitcase and known exactly what the score was.

The question was, did she do anything about it?

———

I FOUND BETTY PALMER'S ADDRESS WITH A SIMPLE SEARCH on my phone and shook my head at how limited privacy had become. I could be an ax murderer about to knock on her front door and the internet had provided me not only an address but directions, complete with recommendations of the best streets to avoid traffic.

The apartment building was older than me and had definitely seen better days. It was a couple blocks back from the sound, but the salt air had still rusted all the light fixtures, and rusted nails were weeping onto the siding. Betty's unit was on the second floor on the end, so I made my way upstairs and headed to her door, hoping she would be willing to talk to me.

She answered the door quickly and holding a dishrag, so I figured I had caught her doing the dishes. She stared at me several seconds, trying to place me, but apparently couldn't.

"I don't need magazines, cookies, or Jesus," she said.

"Everyone needs cookies," I said. "But that's not why I'm here."

I pulled out my card and handed it to her, giving her the same story I'd given Cynthia. I kept pausing as I went, thinking she might invite me in at some point, but apparently she didn't care who saw me standing outside her door.

"What's this got to do with me?" she asked when I finished.

"I'd like to ask you some questions about Otis."

She shrugged, trying to appear nonchalant. "I work the office at night, processing receipts and stuff from the day shift and helping with check-in when needed. All I know about Otis Baker is that he's dead."

"Then why did you give him ten thousand dollars?"

"I didn't."

"I saw a copy of the check."

Her eyes narrowed and she studied me for several seconds. "I don't think you've seen anything of the sort."

I pulled out my phone, accessed the image of her check, and turned it around to show her. "I'm pretty sure the bank will verify that's your account."

Her shoulders slumped. "You working with the cops?"

"Heck no! I wouldn't work with Benton if my life depended on it. That guy's an idiot."

"That's a fact. Does he have a copy of that check?"

"Probably. I mean, Otis had them and the police searched his room, so..."

She sighed. "Then I suppose he'll be along here accusing me of all manner of things soon enough."

"He can accuse all he wants, but if you didn't do anything, he can't prove it. I'm not looking to prove anything except that Otis was a big fat liar."

She put her hands in the air. "Fine. What do you want me to say? That I was a damned fool and that man took almost all my savings?"

"You're not the only one," I said. "Otis scammed a lot of women out of money. In fact, he made a career out of it."

"Is that supposed to make me feel better? That a bunch of women are just as stupid as me? Well, it doesn't."

"It doesn't make my client or her aunt feel better either. Mostly, it just makes them mad, which is why I'm still pursuing this."

"I don't see the point. The man's dead, and good riddance. Even if you knew everything there was to know about Otis, it still wouldn't give any of us the answers we really want."

I knew she was right. Victims wanted to know why and sometimes there just wasn't an explanation good enough for them to accept. It was really hard for good people to fathom the depth of depravity that criminals could stoop to without a moment's hesitation. There was an answer, of course. People like Otis were simply wired differently. But I doubted that answer would give her any comfort. The problem with people like Otis was they didn't look like they were wired differently, which meant they were uniquely suited to do a lot of damage.

"Quitting my investigation now would be like closing a book or turning off a movie five minutes before it finishes just because you know how the ending is going to go," I said. "There's some satisfaction to be gained by following something through all the way. I think it's good for healing because there's nothing left to wonder about if you have all the facts."

"And you think me airing my dirty laundry will help your friend's aunt? I honestly don't see how and it sure as heck won't help me to rehash it."

"I'm not trying to cause you any more grief. Maybe you could just answer a few questions and then I'll get out of your hair."

"Ask 'em and I'll decide."

"Okay. Did Otis pitch the restaurant business to you?"

She nodded. "That's what the money was for. He guaranteed he could double it in a year. I know I was stupid to give it to him, but if I could have doubled that money, I could have gotten out of this crap place and not worried about making rent every month. My husband had second-mortgaged the house and didn't tell me about it. I couldn't afford to keep it after he was gone."

My heart clenched and I hated Otis/Martin all over again. I also wasn't overly thrilled with Betty's husband for leaving her in such a financial predicament.

"I'm really sorry," I said. "That must have been tough, especially when you were already dealing with his death."

"Wasn't the best time of my life, that's for sure. But now is worse and this time it's all of my own making. What else do you want to know?"

"Did you ever go into Otis's room?"

"No. He always said he was too messy to have anyone to his room."

"Did you know the security cameras were broken on Otis's floor?"

She gave me a wary look. "Yes. But I don't see why that matters. Can't get in those rooms without a key card and they're all assigned to the user."

"You can't just make one up when you're filling in on the front desk?"

"I suppose I could have, but as I was out sick the night Otis was killed someone might have noticed if I'd traipsed in and made myself a key card."

"I'm sure you're right," I said. "So how did you know the cameras were down? Was it general knowledge among the staff?"

"I don't think so. I mean, it's not the sort of thing one rushes to the watercooler to gossip about. I knew because accounting left me the work order for the replacement parts to get the manager's approval. It had been sitting on his desk for several days and security was bugging them about it. Fletcher was coming in that night to oversee a banquet and they asked me to get a signature."

"I guess this Otis thing has been a mess for him."

She nodded. "He tried to get Otis kicked out. I think he'd gotten wind of the things Otis was up to and didn't want to deal with the fallout. I know he checked with accounting about his bill but Otis prepaid."

"And since he couldn't get rid of Otis, now he gets to deal with a murder investigation. That can't be good for business either."

"Fletcher is fit to be tied. Can't say that I blame him. I think the owner came down pretty hard when they met this morning. He came back to work white as a sheet."

"Probably worried he'll lose his job."

"Wouldn't you be?"

I nodded. "So when you and Otis met, did you go out to eat or to the beach?"

"Mostly we grabbed a late dinner on my break at the resort."

She said it casually, but I could tell I'd touched a nerve. I held in a sigh. Otis must have had charm that I didn't see in our short interaction, because both Betty and Cynthia had enough indication to question his intent and both had stuck their heads in the sand. I doubted Otis had discovered Love Potion Number 9, so I had to go with superb targeting skills. He knew how to spot a potential victim and exactly how to work her.

With Cynthia it had been emotional, launching off the death of her friend. With Betty, I got the impression that while the romance end of things wasn't unwanted, her investment was more financial. I struggled not to sigh. Even when alarms should have been going off, these women had stuck with him. It was a sad commentary on what loneliness and financial burden could do to some people.

"You never went out during the day?" I said, continuing to press.

"Once. I kept complaining about never going out and he took me on one of those fishing charters. Worst day of my life. The swells were high and I ended up green as grass. Otis didn't even fish. Said he just liked to be out on a boat in the deep water and the sunlight."

"I'll bet the boat captain thought he was crazy spending all that money to sit around."

She shrugged. "Mikey Marlin. That's a name for you, right? A rough-looking sort and a bit odd. Didn't say a word the entire time. Just followed Otis's directions and anchored when he got there. Then baited up his own rod and set to fishing while Otis did his thing with that fancy camera."

"Fancy camera?"

"Taking pictures of dolphins. He liked to watch them playing. Bunch of big fish flopping around as far as I'm concerned. I don't get the attraction, especially when my stomach is rolling."

"Oh, was that the day Otis was killed?" I asked, even though I knew it wasn't.

"No. A couple days before. I was fine the next morning but then that night I managed to latch onto a whole other round of stomach problems. One of those women from housekeeping left brownies for everyone—all wrapped up in pink netting and bows with our names on them. I should have known better than to eat it, especially with my stomach still unsettled from all that boat rocking. Had to go home early that night and missed the whole next day because of it. Like I can afford to lose shift money."

"Maybe you should see a doctor and get checked out," I said. "You might have an ulcer or something."

"I suppose that's possible. My mom had them. Would need money for the doctor, though. Anyway, I've got dishes waiting and a nap to take before my shift."

"No problem. Thanks for talking to me."

She nodded but didn't even look at me before closing the door.

I headed back to the car, mulling over our conversation. A couple of things stood out. The first was that Betty had known about the cameras. The second was that she'd been out sick the night Otis had died. Was she feeling guilty about her handiwork and hiding or trying to give herself an alibi in case the police came knocking?

I didn't know the answer. But what I did know was that Betty was angry and bitter and she struck me as someone perfectly capable of slipping him some poisoned fish. I frowned, wondering if her claims of seasickness were a setup for when cause of death came out. I could already hear her defense—*I don't fish because I get seasick.*

It wasn't enough, of course, but it was another chink in a prosecutor's case. Of course, she could have lifted the fish from the onsite restaurant, but that came with a whole other set of risks. Surely the resort kept such a dangerous item under lock and key, if for no other reason than to avoid the liability of accidental usage by the terminally stupid. But I had no way of knowing without asking, and that was something that might filter back to Benton. If he found out I was asking questions about puffer fish, he'd figure out what Gertie's medical emergency was really about.

I stared out the windshield of my car and blew out a breath. Something about my entire conversation with Betty bothered me. With Cynthia, I'd known she was lying about being in Otis's room, and I was certain she was aware he'd been moving in on other women. But I got the impression there was something else. With Betty, I got the feeling that the things she'd said were true enough, but she definitely wasn't saying everything.

Something was missing from both stories.

But for the life of me, I didn't know what.

CHAPTER TWENTY

As I PULLED INTO THE RESORT, I GOT A TEXT FROM IDA Belle telling me they were in the bar having a drink. I wondered briefly if Gertie had gotten into trouble again and sent Ida Belle straight for the bottle, but at least there wasn't an ambulance or police car in the parking lot. That was encouraging.

I headed for the bar and found them sitting at a table in the corner, sipping on piña coladas and picking at a bowl of snack mix. They waved as I walked in and Ida Belle motioned for the server, who happened to be the same guy who had served me the other night.

"Chance, right?" I asked as he hurried over.

He flashed me a big smile. "That's right. What can I get you?"

"I'll have the same as them," I said.

He nodded and hurried off.

"He wasn't nearly as enthusiastic when he took our drink order," Gertie said.

"That's because we're not nearly as young and good-looking as Fortune," Ida Belle said.

"Or I gave him a really big tip the other night," I said.

"That works too," Ida Belle said. "But I don't think your looks are hurting anything."

Chance hurried back with my drink and a menu, "in case you wanted a snack." I waited until he was out of earshot, then asked if they'd found out where Otis acquired The Last Supper.

"Oh, we're on our third drink already," Gertie said. "It didn't take us long to get the information."

"Your third drink? Really?" I asked. "That's fast working. Did you hold someone at gunpoint?"

"Since I don't have my weapons with me, no," Gertie said. "We just had a bit of luck."

Ida Belle nodded. "We walked into the restaurant as a server was storming out, yelling at the restaurant manager, who'd just fired him. I followed him into the lobby and offered him cash in exchange for information."

Gertie laughed. "He told us the restaurant manager was cheating on his wife with one of the beach servers before Ida Belle even told him what kind of information we were looking for."

"Maybe the manager should have thought about that before he fired him," I said.

Ida Belle nodded. "He probably called the wife as soon as he got into his car."

"So what was the verdict?" I asked.

"Otis ate dinner there the night before he died and had the étouffée," Gertie said. "Unemployed guy was his server."

"Was he dining with someone?" I asked, getting excited. "Did the server know who it was?"

"Yes to both," Ida Belle said. "He was having early dinner with Betty before she went on shift."

"Isn't that great?" Gertie was practically bouncing in her seat.

"How early?" I asked.

"Around five," Ida Belle said.

I frowned. "Which means that Cynthia could have easily seen them when she got off work."

"Oh," Gertie said, her excitement waning. "I didn't think about that."

"Were you able to speak to both of them?" Ida Belle asked.

I nodded and told them about my conversations with the two women. When I was done, they were both frowning.

"Crap," Gertie said finally. "They're both still equally possible."

"Did you get a feel for one over the other?" Ida Belle asked. "Your intuition has always been spot-on."

"I wouldn't say always," I said. "A few people in Sinful have managed to fool me."

"Not for very long, though," Gertie said.

"I wish I could tell you differently," I said. "But my honest answer is no. Both of them have history that made them vulnerable. Both are angry and embarrassed about being taken—I just think Cynthia was better at hiding the anger part. I think either is capable. And given that they both live here and work at the resort, I'm sure they both know how dangerous puffer fish are."

Ida Belle nodded. "Either could have stolen the card from Otis. And apparently both knew the security cameras were down."

"Betty knew for certain," I said. "And Cynthia didn't so much as flinch when I mentioned it, so I'm sure she knew as well."

"Maybe someone saw one of them on the tenth floor that day," Gertie said. "Should we ask around?"

"If it was another guest, I don't know that they would have paid enough attention," Ida Belle said. "How hard do you look at strangers passing in the hallway?"

"What about other employees?" Gertie asked.

"I still don't think we'd get anyone to bite," Ida Belle said. "Cynthia could have been on the floor dealing with a housekeeping complaint and no one would have registered it, as it's common. And I'm going to hazard a guess that if Betty put on some touristy-looking clothes, a big floppy hat, and sunglasses, an employee wouldn't have looked twice."

"Probably not," I said. "Betty was a very average-looking person. No scars or limp or tattoos that I could see, so nothing about her would have stood out. And with her working the night shift, a lot of day employees probably don't know her anyway."

"So we're right back to where we started," Gertie said. "All we've really done is verify what we already suspected. This investigating thing is not nearly as exciting as I thought it would be."

I stared. "You've been out on a date with a man who was murdered, assaulted by a plastic flamingo, and single-handedly taken ten years off the life of a douchebag deputy. How much more excitement do you require?"

"Fine," Gertie said. "There's been a little excitement. But you have to admit that the investigating part is somewhat tedious."

"So what now?" Ida Belle asked.

"We head upstairs and do some research on Martin Hughes," I said as I waved to Chance for the bill.

He hurried over to the table and I signed the bill, leaving him a healthy tip. He flashed the huge smile and made us promise to come back and see him again as we got up to leave.

"I know it might not have anything to do with the

murder," I said as we walked, "but I still think we ought to know more about the man who was pretending to be Otis Baker."

Ida Belle nodded. "Who knows? We might turn up another suspect and make things even worse."

"God forbid," Gertie said. "I hope it's not another crazy woman with an affinity for wielding table decor."

"I would say the odds of that are slim," I said. "But although I hate everything about the man, he definitely knew how to pick and work his victims." I looked at Gertie. "What was it about him that made women want to buy his line of bull?"

Gertie shrugged. "He handed out compliments and empathy and only asked questions about me. Never talked about himself. I suppose if I had the emotional baggage that the other women had, I might have been swayed by it."

"But you weren't," Ida Belle said.

"Of course not," Gertie said. "I know a come-on when I see it, even if it's been a while."

I slowed as we walked into the lobby, zeroing in on two men in black suits who were talking to Fletcher. They were too young to be wearing suits on vacation, and the conversation looked serious. Ida Belle followed my gaze and frowned.

"Don't look like your typical tourists," she said.

"No," I agreed. "Looks like Feds."

Gertie's eyes widened. "Feds? What would feds be doing here?"

"I don't know," I said. "But it's never a good thing when they show up."

"Do you think it's about Martin?" Ida Belle asked. "I know the FBI has been cracking down on identity theft."

"Maybe," I said.

"We should find out," Gertie said.

"What would you like to do?" Ida Belle asked. "Walk up and ask them?"

I scanned the room, checking my options, then practically jogged away, sliding to a stop at a palm tree near the entry to the bar. Ida Belle and Gertie hurried up beside me, looking confused.

I pointed to my lips and they caught on. I'd moved where I could read their lips.

Unfortunately, the conversation was ending. A couple seconds later, the two men in suits walked toward the entrance. Fletcher watched them for a moment, looking slightly shell-shocked, then an employee called for him and he walked toward the front desk.

"Did you get anything?" Ida Belle asked as we headed for the elevators.

"Very little," I said. "All I caught was 'Barefoot Key' and 'speak to owner.'"

"Isn't Barefoot Key where the real Otis died?" Gertie asked.

I nodded. "And where I think Martin picked up his identity."

"So maybe it *is* an identity theft thing," Ida Belle said.

"Maybe," I said as we stepped into the elevator. But I couldn't shake the feeling that we'd missed something and that whatever we'd missed was about to blow everything wide open.

I just hoped we weren't caught in the blast.

As soon as we got back to the condo, I grabbed my laptop and we headed for the kitchen counter. Gertie reached for the room service menu and looked over at us.

"Is it too early to think about dinner?" she asked. "Those

bar snacks didn't exactly do it for me and breakfast was a good while ago."

"By the time they get the food here, I'll probably be hungry," I said.

Ida Belle nodded. "Might as well. We don't have anything else to do tonight and I really don't feel like going back out to eat. You never know when another angry woman brandishing a flamingo might show up."

Gertie gave her the finger but didn't look up from the menu. "I'm having fried shrimp and a bottle of wine."

"Sounds good," I said as I opened the internet browser. "Make it two."

"Three," Ida Belle said.

I typed in "Martin Hughes" and searched, then started opening each link and scanning the data for anything relevant.

"I'd like to order three shrimp dinners and three bottles of pinot grigio."

Ida Belle sighed. "We didn't mean three bottles of wine."

Gertie hung up the phone. "Well, you're welcome to split one between the two of you and save the other, but I'm not sharing. This is the most exhausting vacation I've ever been on, and unfortunately, not in a good way."

"You find anything?" Ida Belle asked.

"A couple of news articles with local arrests," I said. "But all the sort of thing Carter indicated. And three obituaries."

Ida Belle shook her head, clearly disgusted. "All listing him as the grieving husband, I assume?"

"And all in different states, so hardly any chance of the families crossing paths," I said.

I pulled up a news article on a charity event and scanned the text but didn't see any mention of Martin. I scrolled back up, looking at the descriptions below the pictures, and found it. And there he was, standing with his arm around the fourth wife—Marsha Hughes—the one who got away. I turned the laptop toward Ida Belle and Gertie.

"Here's the fourth wife," I said. "Does she look familiar to you?"

They both studied the picture for several seconds, then finally shook their heads.

"Not really," Ida Belle said. "I had a momentary twinge, but it's probably because she reminds me of someone I've met at some point. The name is completely unfamiliar, so I'm certain I've never met her."

"Me either," Gertie said.

I turned the laptop back around and made the image larger. "I'm getting more than a twinge but I can't figure out why."

"Someone you ran across when you worked for the CIA maybe?" Gertie asked.

"I've never been to Georgia. And I didn't exactly frequent tourist areas overseas or hobnob with the general public."

I squinted, thinking a shift in focus might make it clearer, and that's when it hit me.

"She looks like Penny."

"The housekeeper who didn't like us gossiping?" Gertie asked.

I nodded. "Take another look."

Gertie leaned over and studied the picture again. "You're right. Penny could be this woman's daughter."

"Maybe she is," Ida Belle said.

"Great," Gertie said. "Another suspect."

I reached for the phone. "Let's find out."

I called the housekeeping department. "Hi, I'm hoping you can help me," I said when a woman answered. "There was a young woman cleaning my room this morning and I need to speak to her about a personal matter. Her name is Penny. Is she still on shift?"

"She's in laundry," the woman said. "Would you like for me to transfer you over there?"

"Actually, I really don't want to discuss it over the phone. If you could just send her up here...it won't take long, I promise."

"Was there a problem with your room?" the woman asked.

"No. The room is fine. Like I said, it's a personal matter."

"Okay. I'll send her up."

"Thank you," I said and hung up.

"How are you going to play this?" Ida Belle asked.

"Simple," I said. "I'm going to show her the picture and watch for a reaction. If she so much as flinches, then we'll know she's related. Then I fire with both barrels."

"Thank God for the direct approach," Gertie said. "I'm too tired to role-play. You think you can wrap this up before dinner gets here?"

Ida Belle stared. "She'll try not to interfere with your busy eating schedule."

"It was more the drinking part that I was thinking about," Gertie said.

"I don't think it will take long," I said. "Penny didn't strike me as particularly good at hiding her feelings."

There was a knock at the door and I hurried to open it. Penny stepped in, looking uneasy.

"Was there a problem with the room?" she asked. "Or the closet?"

I waved my hand in dismissal. "I'm opting for the bathtub these days. Saves time in the morning when I'm ready to shower."

Her mouth opened a bit and she shot a nervous glance at Gertie and Ida Belle.

"Anyway, that's not why I called for you," I said.

"Then how can I help you?" she asked.

I grabbed my laptop and showed her the picture. "Did you tell Marsha that Martin was here?"

She gasped and her hand flew up to cover her mouth. She took a step back as if the laptop were a venomous snake.

"It's rather pointless to deny it," I said. "You look just like her. And even if you didn't, your reaction gave you away. How are you related?"

She shook her head. "I...I'm not..."

I pulled my CIA ID from my wallet and showed her. "Do you want to try again?"

The color rushed from her face and she started to sway. Ida Belle grabbed her by the shoulders and guided her into one of the living room chairs. I took a seat on the coffee table in front of her. She slumped forward, her face in her lap, taking in large drags of air. Finally, she inched up a bit and looked at me, clearly frightened.

"That badge is real?" she asked.

I nodded. Technically, it was expired, but it was definitely real.

"Marsha is my aunt," Penny said. "But then you probably already knew that. The CIA knows everything, right?"

"That's just a myth perpetuated by Hollywood," I said. "Did you tell your aunt that Martin was staying at the resort?"

"No! I wouldn't have...she's been through enough. I was going to tell my mother, but I had to be sure."

And then it dawned on me. The date on the picture was five years before. Martin had gained some weight and lost some hair since it was taken. Combine that with him using a fake name and Penny being a teen when he pulled his disappearing act, and I realized Penny hadn't been sure it was Martin Hughes.

Gertie sat on the arm of the chair and patted Penny's arm. "We understand. You didn't want to upset your aunt."

Penny shook her head. "That awful man put her through hell. He poisoned her and when she didn't die, he disappeared with all their money and the jewelry my grandmother had left her."

"He poisoned her?" I asked. "Are you sure?"

She nodded. "My mom never liked him, and she couldn't understand why my aunt was suddenly so sick when she'd never had anything beyond a cold. She finally got her to go to the doctor, but he never found anything definitive. The doctor said it was probably some horrible virus or reflux, but my mom never believed it."

"So she suspected something?" I asked.

Penny nodded. "My aunt was out sick so much, she lost her job. Two days later, Martin disappeared. Then my aunt started to get better."

"When she lost her job, she lost her life insurance as well, right?" Ida Belle asked.

"Yeah," Penny said. "That's what mom thinks the whole marriage was about. Sick, right?"

"Yes, it is," I said. "Did your aunt have more tests run?"

"Yes," Penny said. "They found small traces of something found in weed killer, but not enough to prove anything. My mom wanted Aunt Marsha to push the police harder, but she refused."

"Why?" I asked.

Penny shook her head. "I don't know. Maybe because she already knew the truth and didn't want to face it? She hasn't been sick a single day since Martin has been gone. And if he wasn't making her sick, why did he disappear with all their money and her jewelry?"

"Surely the police could issue a warrant for the theft of the money and jewelry," Gertie said.

A flash of anger crossed Penny's face. "They said the money was 'marital property.' And even though the jewelry wasn't, it wasn't worth enough money for them to do more than a cursory search for him. Of course, they came up with nothing and told her she was better off pursuing a civil suit as he probably wouldn't get any time on criminal charges anyway. Can you believe that? Like you can sue the disappearing man?"

"I would be mad too," Ida Belle said. "And then you saw Martin here, living it up."

Penny nodded. "I didn't know for sure. But that first day, oh my God, I almost fainted right there on the spot."

"But surely, after two weeks, you had to know it was him," I said.

"I was home visiting my mother when he got here. I just got back a week ago. When I walked into the room and saw him there, I couldn't believe it."

"Did he recognize you?" I asked.

"No. I was just a kid with braces and thick glasses when he left," Penny said. "And besides, Martin was never interested in anything but himself."

"So how did you figure out that Otis was Martin?" Ida Belle asked.

She stared at us for several seconds, then her lower lip started trembling. Finally, she burst into tears, burying her head in her hands.

"I just wanted to make sure it was him before I called my mom," Penny wailed. "I didn't mean to kill him. It was an accident. I've ruined everything."

CHAPTER TWENTY-ONE

I GLANCED AT IDA BELLE AND GERTIE, WHO WERE STARING back at me, equally confused. I'd assumed Penny might have called her aunt or mother, and one of them had come down to do the deed. I'd never figured the pretty young woman weeping uncontrollably in my living room for a murderer.

"Help me understand," I said. "You had to know how dangerous it was, right?"

She shook her head furiously. "I swear I didn't! I just thought if he broke out in welts I'd know for sure and he wouldn't be able to leave. At least, not before my mom could get here and raise hell with the police. He was on the phone when we walked in the room. I heard him tell someone he was leaving just as soon as he landed the big one and it should only be a couple more days. I couldn't let him get away."

I looked over at Ida Belle and Gertie, who shrugged. So we had a confession but not at all the one we were expecting. And something about it was totally off.

"Why don't you tell me exactly what happened," I said.

"I'm going to go to prison, aren't I?" she asked, then started wailing again. "Momma will never get over this. And Aunt

Marsha will think it's all her fault for marrying that horrible man in the first place. Oh my God. What have I done?"

That was an excellent question, I thought. Because one thing I found hard to believe was that Penny had sneaked puffer fish into Otis's étouffée.

"Given the circumstances, the DA will go easy on you," I said. "Don't worry about that. You've never been in trouble before, right?"

The wailing scaled down to sniffling and she shook her head.

"Then you don't have anything to worry about," I said. "But if you tell me what happened, I might be able to help."

She gave me a hopeful look, then nodded. "I rubbed it on his bedsheets and his pillowcase. I figured if he broke out in hives and his eyes swelled shut then it was him. He was really allergic. Wouldn't even walk on grass for fear that some might accidentally touch his clothes. But I didn't know poison ivy could kill someone, I swear."

I relaxed and held in a smile. Penny was definitely resourceful. A little devious, but I admired that.

"Penny, you didn't kill Martin," I said.

"But...but he died, and I put those sheets on that day."

"That's true, but the sheets aren't what killed him," I said.

Her eyes widened and she looked from me to Gertie to Ida Belle, not quite believing her luck. "Are you telling me the truth?" she asked.

I nodded. "I can't tell you how he died because the investigation is ongoing, and I'd appreciate it if you kept this conversation a secret until an arrest is made."

"Of course! Absolutely," she said. "Oh my God, I've been so stressed. I almost went to the sheriff's department and turned myself in today."

"It's a good thing you didn't," Ida Belle said. "Benton is so incompetent, he might have tried you himself, then made you walk the plank."

Her face flashed with anger. "He was so rude when he questioned us. Like we were all beneath him."

"I'm pretty sure Benton thinks everyone is beneath him," I said. "I wouldn't take it personally."

She started to speak, then hesitated, then finally started again. "Are you going to tell my boss what I did?"

I shook my head. "I don't think you should be punished for trying to help your aunt. What Martin did to her was reprehensible. Besides, your boss has enough trouble to deal with already. No sense in giving her more."

Penny nodded. "I didn't know about Cynthia and Martin until after I did it. Then I was afraid she'd be blamed for what I did. God, I hope this is over soon. She's been crazy—well, crazier than usual."

"What do you mean?" I asked.

"She's always been moody, you know?" Penny said. "But a depressed kind of moody. But when I got back, she was all smiley and perky. Then the next day, she was angry again. Then the day after that, she baked brownies for the staff. Tied them up in pink fabric. Then Otis—Martin—was killed and she's back to being depressed again, just even more so than usual."

"Sounds like she's having trouble processing all of this," Ida Belle said. "Give her some time. She'll be back to her normal depressed self soon enough."

"I hope so."

A thought occurred to me and I frowned. "I hope you wash all the sheets in bleach."

Penny grimaced, immediately understanding what my concern was.

"Not exactly," she said. "The police still have the room closed off. I was hoping when they allowed us back in, I could get in there and get the sheets out before anyone touched them. I didn't think about someone else being allergic until after I'd already done it, and I was afraid to go back into the room."

"I'm sure it will be fine," Gertie said.

I nodded. "But in the meantime, maybe we request no bed change until we leave."

"I can do that for you," Penny said. "I, uh...can I go now?"

"Sure. I hope our conversation didn't get you into trouble," I said. "If anyone asks, tell them I wanted your help getting a stain out of a dress."

Penny gave us all a grateful look. "Thank you. I can't tell you how much I appreciate you keeping my secret."

"No problem," I said.

She rose from the chair and hurried out the door, probably anxious to get away before we changed our mind.

"So?" Ida Belle asked when the door closed behind her. "Do you believe her?"

"I don't see any reason not to," I said. "She did confess."

"To a murder she didn't commit," Ida Belle said.

"She didn't know that," Gertie said. "She seemed genuinely distraught. I don't think she was faking."

"Me either," I said.

Ida Belle nodded. "I believe her too. But we've believed some people in the past on things and been wrong, so I figured it might be a good idea to get a vote. What are you thinking so hard about?"

I looked over at Ida Belle and let out a single laugh. "I think I just put something else together. Not anything to do with solving the murder, but one of those things I couldn't put my finger on after my chats with Cynthia and Betty."

"Well, don't keep us in suspense," Gertie said.

"Remember how I said I was sure Cynthia knew about the

other women? Well, I think she baked something in the brownies to make Betty sick. Why wrap them all up with name tags unless you needed to make sure the right one got to the right person?"

"Ex-lax," Gertie said. "It's an old trick, but it works."

I cringed. "That's horrible."

"It depends on who eats the brownie," Gertie said.

I smiled, an idea forming.

"What are you so happy about?" Gertie asked.

"I had a thought," I said. "I'm going to have Byron get in touch with Benton and tell him he'll want to test the bedsheets in Otis's room once Benton has processed them."

Ida Belle laughed. "The longer I know you, the more I like you."

"But what if Benton just has someone else get the sheets?" Gertie asked.

I shook my head. "Chain of evidence. If Benton thinks the sheets are relevant to the case, they have to be collected by a law enforcement agency. And since Benton won't allow anyone else to work the case, that leaves him to collect the sheets."

"God, I hope he's allergic," Ida Belle said.

"Me too," I said. "*So,* it appears we're back to two suspects."

"I wonder which one of them did it," Ida Belle said.

Gertie sighed. "I wonder where our dinner is."

———

DINNER FINALLY ARRIVED AND WE POLISHED IT OFF, ALONG with two bottles of wine, and then sat on the balcony in a carb- and sugar-induced stupor. Gertie finally headed to bed and Ida Belle was close behind. I sat in my chair, staring out at the moonlit surf, mulling over everything that we'd found out that day. It was a lot to mull about. But unfortunately, none of it was forming a complete picture.

My cell phone rang and I answered Carter's call.

"Well, since you answered your phone, I know you're not in jail," he said.

"Maybe they don't have cell phone jammers here and you know I have ways of getting a phone behind bars."

"Not without your usual cast of characters. Half the people in this town love you and the other half are scared of you. Most would do you a favor, even if it meant going against me."

"I doubt that many people love me. I'll agree a lot are scared."

"So can I assume the troublesome twosome are also in residence?"

"Yep. They went to bed a little earlier."

"It's only nine o'clock. I can't believe you managed to wear them out."

"It's been a really, really long day," I said. "This is officially the most exhausting vacation I've ever been on."

"And how many vacations *have* you been on?"

"Not a lot. Okay, two that I can remember before my mom died. I didn't have time for such things once I was an adult."

"Well, you're doing a bang-up job of it so far," he joked. "Did you manage to find out anything of consequence today?"

"Plenty. Unfortunately, none of it adds up to a single suspect." I told him about our day, and all the information we'd gotten, ending with our very interesting but not-in-the-least-bit applicable conversation with Penny.

"Jeez, you guys *have* been busy," Carter said when I finished. "I'm surprised you haven't crashed already, especially since I'm sure you carb-loaded for dinner."

"I'm tired, but I can't sleep yet. If I go to bed, I'll just lie there staring at the ceiling."

"Can't stop your mind from rolling through the data, huh?"

"No. I have to be honest, in a lot of ways my old job was easier. Other people figured it all out. I had a single function and didn't need to know all the particulars."

"Yeah, I get it. I don't suppose it helps if I tell you it gets better."

"Actually, it does," I said. "Although I'm surprised you said it since it's almost an endorsement of my new profession."

"You're going to do it whether I endorse it or not. Might as well do the best job you can, and if my advice can help, then I suppose I should give it."

"Who are you and what have you done with my boyfriend?"

He laughed. "Maybe I miss you."

"I'll take it but I'm still suspicious."

"I wouldn't expect anything else. So out of your two suspects, do you favor one over the other?"

"At this point, no."

"Which one of them is lying?"

"Both. I mean, I think they were mostly truthful when we talked but it's all the things they didn't say."

"It usually is. So what's your next move?"

"Honestly, I have no idea. That's why I'm still sitting on the patio instead of snoring in my pillow. Hey, there was one thing I forgot to tell you. Something you might be able to help with."

"I'm almost afraid to ask."

"There are Feds here."

"Feds?" His voice changed from casual to serious. "You're sure?"

"They had that look."

He sighed. "Any idea why they're at the resort?"

"I didn't spot them until we were on our way back to the

room. They were talking to the resort manager. I got close enough to read their lips, but all I caught before they left was 'Barefoot Key' and 'speak to owner.' I'm going to be on the lookout for them tomorrow or maybe see if I can get something out of the manager, but I was wondering if maybe you could put out some feelers among your people."

"I was afraid you were going to ask that. Do you know how vague your information is?"

I knew exactly how little I had. Calling up contacts and asking if they happened to know of an agency that might have two men on Quiet Key mentioning Barefoot Key was just short of nothing. And if they were here about the identity theft thing, then likely no one would be gossiping about it. Identity theft simply wasn't sexy enough for bar conversations.

"What about you?" Carter asked. "You can't tap anyone at the CIA?"

"They weren't CIA."

"How do you know?"

"I just do. We have a certain look. It's hard to explain."

"No. I get it. I'll make some calls, but I wouldn't expect much."

"I don't expect anything, so we're good. Thanks, though. It means a lot to me that you trust me enough to do this."

"I have no problem trusting you on the big things. It's the medium things, like Ida Belle and Gertie, that I'm wary of."

"That makes two of us."

CHAPTER TWENTY-TWO

I N AN ATTEMPT TO RELAX, I TOOK A LONG, HOT SHOWER
and then put on my usual sleepwear of shorts and a tank top,
hoping it would trick my mind into shutting down. My body
was on board, but unfortunately, I lay staring at the ceiling for
hours before my body finally gave my mind the finger and took
over.

It didn't last long.

That morning I couldn't even blame the sun for waking me
because I rose before the sun did. I could see the dim glow on
the horizon and decided I might as well fix coffee. If I
managed to drink it all before Ida Belle and Gertie got up,
then I'd just go for round two. But as I walked into the
kitchen, I saw I wasn't the only one up before the chickens.
Ida Belle had already brewed up some morning glory and was
sitting on the balcony with a cup.

There were worse things than watching the sun come up
over the ocean, so I poured a cup and joined her.

"Did you manage to sleep?" Ida Belle asked as I stepped
outside.

"Kinda. But I dreamed the whole time, so I don't feel like it."

"Did you dream the solution to our mystery?"

"I wish. But there is something that's been bothering me. Something we never really addressed. We've been so focused on Cynthia and Betty as the two best suspects, but we have multiple sources saying Otis planned on leaving soon and two saying he was about to make a big haul. So who was the big haul? It couldn't be Cynthia or Betty, and as of yet, no other name has surfaced."

Ida Belle nodded. "That *is* odd. If he had a big paycheck on the line, then you'd think someone would have seen or heard about it. Someone from the mainland, maybe?"

"Maybe. But the old guys in the bar were under the impression that he'd tapped out his audience over there."

"If it really was the paycheck that was going to set him up big time, then maybe he changed up his routine. Kept everything quiet."

"I guess so. But still..."

"Yeah. Still."

"I talked to Carter last night. He's going to see if he can find out something about the Feds."

"You think he'll be able to?"

"I don't know. It's a long shot. The information I have is so vague—two guys in suits, the two Keys. I don't even know which agency it is."

"And you're sure they're Feds?" Ida Belle asked. "They couldn't be lawyers or real estate developers?"

I shook my head. "Lawyers and real estate developers rarely wear guns with their suits. And the good ones have custom-made suits. Not off the rack, which is what you can afford on a Fed salary."

"They were strapping?"

"Yeah. That I'm sure about."

Ida Belle nodded. "You would definitely know what to look for. You think we should try to shadow them? Assuming we can find them or that they're even still around?"

"Maybe. I'm a little worried that we might be busy avoiding Benton."

"You think he's going to get the okay from the DA to arrest Gertie?"

"I think he's pushing hard for it. He'll never get the DA to press charges. Especially not when Byron produces an entire list of better suspects, but he could tie her up for a day or two."

"This vacation is far more work than I thought it would be," Ida Belle said. "Maybe next time, we should go on separate vacations."

"Then who would keep Gertie out of jail?"

"We could try leaving her in Sinful."

"Carter would never forgive us."

"Probably not," Ida Belle agreed. "So what's on the agenda for today then?"

"First, sunrise over the ocean. Then breakfast. Then hopefully anything but running from Benton.

Ida Belle sighed. "I wish the pieces formed a clear picture. Hell, even a fuzzy one would be nice."

"Me too. I'm sure there's something we're missing. And I don't mean things we don't know. I'm talking about in the things we do know."

Ida Belle nodded. "I agree. I feel like when you can't think of the right word. It's there and you get a tiny flicker but not enough to latch onto."

"I hope that flicker becomes a flame before Benton gets the DA's approval."

"You and me both." She pointed to the ocean. "But in the meantime, the view is excellent."

I stared out at the ocean, the sunlight making the water sparkle like diamonds. Boats were already headed out to sea, probably all looking for that perfect fishing spot. Below us on the beach, employees of the resort were setting up chairs and umbrellas, creating long rows of blue.

Just another day in paradise.

Except for the murder part.

———

WE DECIDED AGAINST BREAKFAST AT THE RESORT, JUST IN case Benton came calling, and opted for the café we'd eaten at on the mainland. Since it was a weekday, and after 9:00 a.m., it was fairly empty and we easily found a private table in the back corner. We gave our order to the server, sipped on coffee, and stared at nothing. Finally, we all sighed.

"I can't believe I'm going to say this," Gertie said, "but maybe we should take a day off from investigating and see if something shakes out."

"And what should we do instead?" Ida Belle asked. "Sit on the beach and wait for Benton to show up with handcuffs?"

"We could always go fishing again," Gertie said. "Dave would take us out in a heartbeat."

"When he didn't find us at the resort, that would be the first place Benton looked," Ida Belle said.

"So let him," Gertie said. "The big scaredy-cat isn't going to come out there and get us, and Dave can always pretend his radio stopped working."

"And all our cell phones as well?" Ida Belle asked. "This isn't *Moby Dick*. There are other forms of communication."

"Spoilsport." Gertie looked over at me. "You got any ideas?"

"I'm afraid I'm all out of them," I said. "Except breakfast."

The server sat our plates on the table and headed off. We all picked up our forks and attacked the breakfast, but I knew none of us were focused on our food. Well, maybe Gertie was. But eggs and bacon definitely weren't at the forefront of my mind. My thoughts all centered around my failure on this case. And it brought home just how much of an advantage I had in Sinful, where I had a relationship with the local cops—a strong one—and Ida Belle and Gertie knew everyone and most everything that happened.

I knew cops dealt with the same issues. Sometimes all the trails they followed led to dead ends, and unless a new clue surfaced, they were at a stalemate. It was why warehouses were full of cold case files. But somehow that made me feel worse instead of better. I needed that new clue. No way I could head back to Sinful without knowing, even if Gertie was off the hook.

We had just finished breakfast when my phone signaled a text. It was from Carter.

Feds are DEA. That's all I could get. Be careful.

My pulse rate shot up. That was it. The clue I'd been waiting for. The thing I'd been missing.

I read the text to Ida Belle and Gertie, struggling to contain my excitement.

"This is it," I said. "This is what I've been missing. All this time, we've assumed Martin was killed by one of the women he scammed and that the big payoff he was expecting was another woman. But I don't think it was a woman at all."

"You think it was drugs?" Ida Belle asked.

"Think about it—all those fishing trips into the Gulf, with specific coordinates, but Otis didn't fish. At least, not when he was with Betty, and since Cynthia said he never brought fish back, I'd bet he's never cast a rod. He was prepping for a drop. Plus, he's talking about a big payoff and the DEA shows up at this resort and mentions the Key that the real Otis was at before. I'm certain that's where Martin was as well."

"So what are you thinking?" Ida Belle asked. "That he made connections in the Keys and picked up a route here?"

I nodded. "And came here as Otis Baker to throw the DEA off his trail."

"Then why scam women if he was coming into serious cash?" Ida Belle asked.

"He was waiting for the job to happen," I said. "These things don't occur overnight. They take planning and he would have needed funds to live on while he was waiting."

"Okay," Ida Belle said. "I can buy that but if he was setting up for the big paycheck, why was he getting ready to jet?"

"Because the DEA was onto him," Gertie said.

"Possibly, but I think the answer is probably simpler than that," I said. "One thing I know for certain about men like Martin Hughes is that they're cowards. My guess is he planned on doing one run, collecting the cash, and then disappearing again."

Ida Belle nodded. "And if his drug contacts or the DEA went looking for Martin Hughes or Otis Baker, neither would be here, because he would have already moved on as someone else."

"You really think it would be enough money to set him up for life?" Gertie asked.

"Depends on how big the run is," I said. "But it should definitely be enough to get him fake documents and out of the country. Then he'd have a whole new nation of women to scam if he found himself running short."

"And none of the women he screwed in the US would be able to find him," Ida Belle said.

"Or accidentally come across him like Penny did," Gertie said.

I nodded. "And even though she thought he didn't recognize her, it's possible that he did. At minimum, he knew there was a risk of it happening."

"But if he was in another country," Gertie said, "that risk was almost nonexistent. Or he could have chosen an extradition-free one and then it didn't matter regardless."

"All of this seems to fit," Ida Belle said. "But then who killed him?"

"My guess is his drug contacts," I said. "If the DEA was in the Keys poking around, then you can bet they heard about it. No way they would leave Martin walking around. He'd roll in a heartbeat to save his own skin."

"And being new on board, so to speak, they might have even thought he was an informant," Gertie said.

"Entirely possible," I said.

Ida Belle nodded. "So what now? I love your theory and I think you're onto something, but we don't have any proof. Only speculation."

My phone rang again and I saw it was Byron. This could not be good news.

"Bad news, Fortune," Byron said when I answered. "Benton got the okay from the DA to arrest Gertie. He'll be coming for her soon if he hasn't already left. Where are you guys?"

"On the mainland at breakfast," I said. "And I don't guess we'll be returning anytime soon."

"Did you figure anything else out as far as the suspects go?" he asked.

"Yeah, and I'm working on finalizing my thoughts. In fact,

we're off to pursue another avenue of investigation now. I'll let you know when I've got it all wrapped up in a bow."

"I wouldn't be a good attorney if I didn't tell you to be careful. And Carter would kill me as well."

"There's already been too much violence," I said. "I'm just going to get information and then turn it all over to you. But I think the DA will find it compelling."

"Good. Call me if Benton gets his hands on Gertie, and make sure she knows not to say a word to him until I get there."

"We've got to go," I said as soon as I hung up. "Benton has his okay. Gertie is on the chopping block."

I tossed some money on the table and hurried to the front to pay the bill.

"Where are we going?" Ida Belle asked as I practically jogged them to the car.

"Boat hunting," I said. I pulled out my phone and called Dave. "Hi, Dave. It's Landlubber Lisa from the other day."

"Hey, Lisa," Dave said. "You guys want another fishing trip?"

"Not at the moment. I was hoping you might be able to give me some information on another charter. Do you know a guy called Mikey Marlin?"

"Yeah, I've known Mikey since the crib. He's a local."

"Do you know what marina he keeps his boat at?" I asked.

"It's on the mainland. John's Boat Launch and Marina. I, uh...you looking to hire him for fishing?" His voice had changed during the conversation from jovial to somewhat hesitant.

"No. I wanted to talk to him about something else. Why? Is Mikey someone you think I should avoid?"

He hesitated a couple seconds before answering. "Not exactly. I mean, in general Mikey's a good guy. We were best buds for a lot of years. Hell, me and some of the local commercial fishermen took turns staying with him while he had cancer. He kicked it a year ago and was doing good, but lately, he's started acting strange. Wouldn't come out with the guys and when I went by the marina to check on him, he didn't seem happy I was there."

"When did his behavior change?"

"A week or two ago."

About the time Martin arrived on the island and started chartering fishing trips.

"I appreciate the information," I said.

"No problem, and if you change your mind about fishing, I'd be happy to take you out. Half price."

I thanked him and hung up. "Look up John's Boat Launch and Marina," I said as I started the car.

"Got it," Ida Belle said. "It's two miles from here, just down the highway."

I turned out of the parking lot and set off in the direction of the marina.

CHAPTER TWENTY-THREE

"WHAT'S THE PLAN?" IDA BELLE SAID. "MIKEY HAD TO BE IN on things with Otis so he's not going to chat with us. And we can't exactly search his boat. Sounds like he might live on it."

"I don't have a plan yet," I said. "But I'd like to get a look at that boat and at Mikey, assuming he's around. Then hopefully, I'll think of something."

"You always do," Gertie said. "You're quick on your feet."

"That's because being friends with you means she has to be," Ida Belle pointed out.

I pulled into the parking lot of the marina, and parked next to an SUV that blocked us from the pier. I scanned the area but only saw one person—an older man carrying an ice chest to a rusty truck.

I hopped out of the car and waved at the man as I headed over. "Excuse me, sir. Can you tell me where to find Mikey Marlin?"

The man put the ice chest down at the back of his truck and pointed to the pier. "His boat's about midway down. The Magic Marlin. But I ain't seen him in a couple days."

"Thanks," I said. "I was supposed to talk to him about a

charter. I guess I'll go see if he's there. Any place he would be if he wasn't on his boat?"

"He haunts the Shark Bar pretty regular, but I ain't seen him there for a while either."

"Okay. Let me help you with that."

I grabbed one end of the ice chest and we lifted it into the bed of the pickup. "You must have gotten a good haul."

"Pretty good. Got dinner for a week, anyway. You ladies take care."

I set off for the pier, motioning at Ida Belle and Gertie to follow. I scanned the boats as we went, stopping when I reached the Magic Marlin.

"Hello, Mikey!" I yelled. "I got your name from Deep Sea Dave. I wanted to talk about a charter."

I waited for a bit, but no one responded and I didn't hear any movement inside. I looked over at Gertie. "You got any gloves?"

"Of course," Gertie said. "What do you take me for, an amateur?"

She pulled a set of latex gloves from her beach bag and I put them on.

"Just in case," I said.

Ida Belle nodded. "I wish I had my weapon on me. Something doesn't feel right."

I pulled my gun from my waist and handed it to her.

"Wait here," I said and boarded the boat.

I knocked on the cabin door and waited again, but still no response. I opened the door and looked in, but I knew what was in there before I saw it. There was no mistaking that smell. A man who I assumed was Mikey Marlin lay on the bench, a single bullet through his forehead. I backed out of the cabin and looked over at Ida Belle and Gertie.

"He's dead."

"What?"

"How?"

They both cried out at once.

"Single bullet hole through the forehead. No weapon on site."

"How long?" Gertie asked.

"A day or two," I said.

"I don't get it," Ida Belle said. "Why go to the trouble of poisoning Martin but shoot this guy?"

"I don't know," I said. "Maybe because with Martin's scamming they figured the police wouldn't look any further for a motive."

"So this is it?" Gertie said. "The drug dealers killed both of them? It's kind of a letdown on the big reveal."

"I imagine most crime is exactly what it looks like," I said. "Bad people doing bad things." I glanced back at the cabin, something about the whole situation bothering me. Aside from the obvious. "I'd like to take a look around, see if there's anything that supports our theory."

"Do you want us to help?" Gertie asked.

"No. Keep watch and if someone pulls into the parking lot, let me know. The last thing I want is to get caught on the boat with this body."

I headed back into the cabin, careful to breathe with my mouth, and started searching the drawers and cabinets for anything relevant. Fortunately, the bench the body was on had open storage below, so I didn't have to figure out how to shift the body. I made quick work of the cabin, then checked the closet and the bunk at the front. Nothing. What now? I headed back to the cabin and plopped down on the bench across from the body.

And heard a crinkling sound.

I stood up and pulled the cushion off. I had checked the

storage beneath the bench, but I hadn't checked inside the cushions. I unzipped the fabric cover and reached inside, pulling out a piece of paper and an envelope. I opened the paper first and read. It was a letter from an oncologist. And the gist of it was that Mikey's cancer had returned and his only option was an experimental treatment that insurance didn't cover. A very expensive experimental treatment.

Well, that was the answer to a couple of questions—why Mikey was acting weird and why he would take up a risky venture like drug running with a loser like Martin. I opened the envelope and pulled out some pictures. The first few were pictures of fish and although the catch was impressive, I had no idea why it was necessary to hide the pictures in the cushion. Nor did it make sense to take the pictures after they'd been slit open. The next picture was of the Gulf, a tiny speck in the distance that I assumed was a boat. The remaining two photos were closer shots of the boat and I frowned.

I'd seen this boat before.

And then it hit me. I shoved the photos and the letter back in the cushion, zipped it up and ran out of the cabin, startling Ida Belle and Gertie.

"What's wrong?" Ida Belle asked.

"Everything," I said, and practically ran down the pier. "I was wrong about everything."

CHAPTER TWENTY-FOUR

"YOU WANT TO FILL US IN?" GERTIE HUFFED AS SHE RAN after me.

We jumped into the car and I took off out of the parking lot.

"Call the resort," I said. "Ask for Fletcher."

Ida Belle pulled out her phone and did as I instructed, giving me curious glances as she did. "He just headed out," she said when she disconnected. "He's going boating."

"I bet he is," I said. "Probably headed straight for Cuba."

"I don't understand," Ida Belle said.

"Martin wasn't the one running the drugs," I said. "Fletcher is."

I told them what I'd found on the boat.

"So you think Martin was blackmailing Fletcher?" Ida Belle asked.

"I think he was trying," I said. "Remember his record? Martin wasn't exactly new to the extortion game."

"So Fletcher killed him," Gertie said. "You're sure?"

I nodded. "It all fits. Fletcher told us the owner of the resort knew him from where he worked in the Keys and gave him the promotion here. What do you want to bet it was the same resort Martin was at? And both owned by the same guy?"

"You think the owner recruited Fletcher to run drugs for him?" Ida Belle asked.

"Yeah. Maybe Fletcher had a drug route in the Keys and the owner promoted him to manager here to cover a new route. Or replace whoever was handling it before. Think about it—Fletcher knew the cameras were broken. He probably intentionally put off signing that invoice for the parts in case Martin was a real threat and had to be dealt with."

"Genius," Gertie said.

"Fletcher had access to the puffer fish at the resort and no one would think twice if they saw him walking on any floor," I continued. "He could have easily swiped Martin's card while he was on the beach and again, no one would have thought twice about the resort manager walking around."

"And Fletcher knew Martin was scamming women and figured that's who the police would look at," Ida Belle said.

"But scamming women doesn't cover shooting Mikey," Ida Belle said.

"Mikey was a local fisherman and according to Betty, a rough sort," I said. "The locals would look into it as a fight gone bad over a card game or a woman or any of the other sort of nonsense that men get up to at places like the Shark Bar."

Ida Belle nodded. "They definitely wouldn't have leaped to colluding with a known woman scammer to blackmail a drug dealer."

"Exactly," I said. "But now the DEA showed up and ruined everything."

"So you definitely think the resort owner is in on it?" Gertie asked.

"I think he's running the show," I said. "And so does the DEA but they screwed up. They're looking so hard at the owner that they questioned Fletcher. Twenty bucks says they're trying to find him and my guess is he's lying low."

"You think they came right out and told him they were DEA?" Gertie asked.

"I doubt it, but Fletcher would have known they were law enforcement," I said. "People in his line of work can spot a Fed as easily as I can. They probably claimed they were real estate developers or insurance agents...something of that sort."

"And by asking Fletcher questions, they tipped off one of the guys they should have been gunning for," Ida Belle said.

I nodded.

"So why didn't he clear out last night?" Gertie asked.

"Just speculating...because he wouldn't make a move without talking to the boss first," I said. "Maybe the boss told him to wait while he verified the threat, then called today and told him to leave. Or maybe he couldn't reach the boss yesterday and finally got too antsy to wait any longer, so he made the decision to leave."

"Maybe by the time he got an answer from the boss, the marina was closed and he couldn't fill up his gas tank," Gertie said.

I laughed. "The simplest answers..."

"So Martin must have seen or heard something in the Keys," Gertie said, "but wasn't sure what was going on. Then he came here and saw Fletcher, the owner, and the boat and started putting it together."

"I think that's what all the fishing trips were about—him observing Fletcher's boat outings, making notes so he had enough to attempt blackmail. The drugs were in the fish. That's why they were slit open in the pictures. Martin must have found their discards after they'd taken the product out and took shots of them.

"What a moron," Gertie said. "Trying to blackmail drug

dealers. Doesn't he read the newspaper? Watch a movie? Drug dealers do not play."

"Sociopaths always think they're smarter than everyone else," I said as I drove over the bridge and onto the island.

"So what do we do?" Gertie asked. "We can't call Benton with this. He'll just tack another body onto my name. What about calling the DEA?"

"Even if we could convince them of anything, they'd insist on seeing the body and the photos, and by that time, Fletcher will be long gone."

I turned onto the road for the marina.

"We're going after him?" Ida Belle asked.

I nodded. "I don't see any other way."

"In what?" Ida Belle asked. "The only boat guy here we know is Dave and we couldn't catch an Olympic swimmer in his boat."

"It's all we've got." I pulled out my cell phone and dialed Dave.

"I have an emergency," I said. "Meet me at the dock."

"I'm already there," Dave said. "You have a fishing emergency?"

"Sort of. Be there in a minute."

Dave was standing in front of the dock when I wheeled into the parking lot and slid to a stop. He stared, slightly startled as I jumped out of the car and hurried over.

"I don't have a lot of time to explain, so I'm going to go through this fast, okay?" I said.

He nodded, looking completely confused and slightly scared.

I pulled out my CIA identification and showed him. "I'm not here on official business, but I'm showing you this so you know to trust what I'm about to tell you."

His eyes widened. "You're a spook? No lie?"

"No lie. I need you to listen carefully. I believe Otis Baker was attempting to blackmail Fletcher, the resort manager, because Otis discovered he was running drugs on his boss's boat. I believe Fletcher killed Otis." I took a deep breath before continuing. "Unfortunately, Otis got your friend Mikey involved and he's dead as well."

"Mikey's dead? No. You're wrong."

"Trust me, I saw him myself, but that will have to wait. The DEA showed up yesterday at the resort, probably trying to locate the owner, who I think is the boss. They questioned Fletcher, not realizing he was in on the drug running. Now, Fletcher has taken the boat and is running. If we don't catch him, he'll get away with killing your friend."

"Oh, hell no!" Dave said. "That ain't happening."

"Let me borrow your boat," I said. "I'll make sure he pays for what he's done."

"No way!" Dave said. "I'm coming with you."

"I can't let you do that. This man has already killed two people."

"Well, you ain't gonna make it out of the sound without me. You don't know where the sandbars are. And my boat ain't gonna catch that fancy machine Fletcher is on. Give me a minute."

Dave spun around and ran for the marina.

"Where is he going?" Gertie asked.

"I hope to get a faster boat," Ida Belle said.

"Great," I said. "Then we can add stealing a boat to our list of things we've done."

"We've already stolen a boat," Gertie said.

"*You* stole a boat," I said.

"That was in Sinful," Ida Belle said. "You could claim it was indiscriminate borrowing and get away with it."

"You're sure Fletcher is our guy?" Gertie asked. "Not that

I'm against stealing a boat, but we probably ought to be fairly certain about this before we do."

"I guess we'll know for sure when we find him," I said. "If he starts shooting at us, then I'm right."

Ida Belle snorted. "That's a hell of a sniff test."

I tapped my foot, then paced, looking over at the marina and waiting on Dave to reappear. I was just about to go looking for him when I heard a low rumble. A couple seconds later, a long, sleek speedboat appeared past the marina with Dave at the helm.

Ida Belle clutched my arm and her knees buckled a little.

"Oh my God," she said. "That's a Fountain Lightning. Twin 1075s. I may pass out. Pinch me so I know I haven't died."

I glanced at Ida Belle, then the boat, then looked over at Gertie. "If she's this excited, that means that boat is practically unattainable by regular folk. We're going under the jail, aren't we?"

"Maybe we'll get time off for catching a murderer," Gertie said.

Dave pulled up at the end of the dock and motioned frantically at us.

This is a bad idea.

I knew that was true, but the desire to catch the lying, drug-dealing, murdering Fletcher was outweighing common sense.

"How fast does that thing go?" I asked. There was no point in going to jail for stealing a boat if it couldn't even do the job.

"One-ten...one-fifteen," Ida Belle said. "Depends on the wind."

"How fast does the boat Fletcher is in go?"

"Maybe fifty miles per hour," Ida Belle said.

"So half the speed, but Fletcher is moving in a straight line out of Dodge and we have to traverse the Gulf to spot him," I said.

"Unless you can conjure up a plane or helicopter, this is our best chance," Ida Belle said.

"Let's go," I said. "Before I change my mind."

"Look at it this way," Gertie said as we hurried down the dock. "Dave was going to steal the boat and go after Fletcher whether we were with him or not."

"And you don't want him to go to jail alone?" I asked.

"It wouldn't be very Southern of us if we did," Gertie said.

"Hurry up!" Dave yelled.

As we jumped on board, Dave handed us life jackets. I didn't know whether to be thankful he was being responsible or scared that someone like Dave thought life jackets were necessary.

"Dave," I said. "I have to ask. Did you steal this boat?"

"What?" He looked surprised. "No. I borrowed it from Bobby. The guy who owns it owes him a ton of money for fixing it and won't pay. Until he coughs up the cash, the judge said the boat is Bobby's."

That didn't sound completely right, but I'd asked the question so if this went to court, at least I had a defense. A bit flimsy but not a lie.

"I, uh, don't suppose you have any weapons on board, do you?" I asked.

"This is Florida," Dave said. "I grabbed some supplies from my boat and stuck 'em in the cabin."

I didn't ask any more questions because I had the sneaking impression that Dave's "supplies" might be kin to Gertie's handbag contents. It was better for my defense if I could claim I didn't know. I pointed to the passenger seat and told Ida Belle to take it. I knew she would defer to me as point, but I also knew she was dying to see the boat operate, and she had her best view of the driving from the passenger seat. Gertie and I took two of the three back row seats, leaving the middle empty so the weight was balanced.

Dave barely waited for our butts to hit the vinyl before he headed out. His jaw flexed as he moved the boat away from the dock and into the deeper water of the sound, and I could tell he was just itching to gun it. I hoped to God he knew what he was doing. I'd seen a boat like this on YouTube go completely airborne and flip over. That was definitely something I wasn't interested in experiencing.

He increased speed as we moved away from the bank and began the weaving process that was required to properly navigate the sandbars. I hated to admit it, but he was right. I would have never gotten a boat into the Gulf. I simply didn't know the underwater terrain. It seemed as though it took forever, but finally, we hit the channel that led from the sound into the Gulf.

"Which way?" Dave asked.

"South," Ida Belle said.

"You're thinking Cuba?" Dave asked.

"Easy enough to catch a private jet out of there," I said. "Especially if you've got local officials on the payroll."

"South it is," Dave said. "Hold on to your butts!"

I was nestled pretty deep in the seat, but I still braced myself for the launch that was sure to come. But instead the boat bucked, then slammed down repeatedly on the water, tossing Dave clean out of the driver's seat. Ida Belle managed to hold on but she looked a bit rumpled. Gertie had been thrown straight up and had come down sideways across the back seats.

"Are you trying to kill us?" Gertie asked as she pushed herself up.

"Hold on," Dave said. "That was a mistake. I just didn't... uh, I forgot to..."

"You *do* know how to drive this boat, right?" I asked.

"It's a boat," Dave said. "There's a throttle and engines and it floats."

I looked over at Ida Belle. What I knew about boats could fit into a thimble, but I would bet that thimble of knowledge that this boat wasn't even remotely the same as Dave's fishing charter.

"I got this," Ida Belle said, and waved Dave out of the way.

"Are you sure?" I asked.

Ida Belle stared. "I've been waiting my whole life to drive one of these things."

She moved into the driver's seat and looked back at us. "*Now*, hold on to your butts."

CHAPTER TWENTY-FIVE

IDA BELLE ADJUSTED SOMETHING ON THE DASH, THEN I SAW her hand move to the throttle. A second later, I didn't see anything at all. The boat launched out of the water but instead of slamming down, it shot over the top of the ocean like a plane taking off. Wind tore at my face and I'm pretty sure my eyelids turned inside out. Gertie's cheeks were pulled back so far on her face that it looked as though she'd been the victim of really bad plastic surgery. Her eyes were clenched shut, probably in defense against the wind or maybe just so she couldn't see her own death rushing at her.

"Whoohoo!" Dave yelled, and did a move like he was riding a bull. Of course, he had a windshield to block the hurricane-force gale, so it was easier to be so excited. The ocean and the sky blended together in one blue blur as minute after minute of blinding speed ticked off. I began to worry that we'd speed right by Fletcher, but after about twenty minutes of top-end speed, Ida Belle cut the throttle. I lurched forward, barely managing to keep my seat. Gertie flew out of hers and hit the back of Dave's chair.

"Darn it!" Ida Belle said. "We need binoculars."

I looked over the bow and saw a boat in the distance, but it was too far away to tell if it was Fletcher.

"Hold on," Dave said, and went into the cabin. He came back with a duffel bag and pulled a pair of binoculars out of it. "Here ya go."

Ida Belle took a look. "No go. It's a sailboat."

She handed the binoculars back to Dave and we took off again. Two more times, Dave caught sight of a glint of sun off a boat, but neither was Fletcher. I checked my watch as we took off again. We'd already been on the water for over an hour. We should be getting close.

Another ten minutes passed and Ida Belle slowed again. She took the binoculars from Dave, took a look, then shook her head. "It's a fishing boat."

"Fletcher can't be that far ahead," I said. "Approach that boat. They might have seen Fletcher. And approach them *slowly*. We don't want to kill them with our wake."

Ida Belle nodded and moved the boat at a reasonable clip toward the fishing boat. Reasonable for Ida Belle, anyway. When she was about fifty yards away, she cut her speed to a slow cruise.

"That's Sea Bass Steve," Dave said. "He's a buddy."

As Ida Belle pulled closer to the other boat, two older men on the back deck scowled. Dave stood up and waved.

"It's Dave!" he yelled.

The two men stopped scowling and shifted to confused.

"What are you doing on that boat?" the first man asked. Since his hat read Sea Bass Steve, I assumed he was the boat captain.

"I'm borrowing it," Dave said. "Listen, we got an emergency. Have you seen that fancy yacht that belongs to the resort owner?"

"Yeah," the second man said. "It went past about twenty minutes ago."

"Which direction?" Dave asked.

Steve frowned, probably picking up on Dave's anxiety. "Why you asking?"

"Because that manager guy that takes out the yacht killed Mikey Marlin and he's making a run for it. We're thinking Cuba."

Their eyes widened and they looked back and forth from Dave to the rest of us. I didn't blame them for being confused. The entire situation was a *Twilight Zone* episode from where they were standing.

"You been smoking weed again?" Steve asked.

"No. Look, this lady is CIA. I'm telling you the truth."

I pulled out my ID and showed them. Their expressions shifted from disbelief to startled, and then Steve flushed with anger.

"You're serious? He killed Mikey?" Steve asked.

"I'm really sorry," I said. "Will you please tell us what direction the boat was going? We have to catch him before he hits Cuba."

"Due south," Steve said. "You get after him. We'll be right behind you."

"No, thank you," I said. "We don't need any help."

"It's not about what you think you need," Steve said. "Mikey was our friend. Now get going with that ridiculous boat and catch that yacht. We'll be there to help soon as we can."

It was pointless to argue and besides, if Steve even managed to catch up with us, the whole thing would be over. I motioned to Ida Belle and everyone got back in their seats.

"Take it easy until you're some distance away," Dave said. "I don't want to flip Steve over."

Ida Belle eased away from the other boat, but once she was a safe distance, she punched it and hooted when the boat leaped out of the water. I said a quick prayer as we hit warp speed and hoped we didn't come to a stop in an alternate universe. This had to be how fighter pilots felt. Except they had those cool suits and oxygen. I made a mental note to bring a flight suit and oxygen tank next time we went on vacation. My list of vacation needs was getting extensive.

Just when I thought my chest might collapse, Ida Belle cut the throttle and pointed. Dave grabbed the binoculars, then nodded.

"That's him," he said. "Let's go get that, er...bad guy."

I knew it wasn't what he wanted to say. It wasn't what I would have said, either. Fletcher was a despicable human being and it was time he paid for his crimes.

"So what's the plan?" Ida Belle said.

"Pull near him," I said. "Ask him to surrender quietly."

"You really think that's going to work?" Gertie asked.

"Of course not." I pulled out my cell phone and called Carter.

"I have the murderer, sort of," I said when he answered.

"What the hell?" he asked.

"You can yell later," I said. "Right now, I need you to call the DEA and tell them that the drug runner they're looking for is Fletcher Sampson. He's making a run for Cuba right now."

"Please do not tell me you're on a boat chasing a drug runner to Cuba."

"Okay, I won't tell you. Grab a pen. Send the DEA to..." I waved at Ida Belle and she gave me the coordinates.

I passed them on to Carter, who was still grumbling.

"Do not approach this guy," Carter said. "Wait for the DEA to get there."

"No can do," I said. "They'll never make it in time unless they plan on flying in and bombing the yacht. That boat is way too fast."

"And how did you catch it? Because I don't hear the whine of an airplane engine or the thumping of a helicopter."

"We have a Fountain on loan."

"Jesus, Mary, and Joseph! I don't care if he makes it all the way to Argentina. Do not approach. He's probably sitting on a stock of weapons that rivals gun runners."

"I'll figure something out. Got to go."

I shoved my phone back in my pocket and motioned to Ida Belle. "Go ahead and approach. Everyone stay low. He's bound to be armed and I don't want him getting off a clean shot at any of us."

Ida Belle eased the boat forward. With the slower speed, I was able to move into the open space between her and Dave and peer over the bow. I grabbed the binoculars for a closer look and spotted Fletcher on the top deck, driving the boat. He looked back, grabbed a set of binoculars and trained them on our boat. I saw him cursing as he lowered them and reached for something in a compartment below the steering wheel. From his elevation, he could easily see who we were, and I was certain he knew why we were there.

A second later, a shot rang out and the first bullet hit the water in front of the boat.

"Holy crap!" Dave said. "He's shooting at us."

"He's already killed two people," Gertie said. "Did you think he was going to put his hands up and go peacefully?" She looked over at me. "You're armed. Fire back."

I shook my head. "The odds of my hitting him at this distance with a pistol is slim. You got anything stronger?" I asked Dave.

"Only my six-shooter," Dave said. "My hunting rifles are at home."

"Well, then shoot the boat and sink it," Gertie said as another bullet went sailing over us.

"I'm afraid that won't work either," Dave said. "The bilge would take the water out faster than it came in, and that's if the bullet penetrated the hull in the first place."

I wanted to ask him how he knew that, but I was afraid of the answer.

"Well, we can't just keep following him while he shoots at us," Ida Belle said as she cut the throttle to an idle. "As fast as this thing eats gas, we already don't have enough to make it back to shore. We need a plan."

I watched as the yacht drew ahead, growing smaller as it went, trying to come up with some way to stop its progress, but I was coming up empty.

"Maybe the DEA will get here soon," Gertie said.

"I wouldn't hold my breath," I said. "Even if Carter can get information to the right people, then we have to hope they believe him. If we pass muster, they'd still have to arrange a helicopter or boat, and I'm not sure how quickly that can happen."

"What if Ida Belle makes a close pass?" Gertie asked. "Could you hit Fletcher?"

"I honestly don't know. You're talking about a lot of variables—waves, wind, our movement, his movement—I couldn't guarantee anything. And if we got close enough for me to hit him, then he can hit us."

Ida Belle nodded. "Besides, when he saw us coming, he'd go inside the cabin and shoot from one of the windows. He's not going to sit up there in the open."

"There has to be some way to disable that boat," Gertie said. "Where is a grenade launcher when you need one?"

Dave's eyes widened and he bolted upright. "That's it!"

He ran into the cabin and I looked over at Ida Belle, who looked as terrified as I was. Several seconds later, Dave came running out of the cabin with a speargun.

"What's your plan?" Ida Belle asked. "You want to shoot his boat and reel him in?"

"Of course not," Dave said. "We'd need a lot stronger line for that. Here, hold this."

He thrust the speargun at Gertie and I stuck my arm out and grabbed it before she could get her hands on it. She gave me a dirty look but didn't bother arguing. Dave bent over and started digging around in the duffel bag again. He glanced up at Gertie and winked.

"I got in touch with your online guy," Dave said. "He had a contact in Naples that hooked me up."

I felt my back clench and a second later he jumped up, clutching a stick of dynamite and a roll of duct tape.

CHAPTER TWENTY-SIX

"ALL WE HAVE TO DO IS TAPE THIS BABY ON THE END OF THE spear and launch it over into his boat," Dave said.

"You want to blow up his boat?" Ida Belle asked.

"You want to air fire a speargun?" I asked.

"Awesome!" Gertie said.

"What happens if you kill the guy?" Ida Belle asked.

"I'll be happier in prison than if he gets away," Dave said.

Given what Fletcher had done to his friend Mikey, his sentiment had merit, but I didn't know how well it would stand up at trial.

"One way or another, I'm shooting this thing," Dave said. "Even if I have to bail off this boat and swim over there to do it."

There were several flaws in his logic, starting with lighting wet dynamite, but I was pretty sure Dave wouldn't bother to think it through before he leaped over the side and tried to pull a Navy SEAL move that was doomed for failure.

"How far will that thing shoot in air?" I asked.

"Pretty far," he said. "I shot one just like it at a buddy's fishing cabin. We were sitting outside drinking beer that night and a five-point buck just walks right up into the clearing. Since we was fishing, no one had a rifle, so I went for the speargun."

"How did that work out?" Ida Belle asked.

"Not so good," Dave said. "I didn't think about it going farther in air than water. Darn thing went right over the buck and into my buddy's bass boat. Sank it right there at the dock."

"How far away was the bass boat?" I asked.

Dave shrugged. "I don't know. Maybe fifty feet."

I rolled around the variables. "Okay," I said finally. "This plan is not totally without merit."

"Seriously?" Ida Belle said.

"All we need to do is disable the boat, right? So if we can shoot the speargun into the back of the boat, we can take out the engines."

"And a chunk of the hull," Ida Belle said.

"So? If the boat sinks and Fletcher has to bail, then we fish him out," I said.

"Or leave him as really big fish bait," Dave said.

Gertie gave him an approving nod. "I like the way you think."

"It's this or he gets away, because we can't risk driving close enough to lob dynamite in there by hand," I said. "I wish there was another option, but I don't see one materializing."

Ida Belle looked over at Dave. "Are you sure you know how to shoot that thing? Because you're only getting one shot given that we can't attach a line."

"Sure," Dave said. "That deer thing was just a fluke. I grew up using a speargun. I just prefer fishing from a boat because it's easier to drink beer."

"See?" I said. "All perfectly reasonable responses. It's just like we're back in Sinful."

Ida Belle shook her head. "In so many ways. Fine, then let's get this show going."

Gertie hooted, way too excited about setting off dynamite given that we were on a boat and halfway to Cuba. Dave grinned like an idiot as he loaded the speargun. He taped the dynamite onto the tip, then pulled a lighter out of his pocket and looked at us. "Who's going to light this thing?"

I sighed. Ida Belle would be driving the boat. I needed to be firing my pistol to draw Fletcher off so we could get close enough to hit the boat with the spear, as we only had one chance to get it right.

I pointed to Gertie and she started doing a victory dance.

"Okay," I said. "Here's the plan. Ida Belle will pull up behind the boat, then make a sharp right so that Dave can fire over the side."

Dave shook his head. "I don't think I should be standing in the bottom of the boat to fire. At fifty feet away, I'd have to lob it in the air and hope for the best, as this boat is low in the water. But I can stand on the back and get a better shot into the rear deck of the yacht."

"You remember the part where Fletcher will be shooting at us, right?" I asked.

"Yeah, but you're CIA. I figured you could keep him off me long enough for me to make the shot."

I blew out a breath. He was right about the trajectory, but I didn't feel good about Dave being an open target.

"Fletcher's shooting from fifty feet away as well," Ida Belle said. "Unless he has a rifle with a scope, he's probably not going to be very accurate at that distance with a pistol, especially with the movement of the boat. And he's panicked, which will affect his aim as well."

She was probably right. Unless Fletcher was an ace, the odds of him managing a perfectly placed shot were slim, but there was always the risk of the accidental perfect shot. Still, Dave had already said he was jumping out and swimming if we didn't go through with his plan, and I had no reason to doubt his sincerity. The odds of him making it out alive with no boat or backup was less than none.

"Okay, fine," I said finally. "But you wait until we're in position and jump up there at the last minute. You're going to have to aim quickly. Can you do that?"

"I hunt doves with a rifle," he said.

"Nice," Ida Belle said.

"Alrighty then," I said. "Gertie, you and Dave will sit on the back and be ready to move when Ida Belle makes the turn. I'll take the passenger seat and draw Fletcher off."

Hopefully.

Everyone nodded and Ida Belle and I exchanged glances. I could tell she was as skeptical and as hopeful as I was. I said a quick prayer for all our safety, pulled my pistol out, and took my seat. Ida Belle moved behind the steering wheel and glanced around.

"Everyone ready?" she asked.

Gertie and Dave whooped it up. I gave her a single nod and she gassed it.

The yacht had turned into a small blip in the distance, but nothing that the speedboat couldn't make up in record time. With the windshield cutting the force of air across my face, I was able to use the binoculars to zero in on Fletcher. He was still driving the boat from the top deck, but he looked back as we approached.

As we drew closer, he cut his speed and hurried over to the ladder. He was moving downstairs, which wasn't good. God only knew what kind of weapons he had in the cabin. If he came out with a rifle, then all bets were off. A pistol shot might not penetrate the hull, but a rifle should. I motioned to

Ida Belle and pointed down. She nodded and pushed speed up a bit more.

We were closing the distance fast, and I figured in another ten seconds or so, we'd be in position for the turn. I looked back at Gertie and Dave.

"Get ready!" I yelled.

A couple seconds later, Ida Belle made the turn and killed the engines. At the same time, I jumped up from my seat and took aim at the cabin windows, which is where I assumed Fletcher was hiding. The returning fire confirmed my assessment, and I was relieved that he was still firing with a pistol. In my peripheral vision I saw Gertie light the dynamite and fired again as Dave jumped up on the back of the boat.

I fired off another two rounds but didn't want to unload because I didn't have a spare magazine. A second later, I saw the rifle barrel extending out the cabin window.

Holy hell!

I took aim at the cabin window, but the boat pitched as I squeezed the trigger and I was way low.

"Hurry!" I shouted, my pulse spiking as I heard the rifle fire once, then again, both bullets hitting the side of the boat.

Dave squeezed the trigger and let the spear fly. The recoil sent him reeling backward across the deck and into the water. At the same time, another round from the rifle hit the boat, just below where Dave had been standing. I held my breath as the spear hurtled through the air, praying that it hit its target.

Bull's-eye!

The spear arched up and made a perfect landing right onto the back deck of the boat. The rifle disappeared from the window and a second later, Fletcher came running out of the cabin and dived over the side. The blast came right behind him, taking a good portion off the back of the boat.

We all started cheering and then heard Dave shouting behind us.

"A little help here," he said. "I think I blew out my shoulder. Or my face. Maybe both."

Ida Belle and I leaned over the side and hauled Dave up. His face did look a bit worse for the wear, but that and his shoulder would heal. Dave took one look at the slowly sinking yacht and let out a victory cry.

"Where is that piece of crap?" he asked.

"He went over the side," I said.

"Should we pick him up?" Gertie asked.

"Uh, Houston, we have a problem," Ida Belle said. "Is it just me or is the ocean getting closer?"

Crap!

One or more of the rifle shots must have penetrated the hull, and that last one had entered where the engines were.

Ida Belle tried to start the boat but one engine wouldn't fire. She turned on the bilge, but I had serious doubts that it could keep up with the flow in. Especially if we weren't able to get on top of the water and leave.

"Can you get us closer on one engine?" I asked.

Ida Belle nodded and began to slowly maneuver the boat toward the sinking yacht. The entire back was already submerged, and the bow was tipping upward at an ever-increasing angle.

I spotted Fletcher, clinging to a seat cushion. "There he is."

And that's when the second engine cut out. The boat glided to a stop, seeming to sink even deeper as it slowed. Water started to seep in around our feet. This was so not good.

"Do those cushions float?" I asked.

"Yeah," Dave said, then got excited and rushed into the cabin. "I think I saw an inflatable raft in here."

Ida Belle grabbed the radio and sent out a Mayday call with our coordinates. A couple seconds later, a voice came over the radio saying the coast guard had been notified and to hold tight until they got there. Since we didn't have any other options, I thought it was an unnecessary use of words, but I supposed they did it to make people feel better.

Dave emerged from the cabin with a giant piece of wadded rubber. "I hope the pump's wrapped up in here because I didn't see it anywhere."

"Me too," I said. "I really don't want to blow up my rescue raft."

"Gertie can do it," Ida Belle said. "She's got enough hot air to lift a blimp."

Gertie gave her the finger and we tugged the raft apart, letting out breaths of relief when the pump was tucked inside. We made quick work of the inflation, and it was a good thing, because the boat was going down faster than I thought it would. We launched the raft over the side and everyone climbed in except Dave, who tossed his duffel bag to us, then jumped aboard.

"I figured we might need the duct tape for handcuffs," he said.

We all scooted around, trying to make room for four people and the huge duffel bag.

"Maybe you could just keep the tape and ditch the rest?" I suggested as we started rowing. "You know, for a little more room."

"There's a six-pack of beer in there," Dave said. "And my lucky seashell. I can't toss it over."

I shook my head and kept rowing. As we drew closer to Fletcher, I could see the fight was finally gone out of him. Of course, the blast had taken out his boat, his weapons, and likely his hearing, and he was adrift on a seat cushion in the middle of the ocean, which limited his options. We paddled alongside him, and Dave and I dragged him onto the raft while Ida Belle kept my nine-millimeter aimed at his head, lest he get any ideas. I secured his hands behind his back with the tape and we stuck him on one side of the boat.

Then Dave punched him dead in the face.

———

I WAS AFRAID WE'D HAVE TO WAIT HOURS FOR THE COAST guard to arrive and prayed that the tiny raft would hold given its extensive cargo. But I'd forgotten about Dave's fishing buddies. I heard a boat in the distance and scanned the water, trying to locate the source.

"There!" Ida Belle shouted.

I turned around and saw Sea Bass Steve's fishing charter creeping toward us. We all started high-fiving and celebrating as Steve drew up.

"You guys okay?" he asked as he and the other fisherman tied off the raft and helped us onboard.

"We're better than okay," Dave said. "We got the sumbitch that killed Mikey!"

"That him?" Steve asked and pointed to Fletcher.

Dave nodded.

"We could rig him up on the heavy-duty line," Steve said. "We passed a school of tiger sharks about fifty yards back."

"Nah," Dave said. "I want him to rot in prison the rest of his life. Sharks deserve better eatin' anyway."

"All right," Steve said. "But at least let us tie him to the side of the boat and dangle a little."

Fletcher, who'd been silent up until now, started yelling like a five-year-old as they hauled him to the railing and dropped him over the side, securing him with a rope underneath his arms.

Dave opened his duffel bag and handed us all a beer.

"Worked out perfectly," he said. "One for everybody."

"I'm sorry about your friend's boat," I said. "I hope you're not going to get into trouble."

"Nah, he won't care," Dave said. "He never wanted the boat anyway. He'll make out better this way. Had it insured."

I smiled. I'd had a flash of panic when I'd realized we'd almost been caught in a raft with a school of sharks nearby, but it had passed as quickly as it came. After all, we were all alive and the bad guy was tied up and tempting sharks. Ida Belle had gotten to live out one of her dreams of driving a speedboat. And Gertie and Dave got to blow something up.

Best of all, we'd solved the case.

CHAPTER TWENTY-SEVEN

It took a couple days for the DEA to untangle everything. But finally, Fletcher was behind bars and Gertie was off the hook, much to Benton's dismay. The entire mess Benton had made of things was also sweeping the community, and we had no doubt that the sheriff's retirement was not going to go as Benton had planned. The DEA had caught the resort owner in Mexico and hauled him back to the US to face charges, and they'd arrested a whole host of other people along the Florida coast, including a crew on Barefoot Key. It was quite a big takedown and our involvement in apprehending one of the main players had become national news.

Gertie, of course, was thrilled. Ida Belle and I were not.

After a run-in with a particularly pushy reporter and the "unexplained" destruction of ten thousand dollars' worth of camera equipment, the DEA took pity on us and moved us to a private island they used for retreats. The mansion on the island came complete with a housekeeper, cook, and beach butler, which I'd never heard of but was totally cool.

So now, I sat on the beach of a private island, on my recently extended vacation, holding a drink that had just been served to me by the butler. Ida Belle reclined in the chair next to me, a frosty drink in one hand and her e-reader in the other. Gertie had discovered a metal detector among the beach toys and was off searching for pirate treasure.

My cell phone signaled a text. It was from Byron. I read it and smiled.

"Something naughty from Carter?" Ida Belle asked.

"No. Good news from Byron. Apparently Martin didn't spend all the money he scammed. Benton seized a sizable hunk from the safe in his room. It's going to be divvied up among the women they know were scammed by him."

Ida Belle smiled. "That's incredible news."

I nodded. "It won't make them whole, but at least they'll be getting something back."

"And I'll bet they never give anyone money again."

My phone rang and I answered Carter's call.

"Are the reporters and their equipment safe?" Carter asked.

I laughed. "Perfectly. They can't exactly get to us on a private island, especially if they don't know where we are."

"Private island?" Carter asked. "I just thought they were moving you to another resort farther along the coast."

"That's what they said, but then they brought us here. And it's awesome." I described the house and the servant situation.

"A big white house, Caribbean style, with turquoise doors and shutters?" Carter asked.

"Yes. How did you know?"

He started laughing. "That was the compound of a drug lord. They confiscated it several years back."

"Well, I suppose that's irony for you."

"I've got to run, but try not to get into any more trouble before you get home. I hate to say it, but Sinful has been a little quiet since you guys have been gone. Even Celia is moping around like a dog without a fight."

"We'll be home in a couple days and I'm sure Celia has been saving up all her contempt for our return."

I disconnected and told Ida Belle what Carter had said.

"Two more days in paradise," Ida Belle said. "Then it's back home to Celia."

"The devil you know."

"Ha. That's one way to look at it."

"Well, then I feel we must make the most of the next forty-eight hours. I want nothing but peace and quiet and sleeping on the beach with that well-mannered butler bringing us yummy treats and drinks that aren't watered down."

"You and me both."

We both leaned back, and I closed my eyes, ready to enjoy nothing but the sound of the surf. A minute later, I heard pounding footsteps on the sand and a panting Gertie—wearing an evening gown—ran up to our chairs.

"You're not going to believe what I found in the sand dunes," she said. "Barrels of money and a human skull!"

I looked over at Ida Belle and grinned. "So much for peace and quiet."

"Next year," she said. "Separate vacations."

For more adventures with Fortune and the girls, try Cajun Fried Felony.

To receive new release notifications, sign up for my newsletter on my website janadeleon.com.

MORE MISS FORTUNE FUN

Did you know that Jana created a publishing company that allows approved authors to pen their own stories in the Miss Fortune World? For a different take on Sinful and its residents, check out J&R Fan Fiction.

jrfanfiction.com

Sinful, Louisiana has its own website! If you want to escape to a bit of hilarity, check it out!

sinfullouisiana.com

Made in United States
Orlando, FL
13 June 2024

47839736R00161